DON'T TELL YOUR COUSIN

VERONICA E. KELLY

veronica_kelly@att.net

Cover designed by www.jerrosworld.com

ISBN-10: 1461092426

ISBN-13: 978-1461092421

DEDICATION

To Mom and Dad,

Thank you

CONTENTS

CHAPTER 1

"How could that even be possible?"

"Oh it's possible, the man is married!" Amanda said to Stephanie.

"I can't believe this shit," Stephanie sighed while shaking her head. "He was just here."

"Look, I saw the wedding picture on my boss's desk. It was him, dammit."

"I swear if you tell a soul about this…" Stephanie threatened.

"Well what are you gonna do about it?"

"I'm gonna continue doin' what I've been doin'."

"That's a really fucked up decision." Amanda shook her head.

"Look, I'm not obligated to anybody, he is."

"You're jokin', right? This is my boss's husband we're talkin' about."

"You don't even like her!"

Amanda tucked a few strands of her wavy hair behind her ears before folding her arms.

"That's not the point, Stephanie. He's married!"

"Look," Stephanie interrupted, "I really have a lot on my mind and I can't worry about his son of a bitch wife right now. What about me? I should be hurt," she said as she stormed out of the sunlit kitchen into her bedroom. Her cousin, Amanda, followed behind flopping down on the white shag rug beneath her feet. Stephanie ruffled through her jewelry box searching for the perfect pair of earrings to wear with her little black dress.

"So are you goin' with me or not?" Stephanie asked, placing a diamond stud in her ear.

"I'm not sure. I don't have anything to wear."

"Oh you can't possibly be serious. With all the money that man gives me, I have enough clothes for every woman in Chicago." Stephanie chuckled.

Amanda rolled her eyes as she shook her head. "You know you should really be ashamed of yourself."

"Ashamed? Amanda, what exactly do I have to be ashamed of?" she challenged her younger cousin. Amanda stood up and walked out of Stephanie's room and down the hall into her own. She had the smaller room of the two bedroom condominium. She opened the sliding doors to her walk-in closet and removed a pair of jeans and a black collard shirt from their hangers. She slipped into a pair of size eight jeans and buttoned her shirt to the top button before pulling her full head of shoulder length wavy hair into a pony tail. She was just about to apply a little lip gloss to her pair of full lips before Stephanie walked in. Amanda turned from the full length standing mirror to her cousin who stood leaning against her doorway with her arms folded in front of her chest.

"Are you goin' out or to work?" Stephanie teased, staring at her cousin's ensemble. "You need to loosen up a little and stop bein' so damn conservative."

Amanda examined herself in the mirror.

"What's wrong with what I have on?"

"Everything, sweetie. It's boring and no man wants to be with a boring woman."

"I don't care about what a man wants."

"Please, every woman needs to care about what a man wants. After all, there isn't a woman in the world that can give me what a man can," she winked.

Amanda sighed. "Oh goodness, is that all you think about?"

"No, but its reality honey, deal with it," Stephanie said brushing past Amanda to find something a little more seductive.

"Is this all you have? Where are your…nice clothes?"

"Excuse me? Everything I have in my closet is nice," Amanda snapped while unbuttoning her shirt.

"Right. Honey, conservative doesn't necessarily equal nice."

"And neither does cheap," Amanda challenged.

Stephanie turned to face Amanda and chuckled.

"All right, fine, wear what you want. If you like playin' with yourself at night that's fine with me. I'm ready when you are." Stephanie switched out of the room leaving Amanda facing her honey complexion in the mirror. She let her hair down and shook it out, leaving it wild and untamed. She slipped on her heels, grabbed her purse and followed Stephanie out of the door.

CHAPTER 2

"Are you ordering lunch with us or not?"

Amanda looked away from her computer monitor long enough to glance at Jessica's cranberry colored lipstick. She despised that color on white women.

"I hate that color on you."

"Well I hate that awful looking grandma sweater on you."

Amanda stopped typing and looked down at the pale rose colored cardigan sweater her mother had given to her before she left Chicago for California with her new husband.

"Okay, I admit it's a little dated, but it's comfy," Amanda chuckled as she went back to typing.

"Gosh, you sound like an old woman, you know you could be soooo much more," Jessica said giggling as she ran a hand over Amanda's thick hair. Amanda stopped typing and looked up once more.

"What exactly is that suppose to mean?" Amanda asked with a little hostility in her voice. Jessica's hand fell to her side as she shifted her body weight to her right leg.

"I mean, well I didn't necessarily...well, I meant that you're a really beautiful girl, you're only twenty four and from looking at you right now one would assume differently. But, I mean, hey, to each its own, right?

"Right." Amanda replied dryly, her eyes burning a hole through Jessica's forehead.

"Well," Jessica said, sensing the tension, "Ahh, let me know if you want to order anything." She headed off in the direction of her cubicle before Amanda had the chance to nod her head or give the okay to order without her. Amanda stared off, watching Jessica's slim silhouette as she walked gracefully across the room with her dirty blonde ponytail swinging back and forth with each stride. Amanda opened her drawer to retrieve her compact mirror. She flipped it open, frowning at her reflection. Her hair was disheveled, her bushy eyebrows could use a little waxing and a little facial moisturizer wouldn't hurt, she thought. She closed the compact and stared at her chipped soft pink nail polish from her one month old manicure. She shook her head in disgust as she placed the mirror back into the drawer before closing it. She plopped her elbows on the desk and rested her chin in one hand in deep thought.

"You're on company's time," a delicate sounding voice echoed to Amanda from behind. Amanda immediately removed her hand from underneath her chin and returned it to the keyboard. Embarrassed she had been caught in a daze, she turned her torso sideways and scanned Melanie, her boss, dressed in a cream satin blouse and olive colored tweed skirt. Her perfectly French manicured hands were placed on her hips, her head slightly tilted to the side.

"I guess I'm just a bit disoriented," she mumbled loud enough for Melanie to hear. Melanie stepped in closer and Amanda's eyes zoomed in on the huge diamond planted on her ring finger.

"Well I need you to become more alert. We have tons of work to complete. Did you get to the faxes? Send out the emails?" Melanie asked, her pearl earrings commanding attention.

"I'll get to it right now," Amanda replied turning to face her monitor and rolling her eyes when she was certain her boss could no longer see her face. She heard Melanie walk off in her high heels. She looked over her shoulder to make sure she was alone before picking up her cell phone to view her inbox text. Three new text messages, all but one from Stephanie. Stephanie: Hey what's up. Stephanie: Is she there? Mother: Hey my sweet daughter, call me, I love you. Amanda chuckled to herself as she dialed her mother's phone number from her work telephone.

"Hello, hey dear, how are things?"

"Mom, you could at least let the phone ring twice, geez."

"Well if I spoke to you a little more often I could let it ring longer."

Amanda smiled her first smile of the day. "Mom, I'm feelin' down."

"Well how could such a bright and beautiful woman as you feel down?" her mother asked concerned.

"Aw please, mom, I look terrible right now."

"Well, why leave the house looking terrible? You know how many women would love to have that pretty face of yours."

Amanda examined her reflection in her compact mirror once again. She knew her mother was referring to her long, full wavy hair, flawless skin and almond shaped eyes. People often wonder which parent of hers was of Latino descent. Surprisingly, neither one of them were. Amanda licked her left index finger before rubbing it across her bushy eyebrows.

"I don't know why," she chuckled, rubbing in the Chap Stick on her lips.

"Don't be so modest. You know you're a beautiful woman, start acting like it."

"What is that suppose to mean?"

"Well, are you dating anyone right now?"

"Now what does that have to do with anything?" Amanda rolled her eyes.

"I mean you're just so—"

"Mom, I have to go," Amanda whispered before slamming the receiver to its cradle. She returned her hands to her keyboard, clicking on documents.

"Feeling a bit more focused now?" Melanie asked peeking into Amanda's cubicle and then inviting herself into Amanda's space. Amanda continued to stare at her computer, fingers typing away.

"Yeah, I am," she said forcing herself to sound chipper.

"Well," Melanie began, leaning her backside against the end of Amanda's desk, "that's awfully pleasant to hear."

Amanda continued to stare at her computer, pretending to be focused on her tasks.

"You know," Melanie continued, "we're having a dinner for the entire department in a couple of weeks, will you be attending?"

"Sounds interesting," Amanda said finally turning to the side, acknowledging her boss's presence. "I'm pretty sure I'll be there."

"Great! Well, I'll let you get back to work." She smiled her award winning toothpaste commercial smile and walked out of the office.

****

"I've been callin' you all day. What's wrong with your phone?"

"Nothin'," Amanda answered sampling her bowl of chips and salsa.

"So you just ignored me?" Stephanie accused, sliding her suit jacket off of her petite torso and tossing it over the ivory love seat. She walked into the open kitchen joining her cousin who was seated on a barstool at the island, her hair and makeup a little scruffy.

"Well, I didn't quite ignore you," Amanda responded before stuffing a potato chip smothered with Salsa in her mouth. "I was just busy, that's all."

"Yeah, busy feedin' your face," Stephanie remarked shaking her head in disgust. "So, did you see that bitch at work today?" she asked wearing a playful grin.

"I knew that's all you wanted. That's why I didn't answer the phone in the first place." Amanda popped another chip into her mouth before grabbing the entire bowl and walking off into the living room with Stephanie following right behind. She flopped down on the L shaped sofa and flipped through the channels on the television.

"Just tell me if she was she there or not?"

"Stephanie, why does it matter?"

"I mean I'm just curious. What does she look like? She got any swagger about her? Well, obviously not because her man was all over me today and the day before that and the day before that." Stephanie pranced around the living room smiling and stopping to do her famous booty dance in front of the television screen, blocking Amanda's view of the TV show The Hills. Amanda sighed and placed the chips and salsa dip on the wood coffee table in front of her.

"Look sweetheart, I could care less about your little excursions to random hotel rooms with her husband. You don't know what it feels like to look at that lady and that son of a bitch rock on her hand and know—"

Stephanie, no longer dancing, made her way around the table and stood in Amanda's face with her head cocked to the side and hands mounted on her hips.

"And know what? Go on finish your little speech, don't let me stop you. It was just gettin' good." Stephanie said sarcastically.

Amanda exhaled and shifted herself comfortably on the couch letting her eyes drop to the floor. She leaned back rubbing the palm of her hand against her forehead in an attempt to clear her mind and calm her annoyance with her cousin. She looked up.

"It's useless, it's really no point. You just continue fuckin' her husband and I'll just continue to barely look her in her fuckin' face everyday," Amanda shouted staring up at her cousin who towered over her looking like she wanted to punch her lights out.

"Well," Stephanie said, undoing her bun and letting her hair fall down her back, "I wouldn't have it any other way." She snatched up her suit jacket and stormed off down the hall to her room. Amanda slouched down on the couch and shook her head before stuffing another chip into her mouth.

****

Amanda giggled like an elementary school girl as she sipped her Long Island, standing within ear shot of a group of guys who stood looking in her direction. She was feeling quite buzzed off of her second drink. It was Friday night and the 52 Lounge was packed as usual with a mixture of young and middle aged, sophisticated and chic group of diverse folks. Amanda decided to let her hair down for the night, her long full and curly mane added to her sexiness along with a red sleeveless V neck form fitting dress she had hidden in the back of her closet. Her gold hoop earrings and red peep-toe heels added a bit more zest to her look.

"Girl you look too hot tonight. Where you get that dress? Let me guess you borrowed it from Stephanie, right?" Tiffany sipped on her third Long Island. She had more of a tolerance than her friend.

Giggling. "It's a little somethin' somethin' I had in my closet. I can get sexy you know."

"Good. You need to try it a little more often."

"Why does everybody give a fuck about what the hell I look like?" Amanda sighed before wrapping her lips back around her straw.

"Because you're much too precious to be lettin' yourself go the way you do, sweetheart. And besides, my girls are a reflection of me. And honey," she looked Amanda up and down, "I like this reflection much better."

Amanda rolled her eyes while cheesing. "Whatever."

Tiffany, 5'7 in her heels, wore a black short tube dress, revealing her gorgeous legs and toned arms. Her hair was in a soft upsweep. Her diamond hoops in her ears sparkled. Unlike Amanda, Tiffany made it a point to stay fit and look fabulous.

She had herself looking right at the tender age of twenty five, a year older than Amanda. She loved to shop, have girl talks, wear designer labels at discounted prices and have sex with whomever she deemed attractive whether successful or jobless. Her friends never understood that about her. Amanda especially.

"So what you gonna do about that dude starin' you down over there?" she pointed. Amanda slapped her hand down. "Ouch."

"Don't point. Dammit, must you be so obvious?"

"And must you be so damn scary? When was the last time you had some dick?"

Amanda seized another opportunity to wrap her lips around her straw. Tiffany placed her free hand on her hip and tilted her head sideways. "I can't hear you. Speak up, what was that? Five months you say?" she teased and laughed at her own joke. Amanda couldn't help but join in. She stumbled over her own foot while downing what was left of her drink.

"Let's have a seat," Amanda insisted.

Tiffany grabbed the glass from her. "Let's answer the question."

"Look bitch, you can stand here all you want, I'm lookin' for a seat." Amanda turned to walk off, but Tiffany grabbed her arm before she could take a step. A frown swept across Amanda's face.

"Easy, you know us light girls bruise easily." Alcohol was notorious for making Amanda say foolish things sometimes.

Tiffany rolled her eyes in annoyance. "Well I ain't yellow so I wouldn't know," she hissed. Tiffany extended her caramel colored arm out in front of Amanda. "Just in case you needed clarification."

"I just need you to clarify why the hell we still standin'," Amanda said with her hands on her hips, scanning the room for an empty chair. Dim lights set the mood and all around the spot, was flirty laughter, hip to hip dancing, drink sipping, men staring and music blasting. The place looked a little dated, but the mood and the atmosphere was always intimate, warm and inviting, a great hang out spot to be after a long and tedious day. Amanda wasn't a regular, but Tiffany often frequented and it wasn't out of the ordinary for her to leave the venue on some random guy's arm.

"I have so many options tonight," Tiffany yelled to Amanda over the music as she nestled herself into a chair near the bar, not too far from where a group of suitors awaited the very moment. Amanda made eye contact with one of the guys. He appeared relaxed, dressed in a striped button up and a pair of dark denim designer jeans, blending in with the majority of the younger men. His hair was cut low, not too short in stature, definitely taller than she, even in her highest pair of heels. He smiled and Amanda smiled back, more in surprise than in awe. She instantly wanted to kick herself. She knew such gestures were practically open invitations. Amanda smacked her lips as he began his cocky stroll in her direction. She looked over to her left at the smile plastered on Tiffany's face.

"Damn girl, I hope he's comin' over here to talk to you because I really don't feel like bein' bothered...ugh look at the way he walks and—"

"Hi," Tiffany smiled at the guy as she extended her hand.

"What's up," he said casually never taking his eyes off Amanda as he shook Tiffany's hand. "What's your name?" he asked Amanda. He was standing so close to her she could feel the warmth of his breath.

Amanda twisted her face up in annoyance before responding "Mandy."

"And I'm Tiffany," Tiffany chimed, inviting herself into the introduction. The guy looked her over before redirecting his attention to Amanda. Amanda smirked and shook her head at her friend's behavior.

"Nice to meet you, Tiffany." He tugged at his shirt collar. "You must not speak much?" he said to Amanda.

"I speak when spoken to."

"You mind speakin' to me over the phone tonight?"

"Please, can you come a little harder than that," Amanda snapped, her hair falling in one direction as she cocked her head to the side. The guy shook his head, leaned against the bar and chuckled. "Easy sweetheart, you havin' a rough night or somethin'? What, yo' man ain't treatin' you right?"

Amanda turned towards the bar. "I need another drink," she said to no one in particular.

"I got you baby, what you want?" the dude asked.

"I need for you to—"

"Get her a screwdriver, it's her favorite," Tiffany jumped to the rescue, staring the guy down with a feisty grin on her face with her arms folded across her chest.

The guy chuckled again. "Whatever man," he said before walking off.

Tiffany's mouth dropped just as her arms fell to her side. "What's up with that? Why do you always have to act so stuck up?"

"Why do you have to always act so desperate," Amanda continued standing with her back to her friend while waiting on her drink.

"You could use some dick in yo' life, I really don't understand why you keep turnin' guys down. That guy was pretty good lookin'."

"Well go get him."

"I swear mellow yellow women have it so fuckin' easy," Tiffany blurted shaking her head in disappointment.

Amanda turned to face her, surprised by what she had just heard. She ran a hand through her hair and leaned her backside against the bar. She folded her arms across her chest.

"Here you are, ma'am," the bartender announced behind Amanda.

"What the hell is that suppose to mean?" Amanda asked, ignoring the bartender and her drink for the moment.

"Lighter women have it much easier and don't even try to deny it."

"How dare you," Amanda unfolded her arms. "You know what, take me home. You just killed it for the night with all this foolishness. I'm so tired of you sayin' that shit! Have you ever considered the fact that maybe I'm just not as loose as you are?" A few heads turned in their direction.

Tiffany picked up Amanda's drink and tossed it in her face before storming off.

CHAPTER 3

Stephanie laughed as she stuffed a spoonful of cornflakes in her mouth. "Hell, I would've thrown a drink on yo' ass too," she said after swallowing. "And then I would've made yo' ass buy me another one." She threw her head back in laughter. Amanda sat across from her on the barstool in her silk robe with her hair wildly about. She couldn't help but join in the laughter with a few chuckles of her own.

"But that's not all," Amanda whined. "She had the nerve to leave me there. Luckily that guy insisted on gettin' my number and was polite enough to give me a ride home."

"So did you give him the digits?"

Amanda grinned. "I gave him the number and—"

"That's what I'm talkin' about," Stephanie cheered. "Somebody finally got a man back in her life," she shouted and clapped.

Amanda laughed. "Girl all I did was give him my number, he'll be lucky if I pick up."

"Don't be foolish, damn, go out with the man." Stephanie slid her bowl towards the middle of the counter. "Girl you never know, his dick may be the bomb!"

Stephanie pulled her long relaxed hair out of her face and let it fall down her back exposing her smooth almond skin, high cheek bones and perfectly arched eyebrows. She smiled, revealing a row of picture perfect teeth. "Are you gonna let him lay it on you?"

Amanda snickered. "Come on, Stephanie, I don't want to talk about that."

"Well what's his name?"

"Reggie."

"Reggie, like Reggie Bush?"

"No, Reggie like I'm nowhere on Reggie Bush's level." They both burst out in laugher. "He's not bad lookin' though."

"Good! You finally got someone to get your mind of Tony's ass." Stephanie said in rejoice. Amanda sipped her orange juice as she reflected on her previous relationship. Tony Ray Phillips, her ex boyfriend of three years had cheated on her with numerous women. While in attendance at Northwestern, a young woman she shared a class with informed her that she was also dating Tony and was two months pregnant. Amanda stopped attending that class and school all together. She moved out of the one bedroom she and Tony shared on the north side and into the two bedroom condominium in the Bronzeville area with her cousin. And although it was certain Stephanie's job in real estate allowed her to live quite comfortably, Amanda still handed over whatever she could to help out, at least to keep herself from being considered a free loader. "I can't wait to see him girl," Stephanie placed a hand over her cousin's. Amanda forced a smile, finally coming out of deep thought.

"You might be waitin' awhile," Amanda teased.

"Honey, I'm not the one finger fuckin' myself at night."

Amanda screwed up her face. "Aw yeah, so who did you have in your bed last night?"

"Mr. Construction worker, also known as you boss's husband." Stephanie smiled in delight.

"He was here?" Amanda asked nearly knocking over her glass of juice. "You had sex with him?" Amanda blurted out realizing it was a dumb question.

Stephanie hardly holding in her glee, smiled from ear to ear. "Honey, he drilled me all night and left a little after sunrise."

Amanda shook her head wondering what poor excuse he gave his wife. "I'm so glad I didn't see him."

"Too bad for you, he's definitely somethin' to see, naked that is." Stephanie faced beamed as she pushed herself away from the counter and off the barstool. She grabbed her bowl of half eaten cereal and placed it in the sink. "I cooked dinner for us last night. I made him the best New York Strip ever. A candle light dinner on the balcony and girl it was so romantic." Stephanie turned to face Amanda. "And when we came in I sat on the counter top, opened my legs and gave him dessert. Amanda accidentally spit her orange juice out in disgust and quickly stood up backing away from the countertop. Stephanie laughed uncontrollably. "Honey, relax, it's nothin' a little Pine Sol and Comet can't handle. My ass is clean," she said in between laughter.

"You are ridiculous. What if I would've walked in?"

"Shit, you probably would've called Reggie over." Stephanie smirked.

"Ugh, I don't even want to imagine it."

"Girl, get over it, somebody in this place gotta get some."

"Yeah, and you get enough for the both of us."

Stephanie leaned over the countertop and looked at Amanda. "I don't mind it one bit."

"Of course you don't, slut." Amanda taunted walking off towards her bedroom.

"I heard that!" Stephanie yelled from behind followed with laughter.

Amanda removed her phone from the charger and noticed three missed calls. Two calls from Tiffany and one from Reggie. "She had the audacity to call me," Amanda yelled towards the kitchen to Stephanie. She kept the call from Reggie to herself, debating on whether she would return the call or not. Secretly, hearing her cousin go on and on about sex aroused her curiosity a bit. Not about Reggie but about her boss's husband. She suddenly wondered what Melanie and her husband were doing at that very moment.

"You say what?" Stephanie was now standing in the doorway.

Amanda, startled, dropped her phone. "Damn girl," she said as she knelt down to pick it up. "I said Tiffany had the nerve to call me…twice."

Stephanie shrugged her shoulders. "Call her back," she suggested before turning and walking out the room. Amanda ignored her and tossed her phone on the bed as she sat down wondering what she should get herself into for the day. When her phone suddenly vibrated, she looked over to see who the caller was. Tiffany, fuck that bitch, she thought as she hit the ignore button and stretched across her queen sized bed. Right before her head hit the soft pillow her phone vibrated once more. "If this bitch don't stop—"

To her surprise it wasn't Tiffany. It was Reggie. She rolled her eyes before placing the phone to her ear.

"Hello," she said pretending to sound chipper.

"Can I speak to Mandy?"

"It's Amanda," she corrected, forgetting she never gave out her full name to guys she didn't know or at least didn't want to know.

"Amanda, I'm sorry," Reggie said chuckling, "You gave me Mandy last night." He sounds much sexier over the phone, Amanda thought. She obviously didn't pay him enough attention last night to even notice the sound of his voice.

"Well," she put on her sweet seductive voice, "I usually don't give out my real name unless I like you."

"Aw, so I guess you don't like me, even after I was nice enough to give you a ride to the crib."

Amanda smiled. "Relax, I don't know you well enough to like you yet," she flirted.

"Well I assume that you want to get to know me."

Amanda lay twirling a strand of hair around her index finger. "Well don't assume," she toyed. "So Mr. Reggie, what are your plans for the day?"

"Well Ms. Mandy, sorry, Amanda, that's where this conversation come in at. I wanted to see if such a beautiful woman as you would be interested in spendin' a lovely Saturday evening with me." he chuckled.

Amanda was shocked at how mature and smooth he appeared over the phone. Don't fool yourself girl, it's just an act, she thought. She remained silent for a couple of seconds pretending to ponder as if she actually had a busy schedule. Men like it when you don't appear so thirsty, Stephanie often said.

"Hello," Reggie said, filling the silence.

"I'm sorry, yeah…yeah, that's cool. What kind of plans do you have in mind and what time?"

"Ooh a little assertive are we?" Reggie teased.

He's seems like a gentleman, Amanda thought to herself. Impressive. "No, I just take my time seriously." she lied, suppressing her excitement. This was one of the few interesting conversations she had in awhile with a man since her and Tony parted ways.

"Okay sweetheart, I can dig that. How about I pick you up at about eight?"

Amanda paused again. "All right," Amanda said suppressing her excitement. She was smiling from ear to ear when Stephanie walked in. Amanda held up a finger for Stephanie as if she was on some important call.

"All right, I'll see you then. Oh yeah, one more thing…wear somethin' sexy."

Amanda's smile faded. "Just jokin'," Reggie continued laughing. Amanda quickly joined in. A sense of humor too, she noted.

"Okay, I'll see you later." Amanda smiled.

"All right."

Amanda hit the end button. "Aaaaaaaahhh," she screamed in excitement as she rose to her feet and jumped on her bed like an eight year old. "I got a date!"

Stephanie shook her head at Amanda's silly outburst. "Honey, please, tame yourself, you were just in the kitchen actin' like the man wasn't even worth your time. What he do, offer to give you a million dollars to go out with him?" Stephanie asked. Amanda smacked her lips and sat back on her bed. Stephanie was right, she had better calm down. For all she knew, Reggie could be just another clown.

****

Amanda pranced around her room to the tunes of Floetry. She was a huge fan of Neo-Soul, Hip Hop, especially underground and R&B. She stood in the mirror wearing a short gray V-neck empire waist dress, with a pair of silver metallic strappy sandals she borrowed from Stephanie. She pulled her hair back into a high ponytail in attempt to retain some of her sexiness. She added a little bronzer, lip gloss, and mascara for a more subtle look. She threw on a pair of cubic zirconium studs and stacked silver bangles. She blew a kiss to her image in the full length mirror.

"You vain bitch," Stephanie joked as she checked out Amanda's get up. "And you have every right to be, honey, you look damn good. My shoes and bangles bring your outfit together quite nicely may I add." Amanda considered herself the most attractive out of the duo. She hated when Stephanie reminded her that she was wearing pieces that belong to her. She made a mental note to update and expand her wardrobe as soon as possible.

"Thanks a million," Amanda said kissing Stephanie on the cheek in an attempt to ease her own tension. "Aw, my phone's ringin,'" she said grabbing it off of the bed. "Hello."

"Yeah, I'm outside," Reggie said.

"I'm on my way out," Amanda said quickly cutting the call short and glancing over at her alarm clock resting on her dresser.

8:02. she scribbled down a number and a description on a piece of paper and handed it to Stephanie.

"What the hell is this?"

"That's his number and a little description of what he looks like." They both burst out in laughter as they walked towards the front door.

"Maybe you'll be able to write down how many inches his dick is after tonight."

"You're nuts." Amanda chuckled as she open the front door.

Stephanie peeked out the blinds. She smirked. "Would you look at that, he drives an Infiniti, how...cute."

Amanda shook her head and closed the door behind her.

****

"I'm surprised you came out with me."

"Why is that?" Amanda asked, stuffing a roasted potato into her mouth.

"You know how you were actin' last night...all stuck up."

Amanda sipped her water. "I apologize, guys can be jerks sometimes and besides, you had no game." They laughed.

Reggie nodded his head. "I mean you're a fine-lookin' woman, it took a lot of nerve just to step to you." Amanda could feel herself turning red. "You're gorgeous," he added.

Again Amanda sipped her water. "So how's the chicken breast?" he asked to kill the awkwardness.

"It's delicious. I love Italian food," she smiled.

"Yeah and so do I. Uh, would you excuse me, I have to use the bathroom," Reggie said as he wiped a few crumbs from around his mouth with the dinner napkin and stood up. Amanda's eyes admired his gray argyle sweater vest over a white button up along with a pair of dark blue wash designer jeans. She liked his style. He walked off from the table with her eyes glued to his backside. When he was out of sight her eyes wandered around the restaurant to the exposed brick walls, stacked high with wine bottles. The slew of young looking couples seated around white-cloth tables giving the atmosphere a lofty feel. So far she was pleased with her date's exquisite taste.

"How's everything going?" the cheerful waitress asked smiling from ear to ear. Amanda smiled and nodded. "It's great. This is such a romantic place."

The waitress laughed.

"I agree, although it's quite loud in here right now."

"Well, it is a Saturday," Amanda smiled before stuffing her mouth.

"Yeah, well great, I'll be back to check on you guys," the waitress smiled again before heading to another table. Amanda's phone vibrated inside her clutch. She looked down and fumbled around with it.

"You All right?" A deep voice asked.

Amanda looked up still chewing, expecting to see Reggie. She swallowed the last bits of her food. It was him. He had a smile that stayed logged into her memory though she had only saw him in numerous photographs with Stephanie as well as the ones displayed on her boss's desk.

"Um, yeah," she stammered over her few words, feeling like the moment was a little too surreal. She smiled. A smile always helps when you're at a lost of words, she thought.

He extended his arm. "My name is Mike." Amanda politely shook his hand, still smiling. "I'm sorry, I don't mean to be rude, I just wanted to tell you that you're absolutely gorgeous. I'm sure you hear it all the time."

"Yeah, I kinda' just said it to her," Reggie appeared from behind Mike. Mike turned his head and glanced at Reggie before returning his attention to Amanda.

"Oh, well, I apologize, I had no idea you were here with someone."

Amanda chuckled through her smile. Damn he is fine. He had a freshly shaved bald head with a low clean cut goatee. The pictures she had seen of him did him little justice. She had no idea he was as hot as he was at that very minute. His fitted black graphic shirt and jeans framed his fit physique nicely.

"Right, I guess you thought she was eatin' two entrees," Reggie said with a bit of sarcasm as he sat in his chair. Mike locked eyes with Amanda, who now had her chin rested in her hand, blushing.

"Enjoy your night, beautiful." he said in a low smooth voice before walking off.

Amanda pretended to search for her phone in her clutch to hide her flushed red face and beaming smile.

"See, I told you you're pretty." Reggie smiled.

"I'm sorry, I didn't—"

"Relax," Reggie held up his hand to silence her. "I mean you had nothin' to do with it. I can't knock a dude for admirin' someone as fine as you. Hell, I probably would've done the same thing."

Amanda glared at him.

"I mean if I didn't have a woman." Reggie said in defense before laughing.

"Why don't you have a woman?"

Reggie stopped laughing and sipped his glass of wine. He looked Amanda over as he chomped away at the food on his plate. Amanda now sat with her arms folded across her chest, patiently waiting to hear the answer to her question. Reggie placed his fork on his plate and wiped his hands and mouth with the dinner napkin. He pushed his plate towards the center of the dinner table before folding his hands in his lap. He looked down before staring her in her eyes.

"It's a long story."

Amanda playfully glanced at her wrist. "Oh I've got time."

Reggie smirked and raised his index finger to the waitress as she walked past. "Check please."

"Sure no problem, I'll be right back, would you like your food wrapped?"

"No thanks."

"Thank you, I don't have much left…I'm fine." Amanda said as she placed her fork in the middle of her plate.

"Okay give me a sec." The waitress strutted off.

Amanda eyes nearly burned a hole through Reggie's face. "So are you gonna tell me or not?"

"Baby, relax, I will. I just don't feel like now is the appropriate time. I'm more interested in relishin' the moment with you."

It might be your last moment, Amanda wanted to say. Instead she took a final sip of water to keep the words from slipping out. The waitress returned with the check, Reggie paid the bill and they headed out into the warm night air to his car. The valet man opened her door, she slid in. Reggie walked over to the driver's side and stood there a moment. The valet man strolled off after Reggie handed him a few crispy dollar bills. Amanda, out of curiosity, leaned over a bit to observe what the hold up was. His fingers were typing away at the buttons on his phone's keypad. Amanda frowned and leaned back in her seat, staring out the passenger side window. After what seemed like eternity the driver's side door opened and he slid in, smiling.

"Excuse me, I'm a pretty important person," he said sarcastically. Amanda continued to stare out her window unamused by his comedy. "You All right?" he asked as he drove off in a route that wasn't towards her home.

"Where are we goin'?"

"Well, I figured we could take a walk or somethin'."

"I'd rather go home."

Reggie looked over at her and then back to the road. "Look, can we please enjoy the rest of the night? I would really like that."

Amanda sat quietly with her arms folded against her chest. Reggie continued to divide his attention between her and the road. Amanda, pretty certain this was going to be her last night with him, decided to just enjoy the rest of her night. "Okay," she finally answered. He smiled, hopped on Lake Shore Drive and headed north.

After the three hours spent walking, talking, and eating ice cream, Reggie finally pulled up in front of her apartment. Amanda's face was beaming as she looked over at him and smiled, happy she had made the decision to continue her date with him.

"I had a great time, Reggie." She smiled and looked over at him. He stared back at her. Soft jazz tunes echoed from the radio, enticing the moment.

"I had a ball, thanks for hangin' out with me. Can we do it again?"

Amanda unlocked her door and opened it. "Maybe, maybe not." She got out and closed the door. She stooped down in front of the passenger window, which was rolled down half way. "Have a safe ride."

"Can I call you?"

"Sure."

"Will you answer?"

"You'll have to call me and find out." She smiled, turned away and walked towards the building. She opened her purse and reached in to grab her keys. When her phone vibrated she pulled it out and smiled at Reggie's name flashing across the screen. She answered it and turned back to look at him. He was starring back at her.

Amanda smirked. "Good night, Reggie," she said.

"Hurry up and get in the house woman," he said jokingly.

Amanda inserted the key into the knob, twisted it and stepped inside. "I'm in."

"All right sweetheart, have sweet dreams."

"You do the same babe."

"Wow, I got called babe. I'm cheesin'."

Amanda laughed. "I was just bein' polite," she teased. "Good night."

"Peace."

Amanda placed her phone back into her purse and removed her shoes at once. She wondered how she made it through the night in those things. All the lights were off. As she crept to her room, sounds of a squeaky bed mixed with moans grew louder and louder. Oh shit, Amanda thought. The noises were coming from Stephanie's room. Luckily the door was closed. She gently pressed her ear against Stephanie's door.

Ooooooooh yes, yes, ooooh it feels so good. She heard her cousin moan from behind the door. Amanda could feel herself becoming moist. She listened in, wondering who the mystery man was. She continued listening as the noises grew louder and louder. The head board knocked loudly against the wall. Amanda was tingling. Stephanie moaned louder. Amanda could hear a few slaps against skin here and there. She knew her cousin was the queen of kinkiness. Ooooohhh shit, oh yes, yeeesssssss, Stephanie sang.

"Get it girl," Amanda said to herself in a low excited voice. She placed her middle finger to her crotch and massaged herself, she was soaked. She could hear skin clapping as the bed continued to bump against the wall. She chuckled to herself. Either Stephanie needed a new bed frame or the mystery man was really handling his business.

Say my name she heard the man say. She leaned in closer to the door for the big reveal. Ooooooh yes yes...whew shit yeeessssss, Mike. Amanda gasped. Oh yea Mr. Construction worker." Stephanie said through her moans. Amanda let her finger fall from under her dress and crept to her room. She slammed her door so loud the noise in the other room died down.

Amanda let her shoes fall to the floor. Her door swung open with Stephanie standing in the doorway wearing only black fishnet stockings with frilly lace at the top.

"You are so nasty, now what if I had company?"

Stephanie laughed. "You need some! I don't want to be the only one havin' fun late at night. Now excuse me while I go and let Mr. Construction Worker finish drillin' me." She smacked her own round bottom before closing the door behind her.

CHAPTER 4

"Maybe if you would've picked up a phone, I wouldn't have had to show up all unannounced and shit." Tiffany walked in and flopped down on the couch like she was exhausted. Her juicy Couture sweatpants and white scoop neck fitted tee framed her shape perfectly. Her hair was pulled back into a ponytail and the lack of makeup made her look a couple of years younger. Her lip gloss highlighted her thin lips. Amanda who still stood standing in the doorway finally closed the door shut. She opened up the blinds and let the sunlight radiate through the place.

"I have my reasons for not pickin' up the phone," she said as she sat down on the couch opposite of Tiffany wearing nothing more than a pair of Victoria Secret boy shorts that had Pink written across the butt with a matching white spaghetti strap tank. Her hair was hanging making her appear exotic and seductive. If only Tiffany was a man.

"Oh yeah, well I had my reasons for throwin' my drink in yo' damn face." She got up and stood over Amanda with her arms folded. "You need to watch yo' smart ass mouth."

"Or what?" Amanda jumped up for a challenge.

"Or else Imma' tell you how fat you look in them little ass shorts," Tiffany teased before shoving Amanda back down on the couch. They both burst out in laughter when Amanda got up and pushed Tiffany onto the couch and sat on her.

"Get yo' big self up off of me!" They wrestled while laughing.

"If you ever..." Amanda bounced on top of her in between words, "throw another drink in my face, I'm kickin' yo' ass!" More laughter. The front door swung open and in walked Stephanie holding two Target bags.

"Oooh, girl on girl," Stephanie teased as she closed the door and stepped into the spacious living room, heels clicking against the hardwood floors. She sat the bags on the couch before heading into the kitchen. "Sooooo, Amanda, how was your date?" Stephanie said from the open kitchen. Amanda stood up while Tiffany straightened her clothes.

"Date?" Tiffany asked with raised eyebrows. "Who in the hell did you go on a date with?"

Amanda rolled her eyes at Tiffany before directing her attention to Stephanie who was sipping a can of Pepsi through a straw.

"The date went well. He's a nice guy."

"Wait, what guy are we referrin' to, dammit? Let me in, I want to know!"

"Well maybe if you didn't throw a drink in her face you wouldn't be so late on the gossip! Now you must suffer the consequences." Stephanie teased. Tiffany glared at Amanda. She hated when Amanda ran back to her cousin telling their business. Amanda paid the look no attention. As far as she was concerned Tiffany was in the wrong.

"Well if she didn't call me out of my name she wouldn't have got a drink thrown in her face. She knows I don't play that shit!" Tiffany snapped daring either one to step up. Amanda turned halfway and smacked her lips.

"Bitch, please! Don't come up in here actin' like you all hard. You were actin' easy and I called your ass out on it. Now what?" Amanda chuckled.

"Whatever." Stephanie sat her can on the counter top, "Amanda, you always callin' somebody easy. Don't be mad because we're gettin' ours and you still sittin' around here actin' fresh! Honey, you ain't foolin' nobody. We all know you're a little freak."

Tiffany and Stephanie erupted in laughter while Amanda shook her head denying the allegations.

"Whatever Stephanie, I heard you last night!"

"I knew you were listenin', freak!" Amanda joined in the laughter.

"That man was so good I damn near wanted to share him! Oh wait...I am!" More laughter filled the air, this time only amongst Stephanie and Tiffany. When they noticed Amanda not laughing they stopped.

"Here we go again. Don't start that sensitive shit about how he's your boss's husband and shit!" Stephanie said before lifting her drink to take a sip.

"I didn't say a thing, you did." Amanda thoughts flashed back to the night before. She decided against telling her cousin. Besides, all he did was compliment her, she thought. Tiffany chuckled to ease some of the tension between the two.

"Whatever," Stephanie walked off towards her room. Amanda sat down on the couch and rested her elbow on the arm rest, while twirling her curly hair around her finger. Tiffany walked over and sat down next to her.

"You didn't tell me she was fuckin' that lady's husband," she whispered.

"Oh, well guess what? She's fuckin' my boss's husband," Amanda said sarcastically. "Oh, and he's a construction worker. His wife is absolutely clueless. Poor thing!" Amanda shook her head.

"Are you kiddin' me? As much as you complain about that bitch you should be laughin' in her damn face." Tiffany stared off in the distance and then turned back to Amanda. "So is he cute?"

"Fine as hell girl!" Amanda blurted out before exploding in laughter.

"So you saw him? Does he know you work with his wife? Tell me."

"He doesn't even know me. Hell, he has no idea Stephanie knows he's married. He's playin' her like he's slick. I saw a photo of him on my boss's desk and he was the same dude Stephanie showed me in the few pictures she has of him. You don't forget a face like his!"

"All right now, girl" Tiffany said reading deeper into Amanda's telling. "He sounds like the one you want to be fuckin'."

"Girl please," Amanda twisted up her face and responded, "I'll pass."

"Hell, well tell yo' cousin she can pass his ass my way."

"See, ya'll some low down bitches!"

"Ain't no fun if the homies can't have none!" Tiffany said in her worst imitation of a man's voice. They laughed.

"So check this Tiff, girl I saw him last night."

"What?" Tiffany said loud enough for the entire building to hear. "I mean what?" she corrected herself in a whisper.

"Damn girl, calm down! I said I saw him last night and—"

"Wait before you continue, who you go on a date with?"

Amanda let out a long exhale. "Reggie," she said to Tiffany like he was a mutual friend of theirs.

"Reggie? Who the hell is Reggie, bitch?"

"The guy from the lounge that night?"

Tiffany eyes widened. "The sexy ass dude who tried to talk to yo' stuck up ass?"

"Yes, him. He gave me a ride home, no thanks to you!"

"Oh please, I see you finally went on a date. You need to be thankin' me! Maybe that can be our thing, throwin' drinks on each other then stormin' out and lettin' some fine ass dude come to the rescue!"

"Or maybe you can shut the fuck up and allow me to finish my story!" They laughed.

"That's a good idea though, you gotta' admit!"

"Like I said, if you throw another drink in my face, it's a wrap," Amanda said playfully. "Let me finish my story, Tiffany."

"Ok go ahead with yo' boring story," Tiffany said.

Amanda pouted. "It's not boring."

"Is there dick involved?"

"Uh no, freak nasty!"

"Well then its gonna be boring, continue," they laughed.

"Okay, so anyway I saw him last night."

"Wait, your boss's husband or the guy from the lounge? Reggie?"

"My boss's husband. Pay attention!"

"I still want to know about you and Reggie!"

"Ok, I'll tell you about that in a minute! Anyway, gosh, you made me forget what I was sayin'…Oh, yeah, I saw him last night while I was havin' dinner with Reggie."

Amanda updated Tiffany on the events of the night before as Tiffany listened in like a little school girl.

"Girl, get out of here! You came home and he was fuckin' her? And this is after you saw him and he basically tried to holler at you?" Tiffany asked making sure she whispered.

Amanda nodded her head. "Are you tellin' Stephanie?" Tiffany continued.

"I mean what's to tell? He doesn't even know who I am!"

"So what happens when he comes over one day and all three of you are here? Oh my God, this is so juicy! I would pay to see the look on his face."

"He needs to be worried about his wife." Amanda added.

"Oh, wow, even more interesting!"

"What's interesting?" Stephanie asked walking into the living room. She had changed into a pair of short shorts and a tank top.

"Reggie and little Ms. Innocent over here." Tiffany grinned, changing the subject.

"Oh yeah, that is interesting, finish tellin' us the story, girl!" Stephanie said as she scooted herself in between Tiffany and Amanda. Amanda, happy Tiffany was such a quick thinker, smiled like she was eager to tell the story.

"Well…." Amanda began.

CHAPTER 5

"So initially I was gonna just dye it darker, you know...a brunette, but..."

"Ladies, how was your weekend?" Melanie asked interrupting Jessica and Amanda's conversation. Amanda forced a smile.

"It was pretty awesome!" Jessica said in her most chipper voice ever. She had a way of sucking up and kissing Melanie's ass. Amanda preferred not to. Perhaps that's why Melanie was much keener of Jessica than Amanda. Melanie smiled and nodded her head.

"And how was yours?" Melanie asked Amanda seemingly uninterested in Jessica's nonsense. Amanda's smiled faded as her thoughts raced back to her encounter with Melanie's husband. She ran a hand through her hair and replaced her fake smile.

"It was pretty cool. I hung out with friends and did a little shopping," she said, teasing her hair.

"Shopping? Really, well, what cool stuff did you get?" Melanie asked full of curiosity.

"You know, the usual…clothes, shoes, a couple of pieces of jewelry," Amanda answered casually. Jessica stood there with a huge smile plastered on her face.

"Wow, from where? I'm so glad you went shopping. You should have called me," Jessica said completely oblivious to the lies rolling off Amanda's tongue. As bad as Amanda wanted to twist up her face at both Melanie and Jessica she chuckled and pretended to be just as excited as Jessica.

"Well mostly the stores on Michigan Avenue and State Street," Amanda smirked. Melanie and Jessica looked at each other and chuckled.

"There are plenty of stores on Michigan Avenue and State Street. You have your Gucci and you have your TJ Maxx," Melanie said revealing a devilish smirk while maintaining eye contact with Amanda. "You also have—"

"Look," Amanda glanced at her watch, "As much as I would love to stay here and finish this conversation, I'd hate to waste the remainder of my lunch." Amanda faked another smile before excusing herself out of the conversation and walking off. She heard Jessica let out a row of giggles behind her and made a mental note to keep her at a distance. She walked back into her cubicle and plopped down in her chair.

"Hey," Amanda spun around in her chair to see Jessica standing there with a smile on her face. She stepped in closer and whispered to Amanda. "What are you doin' a little later?

"Why?" Amanda asked with a raised eyebrow. She and Jessica had never hung out together outside of the work although they often left the premises for lunch. Even then, they either had lunch at a fast food place or window shopped on State Street. As far as Amanda was concerned, there were her work friends and there were her real friends.

"Well, I'm having a few friends over for drinks and games. Just wanted to know if you were interested in hanging out?"

Amanda threw her head back and laughed aloud. "Wow, you're actually asking me to hang out with you. That's...weird."

Jessica folded her arms across her chest and screwed up her face in annoyance. "Oh that's right, I forgot, I'm just the little white girl from work." Jessica said sarcastically while her facial expression remained serious. Amanda's laughter came to a halt. She had never heard such words come from Jessica's mouth. She and Jessica had a stare off contest until Amanda spun around in her chair to face her computer.

"What is that supposed to mean?" Amanda asked offended.

"It's because I'm white you don't want to hang out with me."

"That has got to be the dumbest thing I've ever heard. I can't even believe we're having this stupid conversation."

"I mean come on Amanda, I—"

"Listen up," Amanda rose out of her seat and stood directly in front of Jessica petite figure, "It ain't got shit to do with yo' got damn skin color. I don't even know you like that to be kickin' it with you. Don't get it twisted honey, you cool, but I don't—"

Jessica let out a loud laughter interrupting Amanda's response.

"Chill out! It was a joke, Amanda." She let out another laugh before embracing Amanda. Amanda playfully shoved Jessica away from her before letting out a few chuckles herself. "No, but seriously," Jessica said in between laughter, "you're more than welcomed to come hang out if you like."

"I don't know. I have tons of things to do," Amanda said feeling a little embarrassed.

Jessica, sensing her uneasiness, smiled. "Well whatever, just give me a call if you're up for it." She turned and walked away. Amanda sat down in her chair and shook her head confused. She glanced at her cell phone and thought about calling Reggie. He had called her once over the weekend and she didn't bother to answer or return the phone call. She picked up the phone and looked at the time. Five minutes left before she was to clock back in. She scrolled through her contacts in search for his number.

"Wow that is so thoughtful of him," she heard a colleague say in the midst of a bunch of girlish giggles. She went back to the home screen of her phone deciding to peek out of her office instead. She got up and walked out of her cubicle. She was shocked to see Melanie, surrounded by the majority of the women in the department, holding a dozen pink roses. She was smiling from ear to ear.

"And it's not even Valentine's Day," another worker responded.

"He's the sweetest," Melanie said as she headed towards her office with a few workers following closely behind her. Amanda rolled her eyes before turning away and walking back into her office.

****

Amanda headed home from work in her red Mitsubishi Eclipse. She turned up the radio and let the soft jazz tunes play as she periodically checked herself in the rearview mirror. She leaned her head against the headrest as she drove, replaying the image of Melanie and the roses in her head over and over again. She couldn't wait to get home and chat with her cousin. After finally exiting off Lake Shore Drive she slowed at a red light. Beep Beep. She looked to her left. It was a man in an old black BMW. She hated when people paraded around in old version luxury models like they were still the hottest cars out. He waved at her and smiled before rolling down his passenger side window.

"I just wanted to tell you that I think you are so pretty." The gentleman smiled.

She half smiled at him, annoyed, and made a right turn. After pulling up in front of her home she went running straight to the front door. Before she could pull her keys out of her bag the front door opened and Stephanie appeared.

"Hey girl, I'm on my way to the nail salon, you want to come?"

"Girl yes," Amanda replied after looking down at her nails. "I caught you just in time. You won't believe what happened today."

"Does it have anything to do with that pathetic boss of yours?"

Amanda revealed an evil grin. "You know it does."

"Girl, get to it!" Stephanie said as they headed back out and hopped into her shiny black BMW truck.

After their evening of manicures and pedicures, Amanda lay in bed flipping through old issues of Essence magazines. The soft tunes of music played on her nearby lap top. She climbed out of her bed and walked over to her closet. The drab selection of clothes meant a shopping spree was definitely needed. She shook her head while staring in the mirror. Those darn Essence magazines always made her crave a transformation to become a total knockout. She knew she had it going on and was tired of down playing herself. She stood examining her eyes, skin, and the rest of her facial features closely. She turned away from the mirror when she heard her cell phone ring and picked it up.

"Hey you," she cooed into the phone.

"I thought I wasn't gonna hear from you anymore."

"Now why would you think that?" she asked Reggie, pretending to be unaware of her distant behavior.

"I called you and—"

"Yeah, I'm sorry, I've just been extremely busy," she said cutting him off hoping he bought her lie. "You forgive me?" she flirted as she paced back and forth with a wide grin on her face.

"I don't know, I think you got some makin' up to do," Reggie teased.

"What kind of makin' up?" she asked in a sensual tone of voice.

"How about you let me come over and chill with you for the evening."

Amanda paused and scanned herself again in the floor length mirror before responding. "What time we talkin' about?"

"I'm already in your neck of the woods."

Fuck, Amanda thought. She began rummaging through her drawers. "Ok," she said.

"All right, I'll be there in ten minutes."

"Make it twenty." she said before hanging up and tossing her phone on the bed. She put on a pair of short pink shorts and a white tank. She ran water through her soft tresses, showing off her naturally curly texture, still allowing it to remain wild to give herself that in the house look. She put on a hint of lip gloss and dabbed herself with sweet smelling perfume. She put away the Essence magazines and turned up the volume on her computer. Luckily for her, she had already tidied up her room and washed the dishes in the kitchen sink before she started surfing the web and flipping through magazines.

She made her way towards the front room just as the bell sounded. She scanned the living room and kitchen to make sure it was decent enough for company. She peeked out the window. Reggie stood outside the front gate scoping out his surroundings. She buzzed him in and smiled when she opened the front door. He stared at her and grinned as he made his way up the stairs into the apartment.

"How you doin', sweetheart?" he asked wrapping his arms around her waist as she wrapped hers around his neck.

"I'm fine," Amanda replied smiling up at him still embraced.

"This is a pretty cool pad you got here," he said looking around after they pulled away.

"Yeah, I share it with my cousin."

"Your cousin?" he asked alarmed.

"Yeah," Amanda chuckled. "She's a few years older than me. She ain't here though, so you won't get grilled today," she teased.

Reggie laughed. "Oh she like that? I gotta' pass a test or somethin'?"

Amanda nodded her head as she led him down the corridor to her bedroom. "She's definitely a character."

"Oh really? Well, so am I," Reggie responded his eyes glued to Amanda's behind as he followed like a little puppy dog. She spun around and his eyes darted away taking in other objects. Amanda sat on her queen sized bed.

"So, this is my room," she said. Reggie looked around at the espresso wood colored queen size bed, dresser and night stand. A thirty two inch was mounted on the wall across from the bed. Her bed was decorated with ivory linen and tons of decorative pillows which added femininity and a look of luxury. A few small flower arrangements and candles placed sporadically throughout the room.

"Way too much home network channel for you, missy." He teased.

She burst into laughter. "My cousin helped me out a bit."

"Well you two need to work on my little bachelor pad."

"Oh, is it in need of a woman's touch?" she looked at him and smiled. He sat on the bed next to her and looked in her eyes.

"Yeah," he answered smoothly enough to make Amanda blush and look away. He chuckled and looked up towards the dresser at a framed picture of her and a girl that looked somewhat familiar to him. He reached for the picture and examined it closely. "Oh, this was your little buddy from the spot that night, right?" He chuckled as he replayed the night in his head.

Amanda twisted up her face as she also recalled the night in her head. "Yeah, that's Tiffany silly ass," she laughed.

Reggie shook his head in disbelief. "So have ya'll talked since she threw that drink on you?"

"Yeah, I mean that's my girl and things happen."

"I guess," he replied after putting the picture back on the dresser.

"What you mean you guess?" Amanda snapped. "You act like ya'll had a fallin' out or somethin'!"

"I just think she was a little insane for throwin' a drink on you, that's all."

Amanda rolled her eyes. "Anyway, you ought to be happy. Here you are now."

Reggie laughed. "I'm so thankful she threw that drink on you. It really changed my life." he said staring up at the ceiling. They both chuckled.

"You laughin' but it's probably the truth," Amanda said smiling as she crossed her legs. Reggie eyes scanned over curvaceous frame. Amanda noticed and ran a hand along her thigh.

"I see you bein' a little tease," Reggie flirted.

"A tease, no, of course not," she flirted back before standing up and walking out the room. "You thirsty?" she called out to him as she walked down the hall towards the kitchen. She opened the refrigerator and bent over as she searched the fridge for refreshments. Reggie walked up on her and pressed himself up against her backside causing her to look up. He wrapped his arms around her waist from behind as she turned to face him. A sly smile formed across his face. Amanda nearly burned a hole into him with her bedroom eyes. She made circles with her index finger across his chest as she spoke.

"I asked you a question, Reggie." Amanda smiled.

"What you ask me, sweetheart?"

"Are you thirsty?"

"Yeah."

"What you want?"

"I want you," He replied before he leaned in and kissed her on her lips. She returned the kiss this time making it a little more intimate as her tongue slid partially into his mouth. Reggie's hands cupped Amanda's behind causing her to let out a soft sensual moan. With her arms wrapped around his neck and his arms around her waist they continued with their kissing session. The front door swung opened and in walked Stephanie and her mother. Amanda pushed Reggie back in the knick of time. Stephanie was no fool. She smiled at Reggie and Amanda before sitting her designer bag down and extending a manicured hand.

"Well, who is this fine gentleman?" Stephanie teased as her and Reggie shook hands. With her lips drawn into a thin line, Amanda ignored her cousin as she made her way over to her aunt.

"Hey auntie," Amanda said as she wrapped her arms around the lady's neck. The saying was true in the case of her aunt and cousin. The apple doesn't fall to far from the tree. Stephanie and her mother were spitting images of each other in terms of looks and personality. Amanda's aunt, Sheryl, stayed dressed in designer suits, armed with killer shoes and handbags. A marriage of fourteen years, which ended a year ago, to a very well to do business man allowed her and her daughter to live quite comfortably and help mold Stephanie to the savvy woman she is today.

"Hi dear, how are you, sweetheart?" Aunt Sheryl asked as she hugged her and kissed her cheeks. She pulled back and examined Amanda. "You're still so beautiful."

Amanda laughed and glanced over at Reggie who was engrossed in a conversation with Stephanie.

"Well you make sure you do that," Amanda heard Stephanie say as she made her way back into the kitchen and stood next to her.

"Make sure he do what?" Amanda asked eagerly.

"Make sure he does what?" Aunt Sheryl corrected. "You ladies are far too intelligent to speak like you've had no education."

Reggie looked at Amanda with a smirk on his face. He leaned over and kissed her cheek.

"I'm gonna head out. I'll give you a call later," he whispered.

Amanda frowned at Stephanie before she turned and followed Reggie to the front door. As soon as Reggie was out she turned to face her aunt and cousin who stood side by side in the kitchen looking on at her.

"Reggie is it?" Aunt Sheryl asked, peeling a banana. Amanda walked into the kitchen and planted herself on one of the barstools surrounding the island.

"Yes," Amanda answered annoyed.

"Well we didn't mean to interrupt your little session you had goin' on here." Stephanie smirked. Amanda rolled her eyes and shifted her weight to one leg before shooting her cousin a menacing look.

"Stephanie don't you start with me. What did you say to him?"

"None of your business," Stephanie teased.

Amanda folded her arms across her chest. "It's cool, he'll tell me."

"So how's everything?" Aunt Sheryl asked no one in particular.

"Mom, everything is great, my finances are great, my love life is great, my..."

"Love life?" Aunt Sheryl asked seemingly surprised. "Well, who's the lucky man?"

Amanda chuckled. "Yeah Stephanie, who's the lucky man?" Stephanie reached into the refrigerator and grabbed a can of Coke. She took a sip and sat it on the counter in front of her as she ran a hand along her gray cashmere cardigan before twirling a strand of her hair.

"Well," Stephanie began, her eyes avoiding contact with Amanda's. "A special guy I met some time ago."

Aunt Sheryl's eyebrows rose. "Wow, what's his name and why haven't you mentioned him before?"

"Oh, I was going to, but you know...I just didn't," she lied, shrugged and sipped her soda.

"Yeah Auntie, he's such a secret." Amanda taunted. Stephanie nearly choked on her drink as she placed the can on the counter top once again with a tight lip smile.

"Well mom...his name is Mike, he's a construction worker and he's a very good man."

Aunt Sheryl sat on one of the barstools and smiled. "Well," she said to her daughter unimpressed with Stephanie's summary, "Any children? Where does he live? What's his credit score for goodness sakes?"

Amanda let out a giggle. Stephanie frowned as she glanced at her younger cousin. She folded her arms in front of her and turned her attention towards her mother.

"His credit score, mom? Give me a break."

"Well if you're lounging around with the man I hope you have enough decency to know more than just his penis size!" Aunt Sheryl snapped.

"Humph, I guess she told you!" Amanda said with a huge smile, showing off her pearly whites.

"Shut up, Amanda! The same rules apply to you. I would hate for you to end up like your mother."

The room fell silent. Amanda's smile faded and Stephanie unfolded her arms.

"Mom, you shouldn't have..."

"And what exactly is wrong with my mother?" Amanda interrupted, raising her voice a pitch or two.

"Well honey, she's a wonderful woman, but I think it was an unwise decision to follow that man to California!"

"That man is her husband so what exactly is the problem?" Amanda challenged.

"Well that man still had a wife while she was following up behind him."

"Well sounds just like someone else I know!"

Again the room went silent. Aunt Sheryl sat alarmed as she stared at her daughter and then at her niece confused. Tight lipped Stephanie finally loosened her lips and sipped her Coke.

"Mom, what would you like for dinner?"

"Just take me home!" Aunt Sheryl insisted.

"But mom, I thought..."

"Maybe you should just do what the woman ask for once!" Amanda snapped before sliding off the bar stool and heading down the hall.

"Mom just go wait in the car, I'll be there in a minute," Amanda heard Stephanie yell behind her, followed by high heels clicking against the wooden floorboards. Once in her room, Amanda sat on her bed. Stephanie stormed in and stood over her.

"If you ever pull some shit like that again, it's on!" Stephanie whispered to Amanda. "I don't need her all in my business!"

"Well keep your fuckin' mouth closed!" Amanda got up in her face. Stephanie took a couple of steps back. It was obvious Amanda wasn't dealing with any of her attitudes today. Besides, her mother did get a little out of hand.

"Look, I know what my mother said...you know how she just says things."

"Don't make excuses for her. She was out of line!"

"Well my mother is—"

"Fuck your mother!" Amanda yelled. "I'm so tired—"

"Look, save it! I gotta' go. We can discuss this later." Stephanie dismissed herself leaving Amanda boiling with fury.

CHAPTER 6

"So girl, do you work with any fine men?" Tiffany asked toying with her hair while looking in her compact mirror. She and Amanda were nestled in the back of a taxi cab.

"Not really...I mean hopefully people bring cute friends."

"I wonder if Stephanie's man is gonna be there," she laughed. Amanda smirked at her.   "Stephanie will get in yo' ass! You've been warned."

"I'm not scared of her! She got his wife to worry about!" They laughed. "So does she know about this dinner?"

"No, it would have been a mess especially if he's there!"

"Uh-huh, you sure you weren't on any cock block stuff." Tiffany said flipping the mirror close and looking over at her friend sneering. Amanda looked over at her and smacked her lips.

"Whatever! He fine and all, but I ain't tryin' to be a part of that mess!" Amanda snapped, looking out the window towards lake Michigan as they rode to her job's dinner function.

"What the hell is this dinner for anyway?"

"I don't even know. I think it's an employee appreciation dinner or some crap like that."

"You don't sound too enthused."

"I'm fine, it's no big deal. I see those people everyday." Amanda glanced at Tiffany and back out the window again, resting her head back. "It's so much traffic!"

After finally arriving on Pearson, across from the Water Tower Place, Amanda paid the fare and the two hopped out the cab and strutted towards the entrance of the restaurant like they owned the place. Once inside and directed to there party area, Amanda and Tiffany took seats at a nearly empty table while a number of Amanda's coworkers mingled and socialized with one another. Both Amanda and Tiffany gazed around the room.

"Girl there he is," Amanda whispered to Tiffany while pointing. Tiffany eyes traveled around the room until they landed on Amanda's target. Melanie and her husband stood together smiling and laughing with one another.

"You see him? He's full of shit! Look at him pretendin' to be some devoted husband!" Amanda snapped, not taking her eyes off of Melanie's handsome husband, who looked like he belonged on the front cover of GQ magazine. He cast a glance in their direction. Melanie's eyes followed. She smiled and grabbed her husband's hand as they headed towards Amanda and Tiffany.

"Well, get ready, here they come," Tiffany chuckled as she forced a smile on her face. Amanda ran a hand through her hair. If she were able to reach into her clutch and pull out a compact mirror to check her hair and makeup without looking obvious, she would have. She knew she looked fabulous in her black V neck dress, accentuating her curves with a pair of black patent peep toe heels, courtesy of Stephanie. Tiffany opted for a charcoal gray sleeveless pencil dress with her hair pulled back, revealing her pearl earrings, giving her sassiness a touch of elegance.

Melanie smiled before extending her arm across the table towards Tiffany.

"And you are?" Melanie asked in a chipper voice. Amanda and Tiffany looked at each other and then at Melanie who dropped her arm to her side. Mike chuckled, eyeing Amanda on the sly.

"Excuse my wife. She had a little too much to drink. It's an open bar, feel free to help yourselves."

Tiffany smiled as she looked Mike over. Amanda stared at her and cleared her throat. Tiffany's smile faded. "I'm Tiffany," she blurted out. She stood to give Mike a better view of her frame. He observed and shook her hand. Melanie also shook Tiffany's hand.

"You must be Amanda's friend?"

"Obviously," Tiffany said as she sat back in her seat. Amanda quickly extended her arm and shook hands with the couple to divert attention from her rude friend.

"Amanda, its really nice to see you. I didn't think you'd make it," Melanie replied. Her smile fading with each word she spoke. "Your dress is rather…lovely."

"Thank you," Amanda said through clinched teeth.

"Baby," Mike said to his wife, obviously aware of the tension, "How about you go and order me a drink?"

"Right now?" Melanie asked sounding a little aloof.

"Yeah, I'll be over right after I go to the bathroom." He pecked her on the cheek. She smiled and looked over at Amanda and Tiffany before heading off towards the bar. Tiffany shook her head and Amanda rolled her eyes.

"Some wife, huh?" Tiffany asked cheesing from ear to ear.

"Tiffany," Amanda said surprised by her friend's outburst. "Girl, behave—"

"Oh no, it's cool," Mike said not taking his eyes off Amanda. He looked around to make sure his wife was across the room before kneeling down and speaking in a whisper to Amanda and Tiffany.

"So how are you lovely ladies doin'?" he asked.

"We're fine," Amanda answered, reapplying lip gloss to her pair of full lips.

"You really are," Mike replied not breaking eye contact with her. She couldn't help but smile.

"You are really bold with your wife bein' here and all," Tiffany said before putting her glass to her lips and taking a sip of her water. Amanda and Mike looked over at her in awkwardness.

"Well it's nice meetin' you ladies, I'll see you around." He smiled as if it was his first time seeing Amanda. She watched him as he walked off headed towards his wife.

"Don't drool all over yourself," Tiffany teased. "He has a wife and your cousin."

Amanda laughed. "Girl I'm not studyin' him. He's pure entertainment for me."

"Bitch please, who do you take me for? You were lookin' at him like you were ready to rip his clothes off!"

"No, he was lookin' at me like he was ready to rip mine off."

Tiffany smacked her lip. "Well, whatever the case is, you better watch it!"

"You don't have to warn me! You better watch it. I saw you checkin' him out too!"

"Too? See, you were lookin' at him! Some cousin you are."

Amanda and Tiffany laughed.

"He's a handsome man, but that does not mean I want him. He plays it cool."

Tiffany rolled her eyes. "How about we go and get ourselves a drink," she said as she stood up and made her way around the table. Amanda followed along. After a little dancing and mingling they returned to their seats.

"Maybe I should give him a call. I think he has a big dick too!" Amanda slurred her words after four drinks. Tiffany laughed like it was the funniest thing she'd ever heard. She was still working on her third drink. She has a higher tolerance level for alcohol.

"What's his number? You want me to call him?" Tiffany asked scrolling through Amanda's phone.

"Who?" Amanda asked confused.

A few of Amanda's coworkers were on the dance floor while others conversed near the bar or nibbled away at what was left on their plates. The crowd dwindled the later it became. Amanda and Tiffany both extremely buzzed sat glued to their seats cracking up at each other's nonsense.

"Reggie, ain't that his name?" Tiffany asked, still probing through her friend's phone. You have all these men numbers in here and no man?"

They explode with laughter causing a few heads to turn their way including Jessica's. She smiled in their direction before heading over.

"Oh shit here this bitch come," Amanda moaned. Tiffany frowned.

"Who the hell is she?" Tiffany asked in a whisper.

"Hey Amanda," Jessica said in her happy go lucky voice. "Wow you guys had quite a few drinks!" Jessica said, taking note of the empty glasses on the table.

"Who are you?" Tiffany asked a little harshly. Jessica's smile faded. Amanda laughed, encouraging Tiffany's abrasive attitude.

Jessica looked at Tiffany and back to Amanda waiting for Amanda to speak up and introduce her to her friend. Jessica finally extended her hand to Tiffany while Amanda continued to laugh.

"I'm Jessica, Amanda's coworker."

Tiffany fidgeted with her earring with one hand and wrapped her free hand around her drink. Jessica, feeling slightly uneasy, let her arm fall to her side. Amanda was too out of the loop to address Tiffany's rude behavior this time.

"Nice to meet you Jessie," Tiffany said dryly.

"It's Jessica!" Jessica corrected her.

"Look Jessica, Jessie, or whatever the hell you want it to be, I don't really care." Tiffany snapped. Amanda nearly fell out of her chair in laughter. Jessica frowned up her face and trotted off in her navy satin dress and matching navy heels. Melanie walked over to the girls eager to join in on all the fun. She had one too many drinks herself. Her now unkempt hair no longer matched her brown sophisticated scoop neck dress she was wearing.

"Ladies, ladies what's so amusing?" she asked seating herself in one of the empty chairs at the table.

"You," Tiffany replied before all three ladies bellowed in laughter.

"What about me?" Melanie asked excitedly.

Mike made his way over to the table before Tiffany could respond. "Well honey, it's gettin' pretty late," he said glancing at his watch. The laughter ceased as all three women had a stare off contest. Melanie was completely oblivious to the other sets of eyes taking in every inch of her husband. He wasn't.

"Do we have to go now?" Melanie asked her husband like a little child. She was far more relaxed and less uptight with alcohol in her system.

"Yeah do we have to go now?" Amanda chimed in giggling and twirling a strand of her hair. Mike looked at his wife and then to Amanda. He gave her a smile and took his wife's hand.

"Yeah baby, you need your beauty rest," he said in a smooth seductive voice catching the other two women off guard. He peeked over at them and caught them staring him down. Melanie drunkenly kissed him on the cheek as he helped her out her chair. She wrapped an arm around his neck.

"Wait, how are you ladies getting home?"

"Taxi," Amanda called out and waved her hands in the air as if she was actually flagging down a cab driver.

Tiffany laughed as she stood up and adjusted herself. "Let's go, drunken lady," she said to Amanda, pulling her out of her chair.

"Oh no no no, there's no way we're gonna let you ladies take a cab home. Honey, do you mind?" Melanie asked her husband before kissing him on the lips. Amanda and Tiffany both rolled their eyes in annoyance. Mike noticed and smirked.

"Not a problem, sweetheart."

****

After the foursome hopped into Mike's liquid silver Jaguar, he sped off with Melanie sitting slouched on the passenger side. Amanda and Tiffany sat in the back whispering to one another over the soft music playing on the radio.

"I can't believe he's takin' us home. Some nerve of him!" Amanda whispered to Tiffany as she searched her purse for her lip gloss.

"As long as I didn't have to hop back into a raggedy ass cab, I'm fine with his...kind gesture." Tiffany teased and nudged her drunken friend. "You might want to have him drop you off at the end of the block. We wouldn't want your cousin makin' a scene with your boss." She chuckled. "You better hope she doesn't find out about this."

Amanda gazed at the side of Mike's face, ignoring Tiffany altogether. When he caught her looking at him in the rearview, he glanced back and smiled before returning his eyes to the road. Tiffany carelessly elbowed Amanda.

"Ouch," Amanda said a little too loudly, feeling stupor. Melanie looked back this time with a drunken look on her face.

"I know…I know. You girls are tired," Melanie said to them like they were her younger daughters sitting in the backseat. She was obviously out of her mind. She laughed after everything she said. "Honey would you mind droppin' me off first. I need…to get some rest," she yawned and looked over at him waiting for his response. Mike shook his head annoyed with his wife's behavior. Amanda and Tiffany eyes were glued to him, anxiously awaiting his reply.

Amanda leaned over and whispered in Tiffany's ear. "I see why he sleeps around!" Tiffany smiled as she nodded her head in agreement.

Mike let out a long exhale before responding, "Not a problem, sweetheart."

"Is that your response to everything," Tiffany blurted out from the backseat. Everyone turned their heads to look at her.

Mike kept his eyes on the road. "Not to everything," he said as he turned the corner.

"Oh, so you just like to keep your words to a minimum? Short and sweet." Tiffany continued now smiling as she waited for his response. Amanda couldn't help but shake her head before laughing. The alcohol is the only thing that kept her from going off on her flirtatious friend. Amanda's eyes stayed focused on Mike's every facial expression. She watched his lips curl up when responding to Tiffany. He looked over at Melanie and then quickly towards the backseat. He was only able to view Amanda since she sat behind Melanie.

"Not all the time," he said as he pulled up in front of a beautiful brownstone home. He hopped out walked around the car to Melanie's side. When he opened her door she nearly tumbled out. Amanda and Tiffany looked on as he helped her out out of the car and walked her into what they assumed was their house.

"Girl that is one fine man!" Amanda said loudly.

"I knew you were starin' at him! You checkin' out your boss's husband? What a shame." Tiffany teased, shaking her head in disapproval, roaring with laughter.

"Oh please, like you weren't flirtin' your ass off," they giggled as Amanda did an impersonation of Tiffany's questions to Mike.

"I bet he wants to add my coochie to his list!" Tiffany said, checking herself out in the rearview mirror. She didn't catch Amanda rolling her eyes.

"Ugh, you always think somebody want to freak on you." Amanda teased, holding back a laugh.

Tiffany continued fixing her stray hairs. She blew herself a kiss in the mirror and settled down into her warm seat in the back. She applied more lip gloss to her lips and turned to her annoyed friend and smiled. "Am I sexy or what?" she asked putting her lip gloss back into her clutch and crossing her legs seductively. Amanda was no longer able to contain her laughter.

"You are so fuckin' full of it!" Amanda said staring her friend up and down. She had always admired her Tiffany's confidence.

"And what's wrong with that? Just because you're a modest bitch doesn't mean I have to be one. Hell if you're flyy then you're flyy as simple as that," Tiffany said snapping her fingers mid air in a circular motion. They laughed until they saw Mike emerge from the house. They simultaneously fidgeted around with their hair and dresses like two nervous girls going on a date for the first time. "What you primpin' yourself for?" Tiffany teased. "You plan on messin' with your boss's man?"

Amanda stopped running her hands through her hair and placed them on her lap. She responded with a cold "No."

Mike opened the car door and slid into the front seat. He looked towards the back at the two beautiful ladies and smiled. "Feel free to hop in the front seat," he said to no one in particular. If he had his pick he'd prefer Amanda. The girls looked at each other after he turned away. Amanda, surprising herself and her friend, opened her door and stepped outside the car. Tiffany pouted and folded her arms, shaking her head at her friend who paid her antics no mind. Instead Amanda adjusted her dress as she opened the passenger side door and slid into the front seat. Mike looked her over like a hungry dog and grinned before driving off. She smiled back at him.

"How did I get so lucky?" Mike said looking over at Amanda and then in the rearview mirror at Tiffany. The remark took both girls by surprise.

"Lucky how?" Tiffany asked leaning eagerly towards the front seat.

"How did I end up with the pleasure of takin' two sexy women home?" He smirked. He spoke so casually that for a second even they forgot he had just dropped off his wife.

Tiffany smiled back and responded dryly, "Your wife asked you to."

Amanda wanted to reach in the back seat and give her a good slap in the mouth instead she maintained her composure and let out a flirty laugh. Mike sighed, ignored the comment, and continued driving.

"So where do you stay, Ms. Sassy Mouth?" he asked playfully. Again Amanda let out a laugh. The alcohol still had her and her friend buzzed. Tiffany rolled her eyes. It was apparent he was getting rid of her first.

"Twenty Sixth and Indiana," she said and slouched back into her seat like an angry loser. Amanda always has the hottest guys chasing her and she just lets them all go to waste, she thought.

"How about you just crash at my place?" Amanda suggested like a little school girl. Tiffany paid her no mind. Amanda turned half way in her seat and looked at her friend with a huge grin glued on her face. "You don't want to spend the night with me?" Amanda teased allowing the alcohol to get the best of her. Mike looked over at Amanda. He seized the opportunity to let his eyes roam her curvaceous body. Hell, he wished he had a chance to spend the night with her. He felt himself stiffen in between his legs as he undressed her with his eyes. She thoughtlessly sat back in her seat and looked over at him. She had caught him observing her. She adjusted herself in her seat and crossed her legs causing her dress to raise a couple of inches, exposing her thighs. Tiffany sat quietly in the back staring out the window while nodding off.

When Mike pulled up in front of her apartment building he reached towards the back and tapped Tiffany on her knee. She yawned as she opened her eyes and stretched her arms. She sat still for a moment in a daze.

"Do you mind pullin' up a little further, I'm wearin' heels," she said as she reached for the door handle. She tended to become a bitch when she was tired. Mike pressed his foot on the gas to let the car accelerate a few inches and then stopped. Tiffany smacked her lips as she opened the car door and stepped out. Mike and Amanda watched her from inside as she adjusted her clothes and wobbled off in her heels. She then stopped halfway towards the building and turned back to face the car. Amanda rolled down her window. "Can you at least walk me to my door?" Tiffany shouted struggling to stay balanced in her four inch heels.

Mike looked over at Amanda and then past her out the window at Tiffany. He shook his head highly irritated. "Your friend is somethin' else," he said before opening the door and climbing out. He walked around the front of the car over to Tiffany. She happily placed her arm around him as he escorted her to the entrance of the building. She looked back towards the car and smiled. As they neared the entrance Tiffany tugged on her dress.

"Thank you, I don't think I could have made it in these shoes," she lied.

Mike forced a smile. "No problem, sweetheart." He chuckled. "I'm glad I could be of some sort of assistance."

"Can you assist me upstairs?" Tiffany continued. The thought of ripping her clothes off and climbing on top of her crossed Mike's mind, but he pushed the thoughts aside and shook his head.

"As much as I would love to, I don't want to leave your friend down here by her lonesome. She's just as messed up as you are right now."

"Like you give a damn. Well keep it movin' then," she said, stumbling through the entrance of her building and letting the door close behind her. He watched through the glass door as she fumbled with her keys, jiggling each one into the keyhole until the second door finally opened. He shook his head and walked back towards the car.

"Did she make it in safely?" Amanda asked like she didn't closely observe him and Tiffany from where she sat.

"Yeah she's cool," he said letting out a long exhale. "So, where to?" he asked before pulling off.

"You ask that like we have other options or somethin'." Amanda looked him over. He stared casually over at her.

"We can have options," he said returning his eyes back to the road.

Amanda let out a giggle apparently still feeling buzzed. Without much thought she blurted out her address and leaned her head against the head rest and closed her eyes. Mike took a moment to look her over once again. He let his eyes skim over her thighs and the bit of cleavage showing. She opened her eyes and he returned his to the road, beeping at a slow driver.

"No need to rush," Amanda said, sitting up in her seat.

"I'm not rushin'. I'm tryin' to hold on to this moment."

Amanda felt her face turning red as she smiled. "No need to hold on to this moment when we can have more," she said in a sensual voice. Mike nearly swerved out of his lane in surprise. "Relax. I'm just teasin'," Amanda chuckled. Mike snickered, pulled over, and parked near a small playground located around the corner from her apartment. Amanda stared out the window into the darkness and emptiness of the playground. She turned to face him and smirked. "Why are we here?" she finally asked.

"I told you I'm tryin' to hold on to this moment with you. I figure it wouldn't hurt if we sat and chatted for a bit. I mean if you don't mind. If you do we can leave," he said retuning his key to the ignition.

"Oh no, it's fine," Amanda chuckled slapping his hand away from the steering wheel. "I'm in no rush." She checked the time on her phone. 1:36. she slid it back into her purse.

"Expectin' a call?"

"No," Amanda shook her head. She looked him over admiring his sharp features and sexy goatee once again. He leaned his seat back a little and laid back before looking over at her. Amanda fidgeted with her hands while he rubbed his hand over his shiny bald head.

"So was that your boyfriend I saw you with at the restaurant?"

Amanda shook her head. "We're just friends."

"You sure about that? You guys looked like more than just friends."

"Just friends." Amanda repeated as she turned sideways in her seat to face him.

"You look so good," he said staring at her legs. She smiled while twirling a strand of hair around her index finger. "I'm sure you hear that lot."

"Yeah, I hear it enough," she said confidently. "You're pretty handsome you're damn self."

Mike let out a chuckle and bit his bottom lip as he continued eyeing Amanda's thighs, not caring if she caught him staring this time. "I like your dress, you look really sexy tonight. I couldn't keep my eyes off of you."

Amanda held eye contact. "I noticed."

"I hope you don't mind how straight forward I am. Sometimes I just can't help myself. I mean me and my wife—"

"Shhhhh," she said pressing her finger against his lips. "It's ok…some things are pretty temptin'." She let out a laugh. A mixture of the alcohol and the sight of a sexy man had her moist. She crossed her legs fighting to rid herself of the pulsating feeling that was going on in between her legs.

"What you crossin' your legs for?" Mike teased. "You tryin' to keep me away?" he asked seductively, sending Amanda's kinky thoughts over the edge. She shifted in her seat but nothing helped. Mike observed. A wily grin formed across his face. "You okay over there? Are you comfortable enough?" he asked not really concerned if she was or wasn't.

"I could be better." she said rubbing a hand along her thigh.

Mike let out a quiet laugh before he leaned over and kissed her on the lips. A low sensual moaned escaped Amanda's mouth. She grabbed his chin and returned the kiss with a little tongue action to heat things up. Seconds later he was pulling her towards him with her dress rising little by little until she was mounted on top of him. Her curly hair hung wildly about her head, shifting every time her head moved. Their breathing became heavier and heavier as the heavy petting grew more extreme. "Pull it out." Amanda demanded raising up her dress revealing a pair of red lace thongs and a plump ass. Mike grabbed and caressed it before slipping a finger inside of her. She moaned again while kissing his neck.

"You sure you ready for it, baby?" he asked, unzipping his pants.

"I've been ready for it!" Amanda kissed his lips and brushed his hand away from his zipper. She reached into his pants and pulled out nine inches of stiffness. "Ooooo," she moaned as she massaged him. She placed her bottom on the passenger seat before leaning over and wrapping her lips around his hardness.

"Mmmmmmm," he moaned letting his head fall back against the seat while he grabbed onto the back of her head, pushing her head down further. He let his free hand slide across her ass and placed two fingers inside of her. "Nice and wet just the way I like it." He slid his fingers out and slapped her on her bottom. He watched her as she bobbled her head up and down faster and faster. "Hurry up baby, come sit on it." He slapped her butt again before she let it slide out her mouth.

She giggled. "Hurry up before someone sees us."

He opened the car door, got out, and sat in the back seat. She climbed into the back, ass in air. He pulled her on top of him. She slid her panties off, grabbed his dick, and took him in inch by inch until he was fully inside of her. They both moaned in union. He thrust himself in and out as she bounced on top of him while moaning uncontrollably.

"You feel so good," she managed to say, as her hips gyrated on top of him. He pressed his firm masculine hands against her butt cheeks. She bounced up and down so hard her breast came out of her dress. He sucked and held them as she continued to ride him. No words escaped his mouth, only little sounds of pure ecstasy.

"Bend over," he said after raising her off of him. She propped herself on all fours in the back seat as best as she could while he entered from behind, with one knee on the seat to keep him balanced. Amanda bit her bottom lip and threw her head back in delight. This was her favorite position. Her whimpers grew louder and louder with each stroke. He cupped a hand over her mouth as he watched her behind wiggle to and fro making him even more excited. He gave it a few slaps as he pumped her more aggressively. "This what you wanted, right," he said, taking in the pleasure. "You got some good shit." Smack.

Ooooooooooos and aaaaaaaaaahhhhhhhs were the only noises escaping Amanda's mouth. She managed to lift her head every few seconds to look back at him but kept it buried against the leather seats for the most part. She threw herself against him as he forced himself in, heightening the sensation until he felt himself ready to explode. After watching the sticky substance ooze down her behind, he reached into the compartment between the seats and tossed her a few random fast food napkins. He fell back onto the seat breathing heavily, exhausted from the workout while she struggled to clean herself with no help from him.

He pulled up his pants and left his shirt half way unbuttoned exposing some of his smooth muscular chest.

"God, you're so much better than your cousin," he mumbled.

Amanda tossed the paper napkins out the window before letting her dress fall over her behind as she sat upright.

"What did you just say?" she asked, now giving him her undivided attention hoping he didn't say what she thought she had heard.

"I said you're so much better than your cousin," he responded, turning his head to face her.

His response sobered her right up.

"Wait a minute! You knew who I was all along?" she asked harshly.

"Stephanie is your cousin, right? You do stay around the corner. You gave me your address, remember?"

"Yeah, but I didn't give you the apartment number!"

"I saw a couple of pictures of you around the crib."

Amanda turned away from him in total astonishment. She shook her head in disbelief. "Wait a minute let me get this straight! You're tellin' me that you knew I was Stephanie's cousin all along and you continued to pursue me?"

Mike nodded his head. "I wouldn't quite call it a pursuit. I don't see what your point is!" he said, now buttoning the rest of his shirt totally nonchalant about the situation.

"You just had sex with me!" She snapped turning her body towards him. "You had sex with me knowin' who I was, knowin' that Stephanie was my cousin?"

A scowl formed across Mike's face. "She ain't my fuckin' cousin! Why the fuck would I give a fuck about her bein' your cousin? I'm not married to the bitch," he said opening the door.

"Oh, so now she's a bitch?" Amanda snapped.

"Yeah, what you gonna do? Tell her I said it?"

Amanda rolled her eyes and twisted her face. "I can't believe this shit!"

"Believe what? What's so fuckin' hard to believe? You knew she was your cousin! That ain't stop no show! You knew I was bangin' her, so what's the problem 'cause you confusin' the fuck out of me, sweetheart! Hell and if you didn't know about her you know I got a wife!"

"Well yo' wife don't know about us." Amanda said in a threatening tone.

Mike with one foot in the car and the other on the ground, turned towards her. "Aw, so what you gone do, tell my wife?" he asked chuckling to himself. "Check this out baby," he leaned in closer towards her, "She can't fire me," he said before finally stepping out the car and climbing into the driver's seat. "Hurry up and get yo' ass in the front so I could drop you the fuck off." He stuck the key in the ignition and started the engine.

She remained seated in the back with her face screwed up and her arms folded in front of hert.

"I'm fine back here." She rolled her eyes.

"See that's why I hate fuckin' with young bitches," he said as he backed out of the spot and drove off.

"Bitch?" Amanda said offended. She unfolded her arms and leaned closer towards the font seat. "Yo' wife is the fuckin' bitch!" she cursed.

"Yeah she is and so is your cousin, but don't tell them I said that though," he teased laughing at his own response. "Lets face it sweetheart, I didn't do shit to you. I gave you what you wanted. You already knew what the deal was, so I don't know what the hell you're so upset about. I didn't play any games with you." He glanced back at her and chuckled. "In fact, you were pretty easy."

"You know what, let me the fuck out! I'll walk home!" Amanda demanded.

"What?" Mike said as his foot eased off of the accelerator. "You gonna walk home?"

"I said let me out the car!" she said reaching for the door handle. Mike pulled over a block away from her home. Amanda got out and slammed the door. Her face was red with anger. She tugged on her dress as she wobbled towards her house in her heels. She hugged her shoulders as she walked home in the cool, breezy summer night. Mike drove slowly, yelling random things out the window without an ounce of remorse. She tried her best to ignore him, throwing menacing stares his way every now and then.

"Oh I get it," he yelled from the car as he drove along side her, "I get it, you thought you were special," he teased.

She continued walking.

"Well you know what sweetheart, you have a nice night. Oh and thank you, I got to fuck you and didn't even have to take you home! That's cool and all, I would hate for Stephanie to see us." He rambled on laughing. He honked his horn before hitting the accelerator and speeding off. Amanda hurriedly removed her heels from her feet and continued her hike home.

CHAPTER 7

Amanda's phone sounded for the eleventh time in a row. She glanced at the name and let out a long exhale. "Hello," she said dryly.

"I've been callin' your ass all morning!" Tiffany yelled. Amanda held the phone out from her ear as she sat up in bed.

"Yeah, about a hundred times."

"I want every single detail and don't you leave anything out."

"Details about what? Is this what you've been blowin' my phone up about?" Amanda asked knowing the intent of Tiffany's calls all along.

"Amanda, don't give me that shit! I know you're hiding somethin'…"

"Tiffany, it's nine o' clock in the morning! Nothin' happened! He dropped me off and that was that."

There was a long pause. Amanda rubbed her eyes smearing her eye makeup from the previous night. "Let me call you back when I wake up," Amanda said breaking the awkward silence.

"Oh you can forget it. I'm already in route to your house."

Fuck. Amanda thought as she hit the end button on her cell phone. She hopped out of bed and looked herself over in the mirror. She shook her head at her reflection. Thoughts about the night before raced through her head. She struggled to erase them, but to no avail.

"Girl, what time you get in last night?"

Amanda stood paralyzed. Through the mirror she watched her cousin take a few steps towards her. Her guilt made her too afraid to turn around. She pretended to tussle with her hair while keeping her back turned to Stephanie.

"I don't even remember. It was pretty late though."

Stephanie let out a chuckled. "So I guess you had one hell of a night!"

"Well….yeah."

"Well….what did you do?" Stephanie asked taking another step closer. Amanda continued to face the mirror.

"I was out with Tiffany."

"O…K, you're pretty short on words. What the hell is wrong with you? Don't tell me she threw another drink on your ass," Stephanie said laughing at her own remark. Amanda let out a fake giggle but continued facing the mirror.

"No, it was cool we didn't do much. We chilled and had a couple of drinks. That was pretty much it."

Stephanie stared at her cousin's reflection in the mirror. Amanda gazed back. The silence was so awkward Amanda finally dropped her hands from her head and spun around to face her. Stephanie stood standing in her silk black robe folded her arms across her chest.

"Tiffany called the house lookin' for you last night."

Amanda froze. She was caught off guard. She looked off to another part of the room before returning her attention to Stephanie.

"Well it must've been after I left her. I mean, I wasn't with her the entire night."

Stephanie didn't bulge. She kept her eyes fixed on her cousin, reading her every move. Amanda shifted from one leg to the next. "Don't come in here questioning me like you're my mother or some shit," Amanda said throwing in a light hearted laugh to ease the tension. Stephanie's lips finally broke into a smile.

"Right, don't play me for a dumb ass. I hope you were out finally gettin' some D-I-C-K."

Amanda faked another laugh. "Ok girl, you got me. Reggie couldn't keep his hands to himself."

"I knew it! You nasty ass. I want all the details."

"Girl, look, I don't…."

Stephanie grabbed Amanda's hand and led her towards the bed. "Start spillin'," she laughed.

"I mean what do you…" Ding Dong. The Bell sounded and Amanda jumped up quite relieved. "I'll get it, it's probably Tiff," Amanda said racing to the intercom.

"You're not off the hook," Stephanie said before going into her own room. "I do want details when I come back."

"Where you goin'?" Amanda asked happy to change the subject as she buzzed her friend in.

"Mike wants to have lunch," Stephanie yelled from inside her room. Amanda mouth nearly fell to the floor. She decided not to further the conversation. She opened the door for Tiffany.

"Let's get to it," Tiffany said as she brushed past Amanda, like she was late for a conference meeting, and sat on the couch.

"Shhhhhhhh," Amanda whispered, holding a finger to her mouth. "Shut the hell up."

Tiffany obeyed and stood up. Amanda walked past Stephanie's room down the hall to her own room with Tiffany trailing behind.

"What you so hush-hush about?" Tiffany asked as she sat down on the unmade bed and kicked her feet up. "What are you hiding?"

"Nothin' happened, Tiffany. Give it up," Amanda said avoiding eye contact.

Tiffany stared at her with a devilish grin. "Did he try to make any moves?"

Amanda sat at the foot of the bed facing her. "Why would he make any moves?"

"Amanda, are you fuckin' kiddin' me? The man practically threw himself at us in front of his wife. Don't act like he's Mr. Innocent." Tiffany leaned in closer towards Amanda. "And may I add…he's screwin' your cousin."

Amanda let out a chuckle. She wasn't going to win her battle.

"There's really is nothin' to tell." Amanda said with a straight face. Tiffany rolled her eyes towards the ceiling and let out a long exhale.

"Whatever. Keep it to yourself. It'll come out eventually."

Amanda shifted her body on the bed. She looked down at her French manicure as she pondered on Tiffany's statement. While she may be able to fool everyone else, she knew that hiding the truth from her best friend would only last for so long. She felt the guilt resting in the pit of her stomach. Tiffany snapped her fingers, knocking Amanda out of her train of thoughts. "Look like you have a lot on your dirty little mind." Tiffany teased.

"We did it," Amanda said sheepishly.

Tiffany quickly sat up and leaned in closer to her friend. "You did what?" she asked Amanda, giving her undivided attention.

Amanda exhaled. "You know what I mean, Tiff," she said annoyed with herself for not keeping her mouth shut.

"You did what? Kissed…hugged…sucked him off? What?"

"I fucked him, All right!" Amanda said loudly.

Stephanie's head peeped into the room. They stared at her with tight lipped grins plastered on their faces.

"I want all the details! What size was it?" Stephanie asked in a perky school girl voice. Tiffany looked at Stephanie and back to Amanda with a look of puzzlement. Amanda shot her look, letting her know to keep quiet.

"Stephanie," Amanda said, forcing a laugh. "I thought you had somewhere to go."

Stephanie smirked. "Oh, I guess you don't want to tell me in front of Tiffany. Its fine, I'll wait until later." She looked on at her cousin. "I can't believe you finally got nailed. It's been long enough."

Tiffany rolled her eyes when Stephanie left the room. "She drives me fuckin' crazy sometimes."

Amanda nodded her head in agreement. "I told her I was with Reggie."

Tiffany shook her head in disapproval. "I can't believe you."

Amanda sat quietly for a moment looking down at her fingernails to keep from catching Tiffany's facial expression.

"He's so…"

"Wait, I want to hear a play by play of what happened." Tiffany said, folding her legs underneath her. "Don't leave anything out."

Amanda sat quietly for a moment, summoning up all the horrid details that she so desperately wanted to forget.

"Any time now," tiffany rushed.

Amanda looked up at her frantically, mixed with different emotions. "I can't remember every itty bitty detail, so I'll tell you what I can remember…"

Tiffany listened intently as Amanda recalled everything she remembered from the previous night, accompanied with little reenactments to heighten the story. Tiffany sat bewildered listening to the story. Amanda watched the different facial expressions sweep across Tiffany's face. When she had told all she could remember she let out a long winded exhale before stretching across the bed on her stomach. Tiffany shook her head in disbelief. They sat in awkward silence. Each of them lost in their thoughts.

"So let me get this straight," Tiffany finally spoke up. "Not only did you fuck your boss's husband, you fucked a man your cousin is involved with? And really likes by the way." Tiffany said rubbing the guilt in for her own pleasure. "Personally, I don't think you can get any more triflin'." Amanda turned over in bed to face her.

"Thanks for bein' so compassionate and understanding!" Amanda snapped as she sat up again.

"Compassionate? You actually expect for me to feel sorry for you?" Tiffany asked twisting up her face and shaking her head disapprovingly. "Right now I think you're the scum of the Earth!"

Amanda climbed out of bed and stood over her with folded arms. "Is that right? Who are you to call anybody the scum of the Earth?"

"Somebody who didn't go out and fuck my boss's husband, let alone a guy my cousin is head over hills for!"

"Oh, so now he's the victim? Listen to yourself. He's cheatin' on his wife anyway, he's the scum! Stephanie is well aware she's not first in his—"

Tiffany jumped up. "And that just makes what you did so right," she said sarcastically.

"It's not right, but if you think about it, there really are no victims in this situation."

"His wife is a victim...your boss is a victim. Get that through your absent minded little head."

"Don't act like you give two shits about his wife, or Stephanie for that matter."

"I don't have to care about them to know that fuckin' Mr. Construction worker would be a huge fuck up for an already fucked up situation!"

Amanda ran her hands through her hair and stood in the mirror. "Tiffany, if you had the chance you would have screwed his brains out. But we both know you aren't willing to admit that he simply wasn't interested."

Tiffany stood still with her mouth agape. "What exactly are you implyin'?"

"That if he wanted to fuck you he could have. You can't get over the fact that he just didn't want you."

"What?"

"You heard me! You were all over him last night and he paid you no attention. Remember all the little flirtin' you did?"

"Amanda, whatever! So now you're tryin' to act like you're better than me?"

"I'm simply sayin' if I'm scum, you're scum!"

"I can't believe you. The man treated you like shit Amanda, and all you're gonna do is take jabs at me? You know you're wrong. You can hide behind stupidity all you want, but you're not foolin' me. You're a whore in sheep's clothing!"

"Well, you would know."

Tiffany continued to shake her head in disbelief. "I gave you so much more credit than that. You aren't even the least bit remorseful."

Amanda sat on the bed and looked up at her friend who in return looked off into a corner of the room. Uncomfortable silence made its way back into the room. Amanda felt better justifying her actions as an alternative to the enormous amount of guilt and shame she hid inside.

"I was drunk, Tiff. You know how I get when I drink and—"

"Shut up! Just shut the hell up. I don't care about you or anything you have to say right now." Tiffany yelled.

Amanda stopped talking and focused on reading Tiffany's thoughts. "I'm so confused. I mean what are you really upset about? It's not like I fucked your boyfriend."

Tiffany shot her a piercing look. "It doesn't matter. I just thought I knew you better. I can't fathom why you'd do somethin' like this...to your cousin. You just don't get it. I mean if you did it to your cousin, how in the world am I suppose to feel?"

"Tiffany, I wouldn't—"

"I just don't feel like I can trust you anymore."

"What? Look," Amanda jumped up. "I'm not buyin' any of your bullshit. You blew my phone off the hook this morning and you come over here and act like you're some kind of angel. You of all people, Tiffany! You were more in his face than I was last night. I know what I did was wrong, but who are you to judge me? Please don't pretend to be so upset or all of a sudden care so deeply for my boss's relationship with her husband...or Stephanie's little fling. You're supposed to be my friend."

"Yeah, you keep this kind of shit up and you won't have any more friends!"

"I don't need em'!"

Tiffany flopped down on the bed. Amanda hovered over her looking down, waiting for a response.

"You know what the problem is," Tiffany said finally looking up at her. "You're selfish. All you care about is yourself. I'm no angel, but I do care enough to not betray the people closes to me. True enough Stephanie pisses me the hell off at times, but I wouldn't stab her in the back like you did last night."

Amanda rolled her eyes. "Bullshit. You're so full of it. Were you too wasted to remember how ridiculous you were actin'?"

"This isn't about me, Amanda!"

"Tiff, you're fuckin' trippin'! I can't believe you comin' at me like this. Shit happens! Tiffany, I thought you of all people would understand me. You don't understand how horrible I feel. I feel so horrible, Tiffany."

Tiffany looked away, unmoved by her friend's guilt speech. As far as she was concerned, Amanda didn't deserve any pity. She let out a fake yawn as she extended her arms. "Save it, you're boring me."

Amanda took a seat on the bed next to her friend. Again silence prevailed. Amanda jumped up when her phone vibrated on the wooden dresser. She glanced at the name on the screen before pressing the talk button.

"Hey sweetheart," she chimed into the phone excitedly. Tiffany's neck nearly snapped as she turned her head to face Amanda, wondering who the mystery caller was. "Oh Reggie," Amanda continued with a smile on her face. "I know it's been a long time, I've been so busy," Amanda went on. Tiffany rolled her eyes as she fell back onto the bed with her arms outstretched before sitting up on her elbows. Amanda looked over at her and smirked.

"Speakerphone," Tiffany whispered.

Amanda shook her head as she paced back and forth on the phone. She continued to smile for the next ten minutes of their phone conversation. She was secretly hoping that Tiffany would get bored enough to leave but it was to no purpose. Tiffany continued to stare up at her, listening intently to Amanda's conversation. When Amanda finally hung up, Tiffany let out a long exhale. "It's about time!"

"Girl he wants to go out tonight," Amanda said cheesing, blowing off there intense conversation, as she sat on the bed.

"Where to?"

"I'm not sure. He was tellin' me how much he misses me."

Tiffany shook her head. "He seems to be a great guy."

"So why are you shakin' your head?"

"Because he needs to find himself a better woman!" Tiffany said bursting out in laughter.

"Oh that was supposed to be funny," Amanda said, not laughing.

"Relax," Tiffany said as her laughter quieted. "I mean what you did last night was most certainly scandalous, but you're my girl, and I love you. I'm sorry for comin' at you the way I did."

Amanda smiled. "Aaaawwwwwww," she said smiling, "I love you too." Amanda laid back on the bed and turned her head to face Tiffany.

"I hope Stephanie doesn't find out."

"Girl please!" Amanda said brushing the issue off. "New subject."

"Ok, so what are you wearin' tonight, Ms. Hot Ass?" They laughed.

****

"I don't know, maybe we can chill at your place." Amanda suggested to Reggie, who laid sprawled out in her bed fully clothed.

"Well if all we're gonna do is sit around, why not stay here?" He mumbled with his eyes closed annoyed he made the decision to drop by in the first place when he could be at home resting with no interruptions.

"You look pretty tired," she said, avoiding his question. Secretly she didn't want to risk bumping into her cousin or let alone run into Mike if her cousin decided to bring him home tonight.

"I am, I had a long night last night."

"Oh yeah, what were you busy doin'?" Amanda asked accusingly with a raised eyebrow. The change in the tone of her voice caused Reggie to lift his head and look at her.

"Relax baby," he said in a reassuring tone. "I was just chillin' with some of my guys. We sat around and had a few drinks."

"Oh yeah, and a few honeys too, huh?"

Reggie chuckled. "What you do last night?" he asked changing the subject.

"We aren't done with your night," Amanda said light heartedly vying to keep what she did last night to herself.

"Sweetheart, chill out. I mean it's not like I'm your man or somethin', right?" Reggie said in defense. He wanted to take the words back the moment they slipped from his tongue. He kept his eyes opened and saw Amanda's lips frown up.

"That's understood. Trust me, I'm not tryin' to make you anything but what you already are."

"And what's that?" Reggie asked rising up and swinging his legs to the floor.

Amanda glanced at her alarm clock that was on her dresser and then looked back at Reggie who was now putting his shoes back on.

"You've been over here less than an hour and you're already on the run." She fussed.

"I came over here to see you, but you on some other shit. Now if you want to hang out, that's cool with me, but I'm not up for the twenty one question game tonight."

"Well I'm not the one who called you and asked you to come over here!"

"I know…you never do. That's why I'm wonderin' where these questions comin' from."

"It's not even that serious. It seems to me you just don't want to be bothered. Perhaps you came over here for other reasons."

"Other reasons like what?"

Amanda paused and rolled her eyes instead. She decided to keep quiet. Accusing him of just wanting some ass might make her look a little foolish. She knew that he really was trying to spend some time with her, but the thoughts of last night had her feeling uneasy around him. She knew her sudden outlandish behavior would make any man head for the door. He stood up. "What's the problem?" He finally asked.

"There is no problem. I'm just not in a good mood, that's all."

"Well, why you have me come over here if you really don't want me here?"

"Because I really wanted to see you," she said trying to sound sincere as possible. Truthfully she really just wanted someone to get her out of the house for awhile to forget her troubles as well as get Tiffany out of her hair for the day. She wrapped her arms around his neck and planted a kiss on his lips. He went in for another kiss. She moved her head.

"Weren't you just about to leave?" She teased.

"You want me to leave?"

Amanda stared up at him as she pondered on his question. She didn't want to be alone if her cousin came back especially if she decided to bring her date back with her. On the other hand she wasn't really up for company.

"I just really don't want to be in the house tonight," she said still trying to find a way to rid herself of seeing Stephanie, or Mike for that matter.

"Well let's go grab somethin' to eat." Reggie said as he went in for a kiss. She returned the kiss before undoing her arms from around his neck. She grabbed a soft yellow cardigan to put over her strapless printed sundress.

"I see you got the little bohemian look goin' on today," He teased. "The wild curly hair and long flowin' dress."

Amanda laughed as she slipped into a pair of embellished leather flip flops. "I guess these just top off the look, huh?"

"Pretty much," he said nodding his head.

After they successfully made it out the house without running into her cousin they hopped in his car and cruised off. She played with the different radio stations until she settled on some soft jazz.

"Here we go?" she smiled to herself, snapping her fingers and bobbing her head to the melodic tunes.

"Wow, is this what you just spent nearly twenty minutes lookin' for?" he asked looking over at her with a smile across his face happy to see her smiling.

She turned the radio up a little louder. "It's so relaxing. Don't you just love how soothing jazz makes you feel?"

Reggie looked back towards the road. "I'm not really a jazz cat myself, but you do you." He teased.

"I can turn to somethin' else."

"Naw, I'm cool. Where you want to eat at?"

Amanda still enthralled in her music continued to weave and bob her head. "Can we just grab somethin' from some kind of fast food joint?"

Reggie looked over at her once again. "Miss Prissy wants to go to a fast food joint?" he taunted and laughed.

"What? Oh come on, nobody's too good for a greasy burger! Besides I'm not that prissy. I don't know what would give you that impression."

"So you don't think you're a little snobbish?"

"Of course not! Me? Snobbish? Stephanie maybe, not Amanda!"

"It's cool. I like my women a little snooty."

"Oh, well I may have a friend for you," she toyed.

"Who, that crazy girl from that night at the lounge?"

Amanda burst out in laughter as she remembered Tiffany's behavior the night she met Reggie.

"That crazy girl is my friend, so you better watch it!"

"Naw, you better watch it."

Amanda let his words sink into her head before she turned to him and responded. "What's the deal with you and her?"

Reggie shrugged. "What you mean?"

"I mean why you always got somethin' smart to say about her?"

"I don't even know the girl."

"My point exactly."

Reggie glanced at her to read her facial expression. She now had her arms folded against her chest glaring at him. "I mean from what I observed about her that night, I just think she might be a little scandalous."

Amanda stiffened as unwanted thoughts of the night before crept into her head. She was scandalous. She turned her head towards the passenger side window to keep from revealing her thoughts. She could feel Reggie's eyes on her.

"I apologize. I know that's your girl and all." Reggie said turning the music down. Amanda continued to sit quietly, staring out the window in a daze. The touch of Reggie's hand on her shoulder startled her and she gasped.

"Whew, you scared me."

"You okay? Forget what I said about your friend. I had no right to—"

"It's okay," Amanda said cutting him off. "I mean after all she does have her ways."

Reggie nodded his head. "To each it's own, right?" He shrugged his shoulders.

Amanda nodded before turning her head towards the window again.

CHAPTER 8

"She was definitely a little rude," Jessica said before biting into an apple. "I mean she had no such reason to act the way she did."

Amanda massaged her temples. Jessica's yapping was giving her a headache. Jessica continued to stand in her cubicle chomping away at her apple waiting for Amanda to take her side.

"Look, that's just how Tiffany is. She's a little blunt sometimes."

"Amanda there is a big difference between being blunt and being rude."

"Ok well how about I apologize for her. I'm sorry if Tiffany made you a little upset that night. She didn't mean it. She probably was a little too wasted."

"As you were," Jessica continued, not ready to back down.

Amanda sighed and continued facing her computer monitor, typing away. "I really don't know what you're expecting from me. I already apologized."

Jessica tossed the remainder of her apple into Amanda's waste basket. "You haven't even looked up from your computer."

Amanda exhaled, swiveled around in her chair and nearly gasped when Melanie walked up and stood alongside Jessica. Melanie smirked.

"Hope you recovered from Friday night," Melanie said grinning. "Mike told me you and your friend drove him crazy with all your silly foolish drunk talk." She chuckled. "I told him I wouldn't torture him like that ever again." She continued in between laughs.

Amanda sat fuming with anger while Jessica laughed like it was the funniest thing she had ever heard. Amanda wanted to punch both of them.

"Wait, so your husband took them home?"

Melanie nodded. "Poor thing!"

"Poor thing is right. They aren't the friendliest when they're intoxicated." Jessica blurted out, not paying any mind to the furious look on Amanda's face.

"You just don't know when to stop do you?" Amanda finally said a couple of pitches to high. Both heads turned to face her.

Jessica's face broke into a smile. "Oh calm down, Amanda we're just having a little fun."

"At my expense!"

Melanie placed a hand on Jessica's shoulder. "Let's go back to work ladies," she said glancing back over her shoulders as she and Jessica walked out. Amanda sat there a few seconds longer before turning her chair to face her desk. She was so teed off she nearly forgot her own wrong doings. How could he just lie like that? She thought as she placed her hands along the home keys of the keyboard. Melanie sure makes it easier to not feel guilty about sleeping with her husband. Bitch. The sound of a nearby fax machine kicked Amanda out of her thoughts. She looked over her shoulders to make sure no unwanted visitors caught her in a daze. She regained focus and returned to some of her daily activities; faxing, typing, filing, answering phones, taking messages, writing memos and creating spreadsheets. When she finally had enough of being confined to her work space she pushed herself back from her desk, stood up, brushed some of the wrinkles out of her pants and headed down the long corridor towards a vending machine in the kitchen. Gathered there were a handful of her coworkers scattered about eating, napping, and just plain old gossiping. Jessica was seated at one of the tables with one of the receptionist from the front desk.

Amanda strolled past avoiding them as they sat eyeing her and snickering. Amanda paid it no mind. Instead she checked out the ass on the Brad Pitt look alike in front of her who was bent over retrieving whatever he purchased out the vending machine. He looked up catching Amanda by surprise. He smiled at her before briskly walking off and out of the lunchroom. Amanda smiled to herself to keep from laughing at the fact that she had been caught checking him out. She eyed the candy bars, chips, cookies and other snacks in the machine before settling on a Snickers bar. After buying a bottled water she turned to head out of the kitchen.

"I mean seriously she was really rude." Amanda heard Jessica say followed by giggles.

Amanda froze in her tracks. She spun around and headed towards Jessica and the receptionist. The two girls ceased there conversation when they noticed her approaching their table. Amy, the receptionist, quickly bit into a banana.

Amanda forced a friendly smile. "Hey Amy," she said as she opened her bottle of water and took a sip giving Amy enough time to swallow her bite of fruit.

"Amanda, how are you?" Amy said in an overly pleasant voice. "We were just talking about you."

"Really?" Amanda said sarcastically. "As if I haven't noticed." She shot Jessica an evil look.

Amy looked from Amanda to Jessica and back to Amanda again. "Well we—"

"I was just telling her about your friend," Jessica interrupted as if the topic was perfectly fine.

"Oh," Amanda continued on in a mocking tone. "Well maybe I should go and tell my friend about you so she come up here and whoop your little beach blonde ass!"

The two girls gasped. A couple of coworkers who had overheard Amanda turned their heads in their direction.

"Excuse me?" Jessica suddenly spoke up.

Amanda felt a hand grab her upper arm. She looked back to see Valerie, a Latina girl who usually kept to herself, shaking her head. "Whatever it is, it's not even worth it girl," she said pulling Amanda a couple of feet from the table.

"You just don't understand—"

"Trust me, just let it go," Valerie said tossing her shoulder length hair out of her face.

Amanda looked at her and then glanced behind her and rolled her eyes at the girls. They stiffened as Amanda walked back towards there table. She snatched up her bottled water and stormed past Valerie and the rest of the onlookers, out of the kitchen.

****

"I swear I just wanted to knock her brains out!" Amanda whined, curled up in a fetal position with her head rested on Reggie's lap. He chuckled and shook his head never taking his eyes off of the television. Amanda lifted her head and looked up at him. "Are you even listenin' to me?"

"Yeah…yeah, I definitely think you should have whooped her ass," Reggie said still focused on the action movie they were watching.

Amanda smacked her lips and planted her head back on his lap as she continued whining. "It makes me not even want to go to work anymore. I get so aggravated every time I see her or my boss."

"Really?" Reggie pretended to be concerned. "What yo' boss do to you?"

Amanda let out a long exhale. More like what I've done to her, she thought. She sulked in silence, avoiding Reggie's question. Reggie nudged her and she lifted her head before sitting up altogether. "What happened, what she do?"

"You know what, enough about me and my depressing work life. Would you like somethin' to drink?" she asked making her way out of the living room into the open kitchen. She sighed as she buried her head in the refrigerator searching for something to drink. She grabbed two cans of Pepsi and shut the door. She retrieved two glasses from the cabinet and walked back into the living room. She opened her can of coke and poured half the can into one of the glasses before lifting it to her lips and taking a sip.

"You too good to drink out of a can?" Reggie teased, opening the other can and taking a big gulp.

Amanda laughed. "You're such a pig."

"Tell me what happened. Don't leave me hangin'," he said finally looking away from the TV and staring her down.

"I'm so tired of talkin' about that lady. Just forget about it," she said as she leaned over and placed a kiss on his lips.

"Oh yeah," Reggie said, pulling her closer towards him. She got up and sat on his lap. The shared a few more kisses before they heard a key being inserted into the front door. They got a few more kisses in before Amanda got up and sat next to him. "I mean what's the big deal, you're grown." Reggie said brushing a few wrinkles off of his shirt.

"That's not the point, I—"

Amanda paused in mid-sentence when the front door finally swung opened and in walked Stephanie and a face Amanda knew all too well engrossed in there own little kissing session. Stephanie broke free, giggling when she noticed two pairs of eyes on her and Mike. Mike glanced over at Amanda and then to Reggie and back to Amanda again. Amanda looked away and towards the television.

"Mike, sweetheart," Stephanie chimed, breaking the uncomfortable silence. "You finally get to meet my cousin, Amanda."

Reggie looked from Stephanie to Mike and then to Amanda in puzzlement. "Oh they've met," Reggie mumbled, sipping his beverage. All eyes narrowed in on him.

"Oh yeah, I knew she looked a little familiar." Mike said to no one in particular before extending his hand towards Amanda. "I actually bumped into these two at a restaurant a little while back." Amanda looked at his hand before forcing a tight lipped smile.

"Nice to finally meet you," she managed to say, ignoring his hand. He dropped it to his side and nodded.

"Really, you've seen each other before? Amanda, why didn't you tell me?" Stephanie asked excitedly.

"Oh, it wasn't important." Amanda said, interlocking eyes with Mike who smirked back at her. Reggie snickered at Amanda's reply.

Stephanie shrugged it off and extended a hand towards Reggie. "Hey Reggie."

"What's up?" he shook her hand and nodded to Mike. "Nice to see you again," he lied. Mike returned a nod. Stephanie grabbed Mike's hand. "Well, I'll leave you two alone," she said before leading Mike towards her bedroom as if it was his first visit. Amanda stared at them with a livid look on her face. Mike glanced back at her before he disappeared into her cousin's room.

"What was all that about?" Reggie asked after they heard Stephanie's door shut.

Amanda looked at him angrily and asked, "What was all what about?"

"That was clearly the same dude that was ready to game you down at the restaurant. Now he's here." Reggie's voice had a hint of hostility.

"I don't know." Amanda shrugged.

"What you gettin' so upset about? You think I ain't peep the little looks ya'll were givin' each other?"

Amanda looked at him. "What looks?"

"What looks?" Reggie repeated. "Right…what looks?" he said as he stood up. "You know what sweetheart, call me when you ready to—"

"Oh, so now you're leavin'?" Amanda interrupted jumping to her feet and standing in his face.

"You want to sit here and act stupid?" Reggie pointed towards Stephanie's room. "That fool tried to cover up the fact that he tried to come at you and you let him."

"I didn't let him do anything. What's the big deal? Nothin' happened between us!"

"Between who? You and him? Who said I assumed somethin' did?"

Amanda's guilty expression caused her to look away. Reggie shook his head, fuming as he walked towards the door.

"Look…he has a wife." Amanda said fighting back tears. Reggie turned the knob and opened the front door.

"So she's fuckin' around with a married man? Is that what all this shit about? And you condone that type of shit, huh?" he asked shaking his head in disbelief.

"I'm not like that!" Amanda yelled loudly wanting to really believe she wasn't.

Reggie stood in the doorway for a few seconds, pondering on her statement. "I'll call you later." he said before closing the door behind him. Amanda flopped back down on the couch and let the tears of guilt trickle down her face.

CHAPTER 9

"He hasn't even called me back yet," Amanda said, sobbing.

"Well how long has it been?" Tiffany asked as she swept a bronze colored eye shadow across her eyelids.

"I called him last night after he left."

"Girl, chill out. It hasn't even been a whole day yet. I mean what's the deal with you two anyway? Have ya'll fucked each other yet?"

Amanda, tired of standing in the doorway, closed the toilet lid and sat down. "Of course we haven't did anything yet." she said defensively.

Tiffany looked away from the large bathroom mirror at her friend and chuckled.

"Don't sit here and act like you've never given it up easily," she said, turning to her reflection in the mirror.

Amanda rolled her eyes. "That's not the point. And stop bringing that up. I'm tryin' to forget about it."

"You can't just forget about it, Amanda," Tiffany said turning away from the mirror again with a twisted look on her face. "You slept with your manager's husband and Stephanie's…fling or whatever you want to call it. That's a double whammy."

"You think I haven't—"

"And speakin' of your cousin," she interrupted as she applied another colored shadow to her eyes, "Has she said anything to you about Mike?"

Amanda pouted and sat silently for a few seconds before answering, "I've been avoiding her all day. By the time that man left last night, I was knocked out sleep. And I came straight over here after work."

Tiffany shook her head in disappointment as she applied a black liquid liner to her eyes.

"So what happened today at work?"

"Nothin'. I barely said a word to anybody."

"How did you pull that one off? Isn't Miss Jessie…Jessica, or whatever her name is, constantly in your face?"

"Ha, I totally forgot to tell you over the phone last night. I damn near went off on that girl!"

"What? What she do? You were so busy cryin' over that fool, you held out on the good stuff." she said eagerly.

Amanda exhaled before she went on to recall the minor lunchroom dispute between her coworker and herself. Tiffany's smile faded along with her excitement as Amanda got further along in the story.

"It took everything to keep me from killin' that girl. She really crawled under my skin yesterday!"

"You better hope I don't see her ass. I'll really give her somethin' to talk about next time!" Tiffany said heatedly. "I swear, she's really askin' for it. I mean what was the point of tellin' the people at your job about me? Why would they care?" Tiffany continued on, now playing with the loose curls in her hair.

"I wish he would call me, Tiff." Amanda said redirecting the conversation.

"Girl please, you haven't even fucked him yet. So who gives a damn, his loss."

Amanda sighed. "Thanks for being so understanding," she snapped.

"I'm just tryin' to keep you from wastin' your time over him."

"Right. You're the same person who jumped down my throat about not givin' him any action and now you're tellin' me to get over it."

Tiffany continued to play with her hair in the mirror as she spoke. "Well I gotta' tell you somethin', right? That's what friends are for." she told her sarcastically.

Amanda frowned up her face. "What kind of friend are you? You act like you don't even care that I'm upset, like—"

Tiffany held up her hand before cutting her friend off. "Look honey, you have even bigger problems to worry about. You can't even go home and look your cousin in the face. And don't think you're about to be runnin' yo' sad little ass to my place after work everyday. You made your bed so lay in it." she snapped, reaching for her curling irons.

"All right, I'm done with you and your smart mouth for the day. I'm out of here."

Tiffany curled a section of her hair and responded, "Good, now I can finish gettin' ready in peace."

"I hope your date doesn't even show up." Amanda said, storming out of the bathroom.

Tiffany laughed aloud. "Honey, I never worry about a man standin' me up."

"Yeah right," Amanda said as she continued on towards the front door of Tiffany's apartment. "Is that why you have to juggle so many of them?"

"Maybe I should give you a few of them," Tiffany yelled from the bathroom.

Amanda rolled her eyes as she reached for the doorknob. "Keep them. I'm sure you need them more than I do." she yelled back to Tiffany before slamming the door behind her. She hopped in her car and drove the couple of blocks home slowly, hoping she wouldn't run into her cousin. Her mouth twisted into a grimace when she spotted Stephanie's truck parked out in front. She shut off the engine and sat in the car with her hands still gripping the steering wheel. She exhaled, removed her keys, and reached into her purse for her phone. No missed calls. She rested her head against the head rest of the seat and closed her eyes. Images of her and Mike crept into her head as she replayed the steamy love scene once more. As much as she despised him she couldn't help but become aroused every time her thoughts raced back to that night. His skills were incredible and she wondered if Reggie would be able to make her envision the same. Her entire body jerked and eyes shot opened when a tap sounded against her passenger side window. She looked to her right.

"Girl, what the hell is wrong with you?" Stephanie yelled from outside the car. She had a baffled look on her face. Amanda hit the unlock button. "Why are you out here asleep in the car?" Stephanie continued, sliding in the passenger seat without closing the door.

"I was just…just—"

"Lookin' like a damn fool?" Stephanie finished her sentence.

Amanda nodded embarrassingly. "I don't know, I thought maybe you had company or somethin'."

Stephanie chuckled as she looked at her younger cousin in disbelief. "You thought maybe I had company or somethin'?" she repeated, "So you decided to sit out here in your car?"

"Well I was about to come in," Amanda replied, realizing how foolish she sounded.

Stephanie shook her head. "Sometimes I really worry about you," she teased.

Amanda forced a quiet laugh as she kept her gaze focused straight ahead hoping to conceal her secret. Stephanie studied Amanda's face. "You look a little tense."

"Who me?" Amanda looked over at her cousin for a couple of seconds before turning away and looking straight ahead again. "Oh, I'm cool. I just have a lot on my mind."

"Like what?"

Amanda looked down. "Like…Reggie." she lied.

"Reggie? What? Already, wow he must've been amazing. He got you sittin' up here day dreamin'. Girl, just pick up the phone and call the man." Stephanie examined her made up face in the overhead mirror.

"I mean it's not like we did nothin'—"

"Wait, I thought you said you guys had sex," Stephanie said, looking over.

"I meant in awhile." Amanda said, quickly catching her slip up. "We haven't done anything in awhile."

"So he sucked?"

"No, I didn't say that."

"Okay, so what's the problem?"

"I...look I just can't talk about this right now." Amanda decided to avoid the conversation.

"Okay, okay, okay, chill out." Stephanie kept her eyes glued to the side of her cousin's face. "You're really buggin' out over this dude."

Amanda let out a long exhale coupled with annoyance. Stephanie didn't budge. Instead she snickered at the look on Amanda's face. "Relax, okay. We can change the subject."

"Actually I'm about to go inside," Amanda said as she reached for her bag.

"So why didn't you tell me you two saw Mike while you guys were out?"

Amanda's body deadened and for a minute her brain shut down as well. She looked over at her smiling cousin who sat waiting for a reply.

"It was no big deal."

"I mean of course not, but come on, you know how crazy I am about that man. Everything about him is a big deal to me. What was he wearin'?"

"I can't remember."

"What did he say?" Stephanie pressed.

"He...uh...he...said somethin' about...I don't know, I can't remember."

Stephanie twisted up her face. "Oh come on. Stop actin' like you have Alzheimer's."

"I was on a date with Reggie, I wasn't concerned about him."

"It just doesn't make any sense. Did he approach the two of you?"

"I don't know." Amanda clutched her purse tightly as she opened the driver's door with her free hand. "Are you done interrogating me?"

Stephanie waved her off and stepped out of the car. "I guess I have to interrogate Reggie the next time he's over," she said before closing the door.

Amanda walked around the car to her cousin. "Let it go already." She slung her bag over her shoulder.

"What are you about to get into?"

"Well, since Reggie isn't talkin' to me at the moment, I guess I'll go stuff my face with some ice cream and turn on some Lifetime movies."

Stephanie chuckled. "Ugh, that's so sad. I'm headed over to my moms. She complains that I don't come see her enough."

"I'm still so upset with her. Speakin' of your mom, I guess it wouldn't hurt to give my mom a ring."

Stephanie sauntered off towards the driver's side of her truck. "Make sure you tell her I said hello."

"Right," Amanda mumbled under her breath as she walked up the front steps and disappeared into the building.

CHAPTER 10

"I just don't understand it." Amanda heard as she typed away at her keyboard. She stopped typing every few seconds to eavesdrop on her boss's conversation. "I saw this number on our phone bill numerous times and I paid it no mind." Amanda eyes nearly bulged out of her head as she lightly tapped on the keyboard. "I don't want to believe he's running around behind my back." Amanda rolled herself away from her desk and tip-toed out of her cubicle to get a better listen. Melanie's back was facing her and another manager to whom Melanie was conversing with was too engrossed in the conversation to pay Amanda any mind. "Oh dear, I would hate for that to be the case," the other manager replied. Melanie placed her hands to her hips. "I'll get to the bottom of it over dinner tonight."

Amanda cleared her throat, causing the duo to turn their heads in her direction. "I'm sorry to interrupt. I was just wondering if—"

"Oh no, it's fine," the other manager said smiling. "How are you Amanda?"

"I'm fine," Amanda answered with a smile. That same smile nearly turned upside down when Melanie opened her mouth.

"Amanda, just the lady I wanted to see. Can you step into my office?" Melanie said more as a statement than a question.

A look of concern swept across Amanda's face as she walked slowly towards Melanie's office.

"Excuse me for a sec," Amanda heard Melanie say to the other manager before following behind her and closing the door once they were in the office.

Amanda glanced around the room as if it were her first time seeing it. There were so many photos of her and him. One would assume they had a picture perfect marriage. Amanda could barely tolerate being in there. "We were vacationing in Hawaii on that one," Melanie said boastfully.

Amanda looked up and smiled. "Wow, you guys sure are one happily married couple."

Melanie smiled. "Yeah, we like to think so." She folded her arms in front of her.

The room was silent for a couple of seconds as Amanda pretended to be interested in the photos scattered about the expensively decorated office.

"Wow," Amanda continued.

"About the incident that occurred between you and Jessica, do you care to explain?"

Amanda looked up at her boss bewildered. "Nothing to explain. I had no idea she even mentioned it to you." she emphasized with a shoulder shrug.

"Well, it is the appropriate thing to do."

Amanda nodded her head, concealing her rage. She couldn't believe Jessica would stoop so low as to bring a minor incident to Melanie. Then again anything was possible with Jessica. If their friendship wasn't over before, it was definitely over now.

"It was just a petty little argument."

"Well according to her and a couple of other coworkers it was a bit of commotion and you were described as being very improper. I don't want any unnecessary tension going on. This is a professional environment and I need you two to behave accordingly. I don't want to have to give out write-ups or terminate anyone's position over nonsense."

Amanda continued nodding her head. "That's totally understood."

"Good." Melanie said sternly, deciding not to drag the conversation out any further.

"Is that all?" Amanda questioned, brushing past her and reaching for the doorknob to let herself out.

"About that night," Melanie continued. She saw Amanda's frame harden. Amanda's hand dropped to her side as her head slowly turned slightly back towards her boss. Melanie smiled, walking around her to a drawer. She retrieved a small object and cupped it in her hand. Amanda's mind raced back to the night with Melanie's husband. "One of you young ladies left this in the backseat," she said as she raised a small oval diamond hoop earring.

"Oh," was the only word that managed to flee Amanda's pursed lips. She examined the earring before taking it from Melanie's hand.

"It is one of your earrings, right?" Melanie asked noticing the perplexed look on her employee's face.

"Yeah…yeah," Amanda spoke up. "Tiffany is always losing somethin'."

"Tiffany, is that her name? Your friend, the one you brought along that night?"

"Yeah, that's her. She's quite—"

"Rude," Melanie interjected.

"Rude?" Amanda questioned.

Melanie chuckled. "I'm just teasing."

Amanda peeked at the earring. "Well thanks. I'm sure Tiffany will be glad you returned it."

"Well of course I wouldn't keep it," Melanie said as if the earring had mutated into some pesky little bug right before her eyes. "I have enough diamonds."

Amanda turned away before rolling her eyes and opening the office door. "Is that everything?"

"For now," Melanie said before walking around her desk and flopping down in her leather chair.

Amanda seized the chance to escape before Melanie could bother her with more of her shenanigans. She opened her palm and eyed the object in hand. She dialed Stephanie's number as soon as she settled in her workstation.

"Yeah?"

"Don't you yeah me. You left your earring in his car," Amanda whispered in the receiver.

"What?" Stephanie asked from the other end.

"My boss just handed me your earring. An oval diamond hoop."

"Oh, is that where it was?" Stephanie chuckled through the phone.

"You intentionally planted your earring in the backseat, Stephanie?" How—"

"Well I didn't exactly plant it there, maybe it came off while we were busy havin'—"

"Ok, I get it. I have to go." Amanda said, slamming down the receiver. She groaned as she rubbed a hand across her forehead. It was too early in the day for so much foolishness. The sound of Jessica's voice further irritated her and she shook her head determined to get some work done.

"Yeah I heard the news," she heard Jessica say, followed by a couple of giggles right outside her office. Amanda removed her hands from the keyboard.

"Well it's not confirmed," she heard Melanie say before she appeared in her cubicle holding a stack of papers.

"What's not confirmed?" Amanda jumped in.

"Oh, nothing much, just that I may be expecting…"

"Expectin' what?" Amanda asked dumbfounded. There was no way it could have been what she thought.

"A baby," Melanie said quietly as she handed Amanda the stack of papers. "I need you to take care of those for me."

"A baby?" Amanda repeated a couple of pitches too loud unsure if she had heard Melanie correctly.

Melanie nodded her head. "Until we go to our doctor, it's not for certain, so relax."

"Relax," Amanda went on in the same loudness. "Are you sure?" Amanda wanted to slap herself for letting those last three words slip out. Melanie screwed up her face.

"Excuse me? Is there a problem?" Melanie asked defensively before cracking a lighthearted smile. "I'm only a few years over thirty. Women can have children after thirty."

"Right," Amanda said before turning to face her computer screen. She cupped a hand over her mouth to keep it from dropping to the floor after Melanie walked out of her space. "I can't believe it," she said to herself as she placed her hands over the home keys of the keyboard.

****

"So what made you decide to finally pick up the phone?"

"I'm just tryna' see what's up with you," Reggie said after a long pause.

"I'm fine," Amanda said through the phone as she poured herself a glass of lemonade.

"You down for a little company?"

"You can't just leave and pop up when you want to."

"So I guess that's a no?"

Amanda hit the end button on her cell phone as she placed herself in the barstool at the table.

"What are you out here yappin' about?" Stephanie asked as she walked into the kitchen securely tying her robe around her small waist.

"Reggie. He had the nerve to—"

Amanda's cell phone began to vibrate in front of her on the granite countertop with Reggie's name flashing across the screen. Before Amanda could lift her hand to press the ignore button Stephanie had already grabbed the phone and pressed the talk button.

"Well hello, Reggie," Stephanie sang into the phone all the while cheesing at Amanda who sat leaning on the counter rolling her eyes.

"Would you cut it out and give me my phone," Amanda said in annoyance.

"So Reggie, maybe you'd be better at answering my questions than—"

"Give it to me Stephanie," Amanda said sliding off the barstool, wrestling Stephanie for her cell phone.

"So, Reggie," Stephanie continued, giggling as she spoke. "What exactly did Mike say to the two of you when you guys ran into him?"

Amanda eyes widen. Stephanie held a tight grip on the phone and circled the island in the kitchen as she continued to quiz Reggie.

"Stephanie!" Amanda yelled frustrated.

"He did what?" were the next three words that rolled off Stephanie's tongue. The menacing look on her face stopped Amanda in her tracks. "Oh really?" Stephanie said, carrying on with the conversation like Amanda wasn't there.

"Stephanie, just let me—"

Stephanie held her left index finger in mid air for Amanda to quiet down. Amanda sighed as she leaned her backside against the countertop. Her mind raced over countless excuses, but she knew she wouldn't make it out of this one. She wanted to punch Reggie in the face.

"Oh, gorgeous, huh?" Stephanie said, shaking her head disappointed. "Well, someone seems to remember that night quite well," she said forcing a laugh while eyeing Amanda's backside. Amanda turned to face her and caught her threatening stare. Amanda looked off into space.

"Well, thanks." Stephanie placed the cell phone on the counter and walked over to the refrigerator. Amanda reached for her cell phone and without saying a word to Reggie, ended the call. As she stood watching Stephanie dig through the refrigerator she wondered for a second if she was really searching for something, or simply hiding the look of grief on her face.

"Stephanie I—"

"Why didn't you tell me?" Stephanie questioned with her head still buried in the fridge.

Amanda shrugged and paused before replying "I just...I didn't think it mattered."

Stephanie voice cracked. "You didn't think it mattered?" she questioned, raising her head and slamming the refrigerator door shut. "The man I'm involved with practically came onto you and you don't think that matters?" Stephanie yelled loud enough for the neighbors to pull up a chair and listen in. Amanda took a step back as Stephanie took one forward.

"I just didn't think—"

"Amanda, save the bullshit! I can't stand to even hear you speak anymore." A frustrated Stephanie turned and stomped out the kitchen with Amanda following behind.

"Stephanie, that's why I didn't tell you because I knew how you'd react," Amanda pleaded.

Stephanie slumped down on the couch and buried her face in her lap. Amanda sat next to her and gently rubbed her back. The place was so silent Amanda could hear her phone vibrate against the countertop. She knew it had to be Reggie.

"You don't deserve him," Amanda said without much thought. Stephanie's neck snapped in her direction as she narrowed her eyes on her cousin.

Stephanie said harshly, "Don't you sit up here and tell me what I don't deserve!" She got up and walked off to her room.

"I'm sorry I was—"

Amanda words were cut short by the thunderous slam of Stephanie's bedroom door. Amanda headed towards her room, snatching her phone off the counter as she passed the kitchen. She punched in Tiffany's number.

"Hey," Tiffany answered.

"I hope you got some time."

"Start talkin'."

Amanda closed her bedroom door and nestled herself in her bed. She let out a long exhale and paused before recounting the day's events.

CHAPTER 11

"Is she still ignorin' you?"

"I guess. I wish Reggie never opened up his mouth."

Tiffany sipped her freshly squeezed lemonade as they browsed through a cosmetic store.

"This color is absolutely gorgeous," Tiffany said holding up a pewter color eye shadow.

Amanda glanced at the eye shadow as Tiffany placed it back on the shelf.

"Are you gonna get it?"

"I have too many colors similar to it already."

"Well, I'll take it," Amanda said reaching around her friend to retrieve the shimmery shadow.

"So has he been back over yet?" Tiffany asked out of curiosity.

"No, but he's been blowin' my phone the hell up."

"Just talk to him. It's not like he intentionally tried to get you caught up."

"He's a prick. He's just so damn cocky at times."

"Well, cocky is good if you're really workin' with somethin'."

Amanda glared at her friend as she placed the shadow and a few other items in her hand basket on the countertop in front of the register. The sales associate smiled.

"And will this be all for you today?"

Amanda smile and nodded her head. "Yes."

"Would you like to open up an account with us today? You'll save twenty percent on your purchases."

Amanda shook her head. "No, thank you. This is all."

The sales clerk smiled and nodded as she rang up the items while Amanda stood scanning the store. Tiffany stood sipping her lemonade rummaging through the items in her basket.

"What you think about this lip-gloss?"

"I like it." Amanda said peeking at the things in Tiffany's basket. "I especially love that blush. NARS really outdid themselves with that."

Tiffany smiled as she placed her stuff on the counter. "I'm so excited about my purchases."

"Your total comes to sixty two ninety six," the clerk smiled.

"Oh that's not bad," Amanda said reaching into her bag and pulling out her bank card. The clerk completed her transaction and handed Amanda her bag.

"These bags are so awesome," Tiffany said to Amanda as she observed the little shopping bag while the clerk started on her order.

"You're such a sucker," Amanda laughed. "I don't think I can do much more walkin' with all of these bags."

"I'm with you. Let's go back to my place. I'm ready to try on some of my new things."

Amanda shook her head. "As if you needed any more clothes."

They laughed as Tiffany handed the clerk her bank card. After they were all set, they strutted out of the store and towards the parking garage to Tiffany's black Jetta. They stuffed all their shopping bags in the trunk and backseat and headed South of Downtown. Tiffany lived in the Bronzeville neighborhood, a few blocks from Amanda. She pulled up in front of her apartment, cut off her radio and air conditioner before shutting off her engine.

"Ugh, I don't feel like luggin' all of these bags upstairs."

"Come on, I want to try on some of my things too," Amanda said hopping out and opening the back car door as Tiffany popped the trunk. "Girl, who is that handsome brother over there," Amanda inquired as Tiffany slammed her trunk shut. Both pairs of eyes gazed across the street at the athletically built caramel colored guy with a low hair cut bent over cleaning out his trunk. He must have felt the pairs of eyes staring at him because he looked up and over unexpectedly and nodded.

"Damn he is fine," Tiffany whispered to Amanda as they walked off towards Tiffany's building, casually glancing behind them. When they reached the top of her stairs Tiffany searched for her keys. Minutes later they entered the building after checking out the hot guy one last time, giggling like little school girls when the doors shut behind them.

Once settled into Tiffany's one bedroom apartment they headed to her room and scattered their bags about. Tiffany kicked off her flats and pounced on the bed. Amanda removed her embellished thong sandals and crawled onto the bed as well. They lay sprawled around, exhausted from all the walking and bag carrying.

"Whew," Tiffany said as she closed her eyes.

"Don't fall asleep on me."

"I'm not, I'm just relaxin' and tryin' to unwind," Tiffany mumbled. "Aren't you tired?"

"My legs are a little sore," Amanda noted as she balanced her head on a pillow and closed her eyes. The room fell silent while both women lay lost in thoughts. Amanda's cell phone sounded. Tiffany looked up and over at Amanda. Amanda reached for her bag and searched until she found her phone.

"Hello," she moaned into the phone as she rolled her eyes. Tiffany snickered at the irritable look on her friend's face. "Let me call you back," Amanda said pressing the end button.

"Who was that?"

"Reggie." Amanda said as she fell back onto the bed.

"Why are you actin' so bitchy with him? Is it really that bad? At least check out what he has to offer before you toss him to the side."

"You want to check it out for me," Amanda snapped. "Mind your business."

"I wouldn't mind, I thought he was sexy as hell," Tiffany teased.

"Yeah I see I have to keep my eye on you."

"Look who's talkin'. Hello!"

Amanda smacked her lips. "I really do feel bad, Tiffany."

"Well you don't sound too sincere."

"It wasn't worth all of the trouble."

"Or was it?" Tiffany quizzed.

"Ok, I don't want to discuss this right now," Amanda said scooting off the bed, searching through her numerous bags until she pulled out a pair of jeans.

Tiffany rolled over and swung her feet to the floor. "I love them."

"I can't believe I found a pair of Jeans that actually fit my butt."

"Did you see the gay guy checkin' you out?"

They laughed hard. "Yeah right. He was pretty damn helpful though."

They each tried on new clothes and accessories and pranced around in Tiffany's full length mirror. "God, I was so tired of borrowing clothes from Stephanie."

"Yeah, it's about time you took yourself shoppin'. Don't waste your pretty."

Amanda looked at Tiffany and smiled. "Awww," she said before throwing her arms around her friend. "Don't waste yours either."

"Trust me, I don't."

"So what's up with that guy you went out with that night?"

"He drove me crazy. All he talked about was his job. I was so annoyed."

"What does he do?"

"He's a cop."

"Yikes, he probably works right down the street off thirty fifth."

"How did you guess? I told him thanks, but no thanks."

"Wow, it was that bad?"

"Girl, I stored his number as don't answer as soon as I got in the house. He still hasn't stopped callin' me."

"You want to go out tonight?"

"Chris is comin' over tonight."

"Chris? Girl I can't keep up with your list."

"Look, I'm single and until Mr. Right comes and sweep me off my feet, I can do whatever the hell I want to do."

Amanda said jokingly, "Don't try to defend bein' a slut."

Tiffany laughed as she removed a pair of new shoes from her feet. "Keep talkin' shit, i'll send your ass home to Stephanie."

Amanda slouched on the bed. "It's just weird between us."

"You think? You made it weird. Normal people don't behave like you do. I love you girl, but I don't have any sympathy."

Amanda turned her head in Tiffany's direction. "Obviously. I don't need you rubbin' it in my face like you're so much better than me. It just happened. I didn't mean for it to happen. I didn't plan on sleepin' with him. I had a few drinks and—"

"Blame it on the alcohol, right? You're so in denial about it. I mean not only was he your cousin's interest, he's your boss's husband. Speakin' of her, did she confirm if she was pregnant or not?"

Amanda nodded her head. "She damn near made an announcement to the entire office."

"Does Stephanie know? Has she said anything about him?

"I haven't told Stephanie. We haven't talked much. As far as he's concerned, when isn't that women talkin' about him. You should have seen her office. There were so many pictures. It's like some kind of shrine of him."

Tiffany shook her head. "You think he's gonna stop seeing Stephanie?"

Amanda shrugged her shoulders. "It'll be best for her."

Tiffany raised an eyebrow. "Best for her, or best for you? Like you really care about what's best for her."

Amanda stood up and walked over to the window and peered out. "She's still family."

"Humph. Not for much longer."

CHAPTER 12

"Yeah, I'm in front of your place. Can you come out and holler at me for a sec?"

"Reggie, you can't just pop up over my crib like that."

"You weren't answerin' any of my calls. I don't even know what I did. Look, can you just step outside for a few minutes and talk to me. I just want to see you."

Amanda hit the end button on her cellular phone. She pressed the power button on the remote and flipped the television off, brushing a few potato chip crumbs off her jeans and white tank as she stood up. She slipped her feet into a pair of tattered flip flops and headed out of the building. She leaned her backside against the front gate and folded her arms. Reggie hopped out of his car and approached her wearing a huge smirk. Amanda couldn't help but crack a smile. "I missed you," he said smiling.

"That's nice to know."

"So what's up with all the attitude? You mind refreshin' a brother's memory. What exactly is the problem between us?"

"You walked out on me remember? You walk around like you're some kinda' big shot or somethin'."

"You sure this ain't about me tellin' your cousin about your little admirer?"

Amanda shook her head and rolled her eyes. "You could've kept your mouth closed."

"Oh, so it is about him. Why didn't you tell her?"

"What was there to tell? He called me gorgeous, big deal."

"Right, so if I walked up to your little friend and said baby I just wanted to tell you that you are so gorgeous, that wouldn't cause a problem?"

Amanda looked away and remained silent while Reggie stared her down searching for a reaction. She finally looked him in the face.

"Think what you want."

"I'm sick of your little attitude. You keep beatin' around the bush about everything."

"So why are you still in my face? I didn't ask to see you."

Amanda ran her hands through her head pulling her hair away from her face. The hot weather had her itching to go back inside and sulk in central air.

"If that's the way you feel, once I drive off that's it. You fine and all, but I could do without all the extras."

Amanda chuckled. "Well, then I guess you better hop in your ride and keep it movin'," she said as she turned and walked back toward the building leaving Reggie standing there. Once inside she slammed the door and collapsed on the couch with tears streaming down her face. She knew Reggie deserved better and it was best to let him go before things came to the light. In the end she knew she'd lose him anyway.

She wiped the tears away with the back of her hands, repositioned herself on her back, and stared up at the crown molding along the white ceiling. She raised a hand to her head and twirled one of her curly strands around her index finger. Moments of solitude often brought back the guilty pleasures of that night. She closed her eyes in an attempt to rid the memory, but it was useless. She could still taste his bitter lips, smell his fragrance, and hear his soft moans of ecstasy in her ear. The thoughts of him still made her moist between the legs. She crossed her legs, but the throbbing sensation was still there. The reason her cousin and boss put up with him was evident.

Her head shot up when she heard the sound of keys jingling in the doorknob. She wanted to bolt to her room, but her legs wouldn't move fast enough. She sat up when Stephanie walked into the apartment and walked straight to her room without as much as a nod. She heard her kick her heels off and toss her keys on what she assumed was the nightstand where Stephanie always placed her keys. The silent treatment among the two was driving Amanda crazy. She wanted to barge into her cousin's room and confess, but her brain or pride wouldn't let her be so dumb. Besides, the man is married anyway so technically he wasn't yours to begin with, she reasoned to herself. When it was apparent that Stephanie was going to keep up her antics, Amanda laid her head back against the cushion and kicked her feet up once more. She closed her eyes, immersed in her thoughts again.

Maybe it was the thought of her straddling Mike that kept her from hearing Stephanie's footsteps head in her direction. The hard blow to Amanda's face surprised her. Her eyes shot wide open and she scurried off the couch before Stephanie could punch her again.

"You think I wouldn't fuckin' find out?" Stephanie yelled, grabbing a hold of Amanda's shirt, forcing her to stumble to her knees. Amanda quickly crawled out of the way and crouched against a nearby wall. She held her aching and bloody nose, looking up at her cousin who stood towering over her. Amanda's tears had returned and were streaming down her face. "All that fuckin' time you spent lookin' me in my face." Stephanie continued, her voice quivering, "He told me. Mike told me every fuckin' thing, right before he fuckin' told me to never contact him again!" Stephanie said with tears now pouring from her own face as she sobbed.

Amanda sat glued to the hardwood floor. Everything from her toes to her brain went numb as she sat looking up at her cousin. No words escaped her mouth. Her lips never even parted. She watched as Stephanie fell down on the couch and cried uncontrollably. She knew she had the perfect opportunity to flee, but her body remained frozen in place. She could no longer run from her guilt. It was right there staring her in the face and she was forced to reckon with it. Tears continued to stream down Stephanie's red face as she sniffled and shook her head. Amanda looked on at her wondering which wounded Stephanie more, the fact that Mike dumped her, or that her own cousin that she loved so much betrayed her.

"How could you do that to me?" Stephanie said sobbing. "I was there for you, I did everything for you."

Amanda sat speechless, knowing she deserved much more than a jab in the face. No words escaped her mouth, just the muffled noises of her crying. Stephanie glared at Amanda unmoved by her tears. "You knew how much he meant to me." she said pointing a finger at herself.

"I was drunk. I didn't know what I was doin'. He took advantage of me. He—"

"Amanda, please, just please…just be honest with me for once," she begged with tears.

"It's the truth." Amanda pleaded, finally finding the courage to raise herself off of the floor and look Stephanie in the face. "Stephanie you know I wouldn't dare knowingly do a thing like that...I—"

"I don't know you at all," Stephanie said, raising her voice. "Because the woman I thought I knew wouldn't dare go behind my back. She wouldn't dare keep secrets and tell little white lies and fuck the man she knew I was in love with. You're not the woman I thought I knew, Amanda."

"In love with?" Amanda questioned confused. "How can you be in love with a man that's already in love with someone else?"

"You tell me, you've been down that rode before," Stephanie said. "Don't you remember how I wiped your tears the day you left Tony's cheatin' ass?"

"But I was his girlfriend! I wasn't his mistress or some—"

"And he was in love with someone else all along," Stephanie said, taking Amanda down memory lane. A place she didn't like to talk about. She knew Stephanie was trying to push her buttons. The situation between her and Tony still hurt her and she had found ways to beat around it, to stop thinking about it, to erase it from her memory, but her cousin was taking her there, making all the bad thoughts and insecurities spring to life again.

"What does that have to do with anything? So what, big deal he screwed around on me. Your point is irrelevant and it has nothin' to do with what's goin' on."

"You know what Amanda, you are one heartless bitch!"

"Well what does that make you? Me doin' what I did don't make what you were doin' right!" Amanda said taking a step towards her cousin.

"Oh, so what, you had to go teach me a lesson? Was that it? Look, bitch," Stephanie said with a twisted look on her face, "We were family and no matter what, you had no right to do what you did."

Amanda took a step back. "I didn't do it intentionally. You can't blame all this shit on me. He was a prick all along. He never loved you. He never gave a fuck about you. Don't get it twisted. You were nothin' more than a piece of pussy."

Stephanie slapped Amanda so hard she stumbled back into the wall. Amanda held her hand up to the stinging sensation on her face. Stephanie took a few steps closer.

"What went on between me and him was none of your fuckin' business. Don't sit here and pretend to care about how much of a jerk he was. He was obviously smart enough to turn your little whore ass out and send you walkin' home. He was smart enough to send you to work everyday with a closed mouth while you stared his got damn wife down. He was smart enough to have you come home and constantly look me in my face and not say a got damn word to me. He was—"

"The only reason I didn't mention anything to you was because I didn't want to hurt you. I didn't want you to—"

"You don't give a damn about me!" Stephanie yelled. "The only reason you said nothin' to me is because you wanted more from him."

"Are you out of your mind? I didn't want anything from him. I—"

"Then why'd you do it, huh? You just couldn't resist, could you? Little Miss Amanda just had to have him."

"Oh if I wanted him, I could've had him."

"Well maybe you still have a chance. Call him up. Maybe he and his sorry ass wife will make room for you at there place."

"What?" Amanda asked shocked. The thought of being homeless made her cringe.

"I want you out! Get the hell out!"

"Just like that? I don't have any place to go. I can't—"

"Call up Mike, maybe you can stay in the backseat of his car. Call up Reggie…call Tiffany, call yo' got damn mama! I don't really give a damn who you call. Just don't ever call me again." she said firmly looking Amanda directly in the eyes. Amanda looked away as a tear drop fell from her eye. Stephanie turned and stormed off towards her room, slamming her bedroom door close behind her leaving Amanda alone with her thoughts. She slumped down on the couch, unable to conceal her hurt, shame and tears any longer. Her entire body quivered as she cried long and hard. She wondered who she'd call. She wondered if she even had a job to go back to. She thought about Reggie and how she had left him hanging. He was definitely no longer an option.

When her head started to ache from all the crying and thinking she got up and slowly walked to her room. She looked around at the space. She climbed in her bed and laid her head on her pillow as she wiped the new set of tears from her face. Through all of the drama, lies, secrets, infidelity, somehow the thoughts of homelessness didn't cross her mind so she made no backup plans. She knew she'd only be able to deal with Tiffany for so long. While they enjoyed each other's company, petty arguments always found a way to challenge their friendship. Amanda heard Stephanie's bedroom door open and she quickly sat up in bed. Stephanie barged into her room wearing a pair of black leggings and an oversized graphic Tee that belonged to a man.

"Oh, you thought I was fuckin' jokin' right?" Stephanie asked walking over to Amanda's closet. She grabbed handfuls of clothing, still on hangers, and tossed them to the floor. Amanda ran over to the pile of clothing, scooping up as much as she could in her arms.

"Stephanie please don't do this," Amanda whimpered. "I have nowhere to go. I just gave you some money the other day. I can't—"

"Don't you get it? Have you not gotten it through your tiny little brain? Well let me remind you. You had sex with a man I'm in love with. You deceived me." Stephanie said as she continued throwing Amanda's clothes to the floor. "Do you really think I give a damn about you not having anywhere to go? Do you honestly think I care about what happens to you after you leave this apartment?" Stephanie questioned, finally turning around to look at Amanda, who stood motionless. Stephanie's words stung her. She toppled on top of the mountain of clothing, new and worn, and wept. Stephanie continued tossing clothes to the floor unaffected by Amanda's sadness. Stephanie treaded heavily out of the room and returned twenty seconds later with the cordless phone in hand. Amanda looked up at her, finally bringing her wet palms down from her face.

"I'm sorry, Stephanie. I'm really sorry. I didn't mean for it to happen. I didn't mean to hurt you. I—"

"I want you out! There's nothin' you can say to me to change that, or anything else between us. I can't even stand lookin' you in the face. I swear if I didn't love you I'd bash your fuckin' face in." Stephanie picked up as many clothes as she could off the floor and headed out the room with Amanda following behind her.

"Stephanie, just give them back to me."

Stephanie let the pile of clothing she was struggling to carry fall to the floor before she turned and looked Amanda in the eyes.

"I was there for you, Amanda. I did everything for you," Stephanie said, as tears began to fall from her own eyes. "When Mike told me about you two I could barely breathe. It was already enough that he flat out tossed me to the side, but you, you Amanda? You have no idea what pain you've caused me. You sure had me fooled. I wouldn't have expected you to do what you did to me." She wiped her tears from her face and walked back towards Amanda's room.

"Stephanie, I'm sorry. Just give me a chance to make it up to you. I'm not what you think I am," Amanda pleaded as she trailed behind her cousin.

"Was it worth it, Amanda? Was it really worth goin' to work everyday, lookin' your boss in the face, knowin' what you did with her husband?

"Well, it was no different than knowin' what you were doin' with her husband."

"So what, I was havin' an affair with a married man, that's not the issue so don't try and make it the issue. The issue is you knowingly and willingly screwed the man I was seeing behind my back. You betrayed me for someone who didn't give two shits about you. How could you do that to me? How could you let me go on and on with him, knowin' what the both of you did? And to make matters worse I had to hear it from him."

Amanda sighed. "I know what I did was wrong. I didn't mean for it to happen. I—"

"Shut up. I'm so tired of you sayin' that. You did mean for it to happen."

"It only happened once."

"Oh don't give me that. Who knows what would have happened had you not hopped out of his car."

"What exactly did he tell you?" Amanda asked out of curiosity. A look of surprise swept across Stephanie's face as she stopped walking in her tracks and spun around.

"Why is that so got damn important? You're just so got damn unsympathetic. All you think about is yourself. You don't care about who you hurt in the process."

"That's not true. I just want to know."

"He told me everything. He told me about how you came on to him, he told me about you bein' upset that you couldn't see him again, he told me that you even tried reachin' him a couple of times, he told me you—"

"And you believed him. Are you fuckin' kiddin' me?"

"Whether I believe him or not is irrelevant. What's done is done."

"So what about me? You're just gonna take his—"

"Did you have sex with him?" Stephanie asked with her hands placed on her hips. The question caught Amanda off guard. She paused before answering the question.

"It just happened."

Stephanie frowned. "Well let me tell you what's about to happen. By tomorrow afternoon I want you and all your shit out of my house." She turned and walked to her room, leaving Amanda standing in the middle of the hallway, speechless.

CHAPTER 13

"She took it pretty lightly if you ask me," Tiffany said over the phone. "I would've kicked your ass and threw all your shit outside."

Amanda smacked her lips. She pulled up into her designated parking area and hopped out of her car.

"I'm about to head in here." Amanda said slowly walking towards the entrance of her work building. "I can barely stand the sight of this place. What if she knows?"

"Come on, you think he actually told her about you or Stephanie? He's ready to be a family man," Tiffany chuckled.

"This is not the time to be a comedian," Amanda mumbled.

"You might as well go in laughin'. You might end up bein' laughed at."

"I can't believe his son of a bitch ass told Stephanie all those lies."

"Does that really matter? I highly doubt it. He got off Scott free."

Amanda stepped onto the elevator hoping she could take the ride up by herself. She made it to the fourteenth floor successfully and briskly walked to her cubicle before anyone could mutter anything to her.

"Are you sure you're cool with me crashin' at your place for a little while?" she asked Tiffany as she pulled her chair out and sat down. She checked the time on the computer monitor. Five minutes before her work shift began. She flipped open her compact mirror and examined her face. Her puffy eyes from the previous night had gone down drastically. She wore her hair pulled back into a ponytail to compliment her casual khaki colored wrap dress.

"Look, we'll discuss all of that after you get here. Is she there yet?" Tiffany asked.

"I don't know," Amanda said as she clicked on her email inbox. she gasped. "Oh my God." She whispered to Tiffany.

"What?"

"I have an email from her. She wants to see me!"

"What exactly does the email say?"

Amanda reread the email in her head and then aloud. "Please see me."

"What you think she wants?"

"Look, I don't know, I have to go," Amanda said nervously. "My shift is about to start."

"Well you make sure you keep me updated. Let me know if you need me—"

Amanda hit the end button on her phone when she heard a pair of high heels headed in her direction. She began shuffling papers around on her desk and scrolling down in her emails to look busy.

"Hey," Amanda heard a recognizable voice say behind her. She spun around in her chair to face Jessica. She was tempted to turn right back around, but hesitated.

"Yeah?"

Jessica took a few steps into her office. "Melanie wants to see you. She asked me to check and see if you had arrived."

Amanda's body tensed up. "What does she want to see me about?" she asked worriedly.

Jessica shrugged her shoulders. "I'll go and tell her you're here."

"Wait," Amanda jumped out of her chair and grabbed Jessica's hand. Jessica looked alarmed. "Is she upset? What mood is she in? Is she—"

Jessica chuckled like they were still good acquaintances. "Relax. I doubt you're getting fired."

Amanda walked alongside Jessica in the direction of Melanie's office. She could feel herself becoming nauseous.

"What's the big deal?" Jessica asked when she caught a glimpse of Amanda's trembling hands.

I slept with her husband, Amanda thought, but didn't dare utter aloud.

"I don't know," she answered, finally reaching the door to Melanie's office. She looked at Jessica one last time before reaching for the knob. Jessica smiled and walked off. Amanda twisted the doorknob and struggled for an intake of breath when she spotted Stephanie seated in front of Melanie's desk. Melanie looked up at Amanda with red puffy eyes. Amanda looked away and at her cousin who smiled and waved her in.

"Come on in," Stephanie said as if she was delighted to see her. "We were just discussing you."

Amanda stood in place, wondering if her mind were playing tricks on her.

"Amanda," Melanie called to her, wiping tears from her face. "Pull the door up."

Amanda snapped out of her daze and closed the door behind her. She walked towards Melanie's desk, unsure what to make of the situation.

"Discussing me?" Amanda questioned Stephanie, unable to look her boss in the face.

"Yeah, since you're here, maybe you can give Melanie your own version of what happened that night. You know, the night you slept with her husband."

Melanie shrieked as if hearing it for the first time. Her body went into a quiver as she cried uncontrollably. Amanda's mouth dropped wide open. She had nothing to say. She had run out of excuses, apologies and alibis. She stood over her cousin with a menacing look on her face. The thought of bashing her head into a wall ran through her head, but she bit her bottom lip instead.

"Stephanie, I can't believe you," she whispered like Melanie couldn't hear her.

"Oh honey, you aren't the victim. Poor little Miss Melanie is," Stephanie answered as she took Melanie's hands in her own. "I'm so sorry you had to hear this. I swear I had no idea he was married, not until he explained everything to me the night he threw me out of his life. Not until he told me about her," Stephanie continued, glaring at her cousin.

Amanda shook her head. "Melanie don't believe her, she's—
"

"Please...please, I can't take it anymore. I can't stand it anymore," Melanie said snatching her hands out of Stephanie's grasp and rolling herself away from her desk. She got up and stood in Amanda's face. Amanda stared off into the corner with her arms folded, humiliated. Melanie looked her up and down. "You can't even look me in the face. Why not Amanda? You were doing such a great job all this time. Do you know what it feels like? Do you have any idea how much you've ruined my life?"

"I'm not—"

"I can't believe you'd do something like this," Melanie continued as tears ran down her face.

Amanda looked over at Stephanie before lowering her head. She felt her lips begin to quiver along with the rest of her body. She felt the tears in her eyes before they trickled down her face. She looked up at Melanie with a wet, red, and sobbing face. Melanie turned away not allowing herself to be touched by Amanda's grief.

"I'm sorry," were the only two words Amanda could manage to say.

"You aren't sorry," Stephanie cut in. "You don't even care. You can't even—"

"Shut up! Shut up!" Amanda yelled loud enough for the entire office to hear.

"Another outburst like that and I'll have security escorting you out." Melanie said looking her in the face. "You ladies can excuse yourselves," Melanie said looking from Amanda to Stephanie before making her way back around her desk.

Stephanie stood up and smirked at Amanda. Amanda paid her no attention. She looked at Melanie who stood examining the framed photos on her desk. More tears rolled down her face. Amanda could barely stand to look at her. Stephanie strutted past Amanda to the door wearing a light gray pants suit with a soft pink lace camisole underneath.

"Don't be late," she muttered to Amanda before letting herself out and slamming the door behind her leaving the two women alone with their thoughts. Melanie sat in her chair, massaging her temples. She looked up at Amanda who stood fiddling with her hands.

"You know, that man meant everything to me," Melanie said to herself aloud. Amanda remained silent. "Eight long years gone down the drain."

"I know its—"

Melanie raised a hand for silence.

"Just leave me alone. You've done enough." Amanda looked at her one last time before turning and heading to the door.

"I'll hand in my letter of resig—"

"Thank you." Melanie said cutting her off.

Amanda took a deep breath to fight back the tears as she opened the door. She knew those would be the last words she'd ever hear from her boss.

CHAPTER 14

"Girl, you knew it wouldn't last."

"I know, but I can't believe you're just up and leavin' like this. It's only been a week."

"It's no point in stayin' here. I might as well leave."

"You sure you want to stay with your mother? That's definitely back trackin'."

"What am I suppose to do?"

"Stay here, find another job, and get your own damn place. Stop bein' a leech."

"I know I sure as hell won't miss your smart ass mouth. I'm goin' to California and that's that. I can start over when I get there."

Tiffany shook her head for the twentieth time. "I can't believe you're leavin'."

Amanda smiled as Tiffany tightened her grip on the steering wheel, headed back towards home. The pair had made a quick errand to the local, Jewel, to pick up some snacks for a movie night.

"You can come visit me as often as you like."

"So there's no gettin' you to reconsider? It's not gonna be the same, Amanda."

Tiffany put on her turning signal as she turned onto the block of the apartment Amanda once shared with Stephanie.

"Now why would you even turn down this—"

The sight of the liquid silver Jaguar caused both pair of eyes to nearly bulge out of their sockets.

"Please tell me that's not—"

Mike exited his car and walked around to where a smiling Stephanie stood. They saw Stephanie wrap her arms around his neck. Her smile faded once she spotted the two driving past. Tiffany's foot pressed down on the accelerator and they sped up, both shocked at what they had just witness.

Tiffany looked over at Amanda and asked, "Did we really just see what I think we saw?"

"I can't believe it," Amanda muttered shaking her head heatedly. "She kicked me out and let that lyin' son of a bitch move in!"

"Well, at least—"

"I can't believe it!" Amanda repeated angrily.

Tiffany twisted up her face. "Well, at least your boss lady was smart enough to let the bastard go."

Amanda folded her arms and sighed.

Amanda said through clenched teeth, "Let's just enjoy this night together. I'm headin' out first thing in the morning."

Tiffany raised an eyebrow "I thought you said you were leavin' on—"

"I changed my mind."

"You changed your mind? Don't tell me you're upset about that shit!" Tiffany said, slamming on her brakes as they approached a red light. Amanda clutched her seatbelt and nearly snapped her neck as she turned her head in Tiffany's direction.

"Can you pay attention please!"

"Girl, don't worry, your life is safe with me," she said chuckling.

Minutes later Tiffany pulled up in front of her apartment building. The twosome hopped out and headed inside.

"I need to call my mother." Amanda said, flinging her purse across Tiffany's dark brown sofa.

"Does she even know yet?"

"Know about what?

"Does she know about you comin' down there? About you and Stephanie?" Tiffany asked as they walked into the open kitchen and placed the plastic bags on the counter. Amanda pulled out a chair and sat at the kitchen table with her face buried in the palms of her hands.

"I'll tell her when I get down there. I don't feel like talkin' about all that crap anymore. It drives me crazy. Hell, I can't believe what we just saw."

"Well believe it, honey. It shouldn't come as a surprise. He's a jerk!"

"Sure he's a jerk, but what about Stephanie? Doesn't she get the point?"

"Don't worry about her. You shouldn't care about her, she kicked you out remember? Let her deal with his raggedy ass."

Amanda exhaled shaking her head in disbelief, with her elbows plopped on the table and her head rested in her hand. Tiffany joined her friend at the table after putting the food up.

"Cheer up! You look like you just came from a funeral. It's not the end of the world."

Amanda sighed. "It's not that easy. I'm really hurt," she said through her palms.

"Hurt about what?" Tiffany asked, finally reaching her boiling point. "About Stephanie kickin' you out, or seeing her with the man?"

Amanda looked up at her a little stunned. "Both."

"Why are you so concerned about it? Get over it, Amanda! You need to be cryin' over bein' broke for the next couple of months, or however long it takes for you to find another job."

"Forget you, Tiffany, " Amanda said, raising herself up. "Can you try bein' a little more sympathetic sometimes?"

"I am sympathetic, but not today. I'm so tired of you mopin' around here like somebody owes you somethin'. Dammit Amanda, you brought this on yourself!"

Amanda sat back down in the chair and wiped a few tears with the back of her hand. Again silence prevailed. Tiffany combed her fingers through her hair, looking on at her troubled friend. "Amanda, I'm not—"

"I don't want to talk about it," Amanda said quietly, staring off into the corner, mulling over her situation.

"Fine, I'll be in the front," Tiffany answered, raising herself from the table and walking out of the kitchen. Amanda tried wiping away her tears, but they continued to overflow as she sobbed. She stood up, went in Tiffany's bedroom, and laid across the bed, still shedding tears. "You All right?" she heard Tiffany ask unaware that she had entered the room.

"I'm fine," Amanda answered as best as she could. Tiffany sat on the bed and rubbed Amanda's back.

"I'm sorry, sweetie. I wasn't tryin' to make you upset, Amanda."

Amanda continued to cry. "Everything is gonna be fine," Tiffany continued.

Stillness remained among the two until Amanda turned over and positioned herself on her back. Her eyes were red and puffy. She wiped away the remainder of the tears and sniffled.

"I really fucked up." Amanda said in a raspy voice.

"Fucked up how, Mandy?" Tiffany questioned as she leaned in closer towards her friend and wiped a couple of tears herself. Amanda sat up brushing out the wrinkles on her light gray jogging suit.

"I can't believe what I did to her. It wasn't worth it. It really wasn't worth it."

Tiffany nodded her head in agreement. "If you would have known better you would have done better."

"Please save that chicken soup talk for somebody else. That's not what I want to hear right now. Besides, it sounds real fake comin' from you." Amanda said, rolling her eyes and chuckling.

"Well, I don't want you to keep beatin' yourself up about this. Look at you," Tiffany said pointing at Amanda's baggy jogging suit. "You really let yourself go this past week."

Amanda looked down at the couple of stains on her top then smiled and looked up. Her wild curly hair went in every direction and although her attire was rather sloppy her beauty remained.

"Tiff, I feel horrible. Last week I had a cousin, a job, a home, and a guy who seemed to really dig me and now I have nothin'." Tiffany contorted her face. "Oh, and you!" Amanda said throwing her arms around her best friend's neck, pulling her closer. They laughed as Tiffany playfully shoved her.

"You better not forget me."

"Tiffany, I feel so horrible right now. What should I do?"

"Do about what?"

"About everything."

"Well first off, you need to stop walkin' around like you're not the beautiful woman you are. Secondly, you're gonna have to let some of your worries go. You can't control or obsess about what Stephanie thinks of you. Obviously, she's content on continuing a fling with that jack ass."

"I screwed up with Reggie too, and—"

"Call him." Tiffany suggested, jumping up from the bed to retrieve Amanda's cell phone from her purse. She reentered the room with her friend's phone in hand scrolling through the contact list.

"I can't," Amanda said reaching up for her phone. "He probably won't answer anyway. I haven't spoke to him since that day."

"So what, he's probably sittin' around thinkin' about you now."

"I highly doubt it."

"Well, we'll see about that, won't we," Tiffany said as she hit the talk button and pressed the speaker phone once the other end started ringing.

Amanda eyes widened. "I can't believe you—"

"Shhhh," Tiffany whispered, bringing her finger to her mouth, plopping down on the bed beside her friend. They both quieted their voices, waiting for Reggie to pick up.

"Hello," a female's voice answered just as Tiffany was about to end the call. Both girls' eyes bulged as they stared at each other with their mouths agape. "Hello," the voice repeated. Amanda quickly snatched the phone from Tiffany and pressed the end button. She tossed the phone on the bed a few inches from where she was sitting.

"You don't even know who it is, Amanda," Tiffany said in response to the look of shock on her friend's face.

"Did a bitch really just answer his cell phone?" Amanda asked, wide eyed while Tiffany continued shaking her head in astonishment. "I really can't—"

Both girls looked at Amanda's phone when it began vibrating. Tiffany reached for it and Amanda took it from her, staring at Reggie's name on the screen.

"Answer it!" Tiffany slapped a hand on Amanda's knee.

"Hello," Amanda said after she hit the talk button, holding the phone with a trembling hand. She quickly put the call on speaker, allowing Tiffany to listen in.

"What's up?"

"Who was the girl that answered your phone?" Amanda asked with an attitude. Tiffany eyebrows rose as she eagerly awaited Reggie's response.

"My sister," Reggie said nonchalantly. "Why you so concerned about who answer my phone? You call yourself leavin' me alone, remember?"

Amanda and Tiffany quickly exchanged glances, smiling at each other. Tiffany nodded her head as if Reggie passed his test. Amanda rolled her eyes.

"Reggie, I just have so much goin' on and—"

"You told me to keep it movin', remember that?" Reggie snapped.

"I did, but I didn't really mean it, and I—"

"And you what? You can't just toss me to the side like that and think shit still sweet between us."

"It's not like that, Reggie." Amanda rolled her eyes in annoyance. "Can you just let me talk? I know you're upset, but—"

"I was headin' out the door, just hit me up later or somethin'," Reggie said in a rush. "Call me later, bye."

"Hello?" Amanda said. She looked down at her phone and saw the call had ended then looked up at Tiffany and shrugged her shoulders. "What's his problem?"

"He just checked you," Tiffany said, erupting with laughter. Amanda cracked a smile.

"He didn't check shit! And I ain't callin' his ass back either."

"Yeah right, I see you tryin' to hide your smile. He didn't have to call you back."

"He sure in the hell didn't. Not with that nasty attitude."

"Girl, please! If I was him I would've reacted the same way. You told him to keep it movin', correct?"

Amanda grinned. "Whatever."

"Whatever my ass. So what you gonna do?"

"Nothin'. I'm definitely not callin' his sorry ass back."

"Oh well, you'll be the one layin' up here trippin', not him."

Amanda stood up and walked over to the full length mirror hanging on the back of Tiffany's closet door. She pulled her hair back from her face and ran a hand over the multiple stains on her sweat shirt.

"Why would you let me leave the house lookin' like this?" Amanda asked, turning away from the mirror to face Tiffany.

Tiffany shrugged her shoulders and giggled. "All we did was run to the store. It's not like I didn't throw a baseball cap over my own head. Joggin' suits, or not, we still got it goin' on."

Amanda looked at her reflection again. "I don't know about all that, Tiff," she said with slumped shoulders.

"So what's up, are we gonna watch some movies or not? All this time we're wastin', we could have at least watched one movie by now." Tiffany asked as she got up and walked out the room with Amanda trailing behind.

CHAPTER 15

"I just don't understand what went wrong," Amanda's mom said for the second time within the first five minutes of their conversation.

Amanda let out a long winded exhale. "Things happen mom. People grow apart."

"Well not you and Stephanie. You guys are practically inseparable. I thought the living arrangement you guys had going on was perfect."

"You thought wrong," Amanda said nonchalantly, shrugging her shoulders and rolling her eyes every few seconds.

"So you're coming down here to stay with me for awhile, huh? Why did you wait so long to fill me in on all of this? How long have you been over Tiffany's? How are things—"

"Whoa mom, calm down. One question at a time please. Geez!"

"Amanda, how do you expect me to react? This is a little too much. I'm still trying to put together the puzzle.

"Mom, I already told you things just got really hectic between us."

"Why hasn't Stephanie called me and mentioned anything to me?"

"For the second time, I don't know! It's not my problem."

"Hold on, now you calm down. Don't get fancy with me. I'm simply trying to rectify the situation."

"Mom, you can't do anything at this point, but help me out."

"How can I help you if I don't know what went wrong between you two?"

"Just be there for me."

"I am here for you, Amanda. Don't—"

"Mom, I'll talk to you a little later. Can you just pick me up from the airport, please?"

"Well, what about your car?"

"What about it? It'll be parked here in front of Tiffany's building. It should be fine."

"You sure you just don't want to move here?"

"Mom, I'll fly there for two weeks and see how things work out. I just need a break from Chicago right now."

"Honey, Chicago isn't the problem."

"Mom, I'll see you later on. Airport, ten thirty your time. Thanks...love you...bye." Amanda hit the end button and tossed her cell phone on the bed as she stood over her suitcase hoping she packed everything she needed for her two week visit.

"Tiffany!" she yelled.

"What?" Tiffany shouted back from the bathroom.

"Are you ready? I have a flight to catch."

"I know. I'm comin'. I'm just fixin' my hair."

Amanda pressed a hand against the top of the suitcase struggling to zip it up with the other hand. "Whew," she sighed heavily after sitting the heavy suitcase on the floor. Tiffany walked in smiling with her long pony tail swinging behind her, wearing a pair of skinny leg jeans and a fun printed top.

"You sure you don't want me to come with?" She cheesed.

"Girl, hush. What you doin' tonight?"

"Why? It's not like you're gonna be hangin' out with me."

"You're right, I'll be in Cali havin' fun in the sun while checkin' out all the hot guys."

Tiffany rolled her eyes. "I'm so jealous. I should've planned a vacation. My boss drives me crazy."

Amanda smiled. "Let's go, chick. I don't want to be stranded in the airport, waitin' around for another flight."

"Yeah, I have company comin' over."

"Company?" Amanda inquired as she lifted the handle on her carry on and rolled it behind her as they left the room. "What company?"

"Alex, the guy we met at the car wash."

"Are you serious? The cute one with the sexy body?"

Tiffany smirked. "Yes. He is so hot."

"Well, have fun and behave yourself young lady," Amanda teased as they walked out the apartment to Tiffany's car. Amanda threw her suitcase in the trunk and hopped in on the passenger side. "Midway. Hop on the Stevenson, it'll be quicker."

"I know where I'm goin', relax. I can't believe you booked an early flight. Someone was a little giddy."

"The earlier the better," Amanda glanced at the time on the radio. "Six in the morning is pushin' it. I just didn't want a flight smack in the middle of the day."

"What airline are you flyin'?"

"Delta," Amanda said, looking over her ticket information.

Tiffany turned the volume up on the radio. "Put in a CD, I'm so tired of these commercials."

"I hope my mama's husband don't drive me up a wall," Amanda said as she slid a random CD into the player.

"Hell, she better hope he doesn't drive you anywhere." Tiffany cracked.

"Are you tryin' to take a jab at me? It's too early in the morning for that shit," Amanda snapped leaning back in her seat and closing her eyes.

"So what are your plans once you get down there?" Tiffany quickly changed the subject.

Amanda shrugged her shoulders with her eyes still shut. "Don't really have any."

Tiffany glimpsed at her and returned her eyes to the rode. "Look, you need to wake the hell up. I'm just as tired as you are. At least keep me company until we get to the freakin' airport."

Amanda's eyes shot opened as she looked over to her left at Tiffany. "I'm tired. I've been up packin' all morning."

"Well, you could sleep on the plane. You was up talkin' to that boy all night on my house phone. You better come back to Chicago with some money."

"Tiffany, for real, calm down. I spent ten measly minutes on your house phone. Besides, he called me."

"You gave him my number?"

"I gave him your address too," Amanda said raising her voice preparing for a debate. "He asked me who I was stayin' with and where I was stayin'."

"Does he know you're gonna be gone?"

"I'll tell him when I make it to Cali. He don't need to know all my whereabouts. He ain't my man."

"You act like it!" Tiffany snickered.

"I do not. You're overreactin'. I called him a little after we were done watchin' movies."

"I thought you said you weren't callin' him."

"I was bored."

Tiffany rolled her eyes. They laughed in union.

"So what did you two talk about?"

"None of your business!" Amanda said, checking herself in the overhead mirror.

"Well maybe you should'v asked Reggie to take you to the airport."

"Whatever. Maybe I'll have him pick me up."

"Have you been over to the his house yet?"

"No," Amanda shook her head.

"What if he stays with his mama or some crazy bitch you don't even know about?" Tiffany said before beeping her horn at the driver in front of her. "Damn, the light turned green how many seconds ago?"

"I doubt he stays with his mama, or another female."

"Why is that? You can never be too sure."

"I just know. He just doesn't rub me that way." Amanda said peeking at the time again.

"He ain't rubbin' you no kind of way. You ain't givin' up no ass to the man, so he has to be gettin' it from somewhere," Tiffany said looking over at her every few seconds.

Amanda smacked her lips and exhaled. "Well why don't you give him some since you seem to be so concerned."

Tiffany chuckled. "Hey, I'm just sayin'."

"How about you just not say anything else and get me to the airport. The clock is tickin', woman. I know you tryin' to buy some time, but I don't have it." Amanda cracked a smile. "I know you're gonna miss me."

Tiffany rolled her eyes. "I'll be fine, trust me."

Amanda smirked and nudged Tiffany's shoulder. "You know you will."

Tiffany smirked. "Okay, maybe just a little."

Amanda smiled as she closed her eyes once more. This time they didn't open until Tiffany's car came to a halt in front of the Delta airline departure.

"I'm so tired," Amanda moaned. "Pop the trunk."

Both girls hopped out of the car and Tiffany helped Amanda pull her luggage out.

"Damn, you sure you're only stayin' for two weeks?" Tiffany teased.

"I know, it's pretty fuckin' heavy," Amanda said as she rolled the suitcase on the sidewalk.

"Aaaaawww, I'm gonna miss you," Tiffany cooed as she extended her arms and embraced Amanda. They both laughed and rocked with each other as they hugged.

"Make sure you tell your mom I said hi. And bring me back one of them fine California men."

"Girl, hush," Amanda said giggling. "Make sure you keep an eye on my car."

"All right honey," Tiffany said as they hugged each other one final time. "I gotta move this car."

Amanda chuckled as she watched her friend sprint around to the driver's side and hop in, turning on the hazard lights. Amanda leaned over the passenger side window.

"All right girl, I'll call you when my plane touch down."

"Okay, don't forget."

"I won't," Amanda said, turning away from the car and grabbing the handle to her roll on. "Talk to you later."

"Don't do anything I wouldn't do," Amanda heard Tiffany yell behind her.

Amanda snickered. "Whatever," she yelled back and entered the airport.

CHAPTER 16

"I'm so happy to see you, sweetheart," Amanda's mother said looking her daughter over before embracing her once again.

"Mom, can we get in the car?" Amanda teased while smiling. "Pop the trunk."

"I was thinking about a few things to do on your stay. You have anything in mind?"

Amanda nodded her head as she slid into the passenger's side of her mother's charcoal gray Acura TL. She leaned her head back against the ebony seat and closed her eyes and said, "Yeah, rest and relax."

"You could've done that back at home," Amanda's mother said as she pulled off and headed towards the west side of Los Angeles in route to the Ladera Heights community.

"Mom, I've been up all morning, so cut me a little slack." Amanda whined opening her eyes and turning her head side ways to catch another peek of her mother. Her hair was pulled back into the usual low pony tail. She kept her French manicured nails on the steering wheel, peering in the rearview mirror every few seconds.

"I cut you enough slack," she said looking over at her only daughter, batting those long eyelashes of hers.

"What's that suppose to mean?"

"Sweetheart, you know how much I want you to be here with me. I don't know what it is about Chicago that has you so hooked."

"The hotdogs," Amanda said chuckling at her own remark.

"Oh give me a break. When was the last time you and that snooty cousin of yours ate a hotdog?"

Amanda shrugged her shoulders. The thought of Stephanie made her want to quickly change the subject. "Who cares what she eats?"

Amanda's mother looked over at her again. "I want to know what the problem is between you two."

"At least you guys have better trees here. The palm trees are absolutely beautiful."

"Amanda, stick to the subject. We're talking about you and your cousin not the damn trees," her mother said shaking her head irritated. "If its that bad, why not move here?"

"Because I don't want to live with you."

"Why not? We have enough room."

"Mom, I'm not gonna intrude on you and Ben's place. That's just—"

"Honey, it's a three bed two bath condo. It's not like we're living in a one bedroom apartment. So of course we—"

"Mom," Amanda interrupted, "I'm not talkin' about the size of your place. I just don't want to move back with my mom."

Amanda's mom exhaled. "Well, baby if that's how you feel then I won't press the issue."

"Thanks," Amanda said dryly.

Her mother shrugged her shoulders and the ride remained silent until they pulled up beside Ben's platinum colored Infiniti sport utility vehicle.

"Oh he's back," Amanda's mom said as she shut the engine off.

Amanda forced a smile as the two climbed out of the car, grabbed Amanda's luggage and headed inside.

"Whew," Amanda said dropping her bags on the Pergo wood flooring. "It sure does feel good in here."

"It's nothin' like central air on a hot summer day," Ben said, wearing a huge smile on his face. Amanda chuckled as Ben held out his arms to embrace his step daughter. "How was the flight?" Ben asked, picking up Amanda's belongings and walking off towards the guest bedroom.

"It was All right," Amanda called to him as she walked towards the floor to ceiling windows and peered outside at the greenery. She slid open the sliding doors leading to the private balcony and inhaled the smell of fresh air. Her mother joined her smiling from ear to ear.

"It's such a nice day out."

Amanda nodded her head and grinned. "Yes, finally, a breath of fresh air compared to Chicago's rainy weather."

Amanda's mother smirked. "I told you to come on over here, but you refuse to listen."

Amanda rolled her eyes. "You said you wouldn't press the issue."

"I know what does need pressin'...this wild hair of yours." She combed her hands through her daughter's curls.

Amanda chuckled. "Very funny."

The two of them walked back inside and joined Ben who had nestled himself on a sofa inside the large living room.

"I guess I better make a run to Ralph's."

"What's Ralph'? Oh the grocery store, right?"

"Yeah, somethin' you guys in Chicago refer to as Jewel and Dominick's," her mother teased. Ben let out a chuckle as he stood up. A ribbed tank covered his potbelly while a pair of blue cargo shorts masked his puny legs. He reminded Amanda of Ronald Isley from the legendary family music group, The Isley Brothers. Only his fine hair that he had pulled back into a greasy ponytail was graying.

"Mom, stop actin' like you weren't born and raised in Chicago."

"Ugh, don't remind me."

Ben let out a chuckle. "I'm runnin' to the store. I'll be back with in a few."

"Honey, maybe you should stop and pick up a couple of movies."

Ben shook his head. "Isn't she just a demandin' little somethin','" Ben asked Amanda teasingly.

Amanda laughed and looked at her mother, "Yeah, tell me about it."

Her mother smirked. "Well, I am the queen of the castle." She nodded before kissing her husband on the cheek. He smiled and disappeared out the front door. Amanda followed her mom into their big kitchen with a breakfast bar that opened up into the dining room. Amanda searched the contents of the refrigerator while her mother began loading the small pile of dishes that were in the sink into the dishwasher.

"Mom, what's up with all of the healthy choice meals?" Amanda mocked.

"That's exactly why Ben ran to the grocery store. So hush."

Amanda closed the stainless steel refrigerator and sat in a chair at the breakfast bar. She put her elbows on the granite countertop and rested her chin in the palm of her hands.

"So, what's on you and Ben's agenda for tonight?"

Amanda mother shook her head as she flipped the switch for the garbage disposal. "Not sure. I planned on spending my evening with you."

"Why, so you can talk me to death?" Amanda teased. Her mother rolled her eyes as she ran a dry dish towel over the wet countertop. "I was just jokin'."

"What's the issue with you and Stephanie? Or do I need to call her to find out?"

Amanda smacked her lips. "Mom, we're grown women, no need for you to go dappin' in our business. Trust we can handle things on our own."

Amanda's mother tossed the towel in the sink and placed her hands on her hips as she faced her daughter.

"You know what, don't give that crap. It's a reason your smart ass is sittin' in front of me and not back in Chicago some damn where."

Amanda said through clenched teeth, "Let's not make an argument out of this."

"Oh, there won't be an argument. I'll be damned if you think I'm gonna sit her and argue with a child," Her mother yelled with her voice raised a couple of notches higher than normal, forcing Amanda to soften the tough look on her face.

"Mom, relax," Amanda pleaded softly, breaking eye contact. Silence invaded the room as her mother rummaged through a few cabinets.

"How's work?"

Amanda raised her eyebrows, thrown off guard by the question. She quickly faked a smile. "Fine."

Her mother placed a box of cornbread on the counter and closed the cabinet. "Just fine?" she questioned, redirecting her attention towards her daughter. "You don't sound too convincing."

Amanda shrugged her shoulders as she stared off into a corner of the room. "It's ok, nothin' special, or worth talkin' about."

Amanda made eye contact and caught her mom raise an eyebrow.

"Mom, I'm on a vacation. Who wants to talk about work on vacation?" Amanda said giggly, trying to lighten to mood. Her mother smirked.

"I guess." Her mother reached in the cabinet below the sink. "Want to make this cornbread?"

"Sure," Amanda said excitedly, walking towards her mother. She was happy to partake in any activity that didn't involve talking about Stephanie, work, or the rest of her problems back at home. She reached in the fridge to grab the eggs and milk.

"Make sure you add a tiny amount of oil to the batter. Not too much."

"What else are we havin'?" Amanda asked eagerly.

"We'll have to see what Ben picks up from the store."

"I hope it's not fish."

"Relax, it won't be fish. Get started on the cornbread and leave the rest to the head chef in charge."

Amanda laughed. "Yeah right."

"I was talking about Ben, not me. Wow, you sure do know how to make your mother feel good." She chuckled.

"Your cookin' is great. I wouldn't call you the head chef. We both know Ben has you faded, hands down."

"I don't have a problem with that. I love a man who knows his way around the kitchen."

Amanda rolled her eyes. "I'm sure you do."

"What's that suppose to mean?"

Amanda shrugged her shoulders. "Nothin'."

"So when are you gonna meet your prince charming?"

Amanda shrugged her shoulders again. She whipped the batter of oil, egg, milk, sugar and cornbread mix, pretending to be focused on the task of preparing the cornbread. A few seconds of awkward silence fell upon the room. Her mother placed a hand on her shoulder. "What's the matter, sweetheart?"

"Its ok mom, I'm just tryin' to make sure the cornbread comes out all right."

The front door swung open and in walked Ben struggling to carry the many bags of groceries. Amanda was thankful for his presence. "Ben, why didn't you just call and let me know you were outside, I would've helped you bring the bags inside," Amanda said leaving the batter on the counter and heading towards Ben to help. She grabbed a few bags and sat them in the kitchen. Her mother took over the cornbread task.

"The lines were out the door," Ben exaggerated as he usually does, stirring up a few giggles from Amanda.

"Were the lines out the door or were they just long?" Amanda taunted.

"Hush, you know what I mean," Ben replied, laughing as he began putting the food away.

"Well, I'm unpack a few of my things and hop in the shower," Amanda said stepping over a few bags as she headed out of the kitchen. Her mother and stepfather giggled amongst each other too engrossed in their own conversation to respond back. She walked into the cozy guest room, where the walls were painted a taupe color. The iron sleigh bed was decorated in fancy and delicate ivory linen topped off with a variety of attractive matching toss pillows. She picked up the framed photo of her and her mother on the nightstand and scanned over it. She smiled. It was a picture from her last visit of when they went to Venice Beach. She put the photo down and unzipped her suitcase then grabbed a few empty hangers and hung up her clothing, leaving the things that didn't need hanging in the luggage.

After her long shower, she threw on a teal, halter bra Maxi dress. She examined herself in the full length standing mirror. She loved her reflection. The empire waist, ruche front, and open cut out back accentuated her curves. She slipped her feet into a pair of metallic gold flat embellished sandals. A knock on the door sounded as she slid a 14 carat gold bangle bracelet on her wrist. She opened the door to see her mother standing in the doorway smiling.

"You're just too cute," her mother said walking into the room. Amanda smiled and held up her wrist. "Oh, you're wearing the bracelet I bought you. Honey, you're a breath of fresh air."

"Yeah Tiffany and I did a little shoppin' not too long ago," Amanda said as she ran her fingers through her hair.

"I think you should wear it wild and curly, it's natural state." Her mother suggested as she took a seat on the full size bed.

"My plan exactly."

"Well it's apparent you want to go out for a stroll today."

"Yeah, it'll be nice to get out and do a little somethin' today. You always cook way too early."

"Well, Ben is in there whipping up dinner for tonight. Maybe the two of us could go out for a drive. Do a little shopping, maybe get manicures."

"Sounds like fun, but let's hold off until tomorrow. A nice drive or walk would be fine for now."

"All right, well I'm ready when you are," her mother said already comfortably dressed in a white collard top and a pair of white Capri's. She exited the room. Amanda rubbed a small amount of Mac's Lip-glass along her lips, grabbed her sunglasses, and joined her mother and Ben in the living area.

"Where are you ladies headed?" Ben asked, turning to the sports channel on the fifty inch Samsung plasma mounted on the wall.

"Out," Amanda's mom said smiling. "We're gonna leave you with your sports."

"Wow, God is good," Ben teased. The ladies giggled as they headed out the door to her mother's car.

"Let's go to an Art Gallery or a museum," Amanda's mother suggested.

Amanda chuckled. "As long as you're drivin' we can go wherever you want."

"Great." Her mother sped off in the direction of Wilshire Boulevard and turned on the radio while Amanda toyed with the game applications on her phone. "It's such a gorgeous day out."

Amanda nodded her head without looking up from her phone. "Yeah."

"Oh, you're too busy to converse?" Her mother teased.

Amanda finally looked up and laughed. "Mom, relax."

Her mother smirked and continued driving while Amanda refocused her attention to the game she was playing. She looked up after her mother pulled up in the parking lot of the Petersen Automotive Museum.

"What in the world—"

"Come on," her mother cut her off as they hopped out of the car and headed inside. Her mother paid and off they were.

"Mom, are you kiddin' me? What possessed you to bring me to an automotive museum?"

Her mother bellowed with laughter. "Honey, relax, it isn't as bad as you think."

Amanda couldn't help but laugh. "Is this your way of gettin' back at me for not payin' any attention to you on the car ride here?" she teased.

"Ben brought me here and it wasn't half bad."

Amanda rolled her eyes. "Mom," she whined.

"Come on, I already paid the twenty, so we're stuck here. Amanda smacked her lips. "Amanda, don't be such a snob. I've raised you better than that."

"I'm in no way, shape or form, even remotely close to bein' a snob."

"It's always fun doing things you wouldn't normally do."

"Yeah, tell me about it," Amanda said sarcastically as they began their tour around the museum. Surprisingly, Amanda found herself amazed and fascinated with the array of ordinary and quirky cars, including the Bat mobile and Rolls Royce with round doors.

"I told you, I couldn't believe it until I saw it." her mother said just as excited as her daughter.

"I'll admit that this place is pretty cool for a person who isn't the least bit interested in cars."

Her mother pointed ahead and said, "The rotating exhibits are pretty cool."

They continued their tour around the museum.

"I how the displays are set up into the different eras using the cars to showcase the time in history."

Her mother nodded her head in agreement. After the two hour walk around the museum they left out smiling and giggling while carrying on a conversation they had begun back inside the place.

"I saw you checkin' that guy out," her mother teased as she hit the unlock button on her keys.

"Mom you're always thinkin' I'm checkin' somebody out. Clearly he was droolin' at me." Amanda said laughing as they got in the car.

"He was a handsome young man."

"Too bad I don't live here," Amanda reminded her.

"Well, I hope he was motivation." They laughed as her mother sped home.

CHAPTER 17

Amanda awoke the next morning, struggling to open her eyes from the blinding sunlight. She lifted her head off the pillow and glanced around the room from where she laid. After the objects in the room registered to her head and reminded her of where she was, she let the back of her head fall back onto the pillow, shut her eyes then pushed the ivory bedding to the side to cool her body down. There was a knock on the door just as she positioned herself on her side. She groaned and ignored the knock.

"Knock knock," her mother said as she opened the door and peeked into the room at her tired daughter. "Amanda," she called.

"Mom, what is it?" Amanda said in a grouchy voice after letting out a heavy winded exhale.

"It's ten o' clock. Do you plan on getting up soon? I made breakfast."

"Not now mom, I'm sleepin'."

"Well it'll be nice if you get up. The sooner you get up, the quicker we can head out."

Amanda moaned as she turned to her other side, placing a pillow over her face in frustration. Her mother shook her head and closed the door. Amanda eased the pillow away from her face to see if her mom had truly left the room.

"Thank goodness," she whispered to herself when she realized she was left alone.

She tossed and turned every few minutes unable to fall back asleep comfortably. Suddenly her cell phone vibrated on the nightstand next to where she rested. She slowly reached for it and glanced at the caller ID.

"Hello?" she answered in annoyance.

"Look, you didn't have to answer the phone if you were gonna have such an attitude," Tiffany snapped.

"What's up?"

"You tell me, Miss California."

Amanda chuckled. "It's cool."

"I see. You haven't even called me!"

"Girl, can I at least settle in first? Don't call me actin' like you're my man or somethin'."

The girls laughed.

"Has Reggie called you?"

"Nope, he sure hasn't."

"Well he called the house."

"Really? What did you say?"

"I didn't answer, I wasn't home. I was out with this really—"

"That's strange. He didn't call my cell phone first, or at all for that matter," Amanda interrupted.

"Maybe he didn't really want to talk to you," Tiffany teased.

Amanda frowned up her face. "Excuse me," she said after rolling her eyes. Laughter erupted from the other end of the phone while Amanda's end remained silent.

"Pucker up, I was just messin' with you."

"So he called the house phone for real?" Amanda asked confused.

"How about you just call him since he's the one you really want to talk to." Tiffany snapped. Amanda rubbed her eyes and sat up in bed.

"Don't be so jealous. I was just—"

"Jealous of what?"

"Tiffany, it's way too early in the morning."

"It really is, so don't test my patience."

Amanda removed the phone from her ear and screwed up her face as if the phone was actually Tiffany itself.

"You want me to call you back later because you obviously aren't feelin' me right now," Amanda said with an attitude. Silence sat on the other end of the phone causing Amanda to roll her eyes. "Hello?"

"I'm still here. Just call me when you completely wake up."

"Ok," Amanda said relieved.

"Or after you're done talkin' to Reggie."

Amanda shook her head before pressing the end button. She placed the phone back on the nightstand beside her then laid her head back on the pillow, twiddling her thumbs as she thought about Reggie and his mysterious call to Tiffany's house phone. She swung her legs around and placed her feet to the floor, stretching as she stood and walked over to the window looking out at the clear sunny day. She opened the door and walked sluggishly towards the kitchen, wearing a pair of pink pajama pants and a pink tank. Her mother was sitting in the dining area with a cup of coffee besides her flippin through a home magazine. She looked up and smiled at her daughter who stood over her.

"Well, look who's finally up."

"Ugh mom, you make me feel like a seven year old." They chuckled as her mother playfully tried to force her daughter to sit on her lap. "Mom, it's too early in the morning for all of this. Go play with your husband," Amanda said after breaking free of her mother grasp and scurrying off into the kitchen. "Where's Ben?" Amanda asked as she piled grits, eggs, and three sausage links on a plate.

"He had some work to do at the office."

Amanda walked back into the dining room and sat down in one of the six seats at the oak table.   "So what do you want to do today?" Amanda asked before placing a spoon of grits into her mouth.

"We can do a little shopping and have ourselves a spa day."

"Sounds like fun."

Amanda's mother closed the magazine and pushed herself up from the table. "I'll be getting ready," she said as she walked off towards her and Ben's master bedroom. Amanda was left alone with her plate of half eaten food and her thoughts of Reggie. She rolled her eyes, annoyed at all the attention she gave to a man that didn't belong to her. After nibbling at what was left on her plate she went into the kitchen and scraped the remainder of the food into the stainless steel garbage can, placing the empty plate in the sink.

She trotted off to her room and stretched across the bed. She thought about calling Reggie, but didn't want anymore nonsense to ruin her day. Tiffany had already pushed a few of her buttons and she needed to unwind before talking to him. She got up and searched the closet where her clothes were hanging and opted for a pair of jeans and a white ribbed tank. She showered, dressed, applied light makeup to her face and slipped her feet into a pair of thong sandals after she tussled with her hair.

"Sweetheart," her mother call from the other room.

"Yeah," Amanda answered as she grabbed her phone and walked into her mother's luxurious bedroom that was painted a deeper shade of taupe than their guest bedroom. The queen sized bed was dressed in a gold dupioni silk bedspread. Her mother was standing in her walk-in closet.

"I was just wondering if you were ready," she said as she slid on a pair of jeans. She scanned her daughter's ensemble as she slid on a white cotton scoop neck shirt and topped it off with a pale pink cardigan. Her mother always maintained a very well to do image. "No dress today, huh?"

"I'm not really in a dress mood," Amanda said sitting on the bed.

"Cheer up, honey. What's the matter?"

Amanda shrugged her shoulders fighting off the temptation to pour her heart out to her mother about Reggie. "Nothin'."

Her mother smiled. "Well a little shopping never hurts."

Amanda cracked a smile. "Yeah, let's get goin'."

The twosome headed out into the sunshine.

"So where to?" Her mother asked as she fastened her seatbelt.

"Rodeo Drive," Amanda said, rolling down the passenger side window. Her mother drove off in the direction of Beverly Hills.

"You must have a ton of cash on you, huh?" her mother teased.

"Uh no, but that won't stop me from checkin' out all the expensive boutiques."

"Like mother like daughter," her mother snickered.

"When was the last time you been shoppin'?"

"It hasn't been that long, maybe two weeks ago."

"Ben spoils you."

Her mother chuckled, shaking her head. "Not all of the time."

"Mom, you're so modest. Remind me to check out your closet when we get back."

"My wardrobe is drab according to you."

Amanda laughed. "I said that?" she teased.

They laughed aloud.

After parking, Amanda and her mother walked along the streets filled with hotels, restaurants, and boutiques of luxury fashion, smiling and laughing.

"Mom, let's check out Jimmy Choo," Amanda said as they walked out of Stuart Weitzman. Her mom sat her three shopping bags on the pavement to adjust her clothing then reached into her purse and pulled out a pair of shades.

"This sun is beaming," she said as she slid them over her eyes. " Much better." She grabbed the handles of the bags and the duo continued their walk along Rodeo Drive. "Honey I want to look in Harry Winston for a bit."

"Mom, seriously, that's such a tease."

"It never hurts to look."

Amanda rolled her eyes. "Lookin' stupid when we walk in and walk right back out will."

Her mother threw her head back in laughter. "Let's go."

They entered Harry Winston and a number of other boutiques including an eatery, before settling down in a nail spa for manicures and pedicures. Amanda rested her head against the massage chair being careful not to chip her freshly French manicured hands while her mother sat beside her being equally as careful.

"So, how's Tiffany?"

Amanda raised an eyebrow, a little surprised by the random question. "She's fine."

"I'm just making conversation," her mother said.

"Well let's change this conversation quick."

"Why? Are you ladies in some kind of feud or something?"

"No, I just don't want to talk about her, or anybody else back in Chicago for the rest of this vacation."

Her mother stared at her, shaking her head. "Amanda, what is your problem?"

"Mom, not here, please."

"Well when will you open up and tell me what the problem is?"

"What problem? I don't have a problem, mom. I just want to relax and enjoy myself."

Her mother sighed. "If you say so."

They continued their pedicures in an awkward silence, making random small talk with the nail technicians every few minutes. When they were finished they headed back towards her mother's car.

"Mom, I'm not tryin' to—"

"You're starting to stress me out," her mother interrupted as she threw her bags in the trunk. Amanda twisted up her face as she tossed her bags in the backseat and slammed the car door. Her mother hopped in on the driver's side and started the engine.

"How am I stressin' you out? You're the one drivin' yourself crazy."

"Amanda, I don't even want to talk about it anymore. You want to be secretive, that's fine. Things always come to the light."

Amanda sighed and rested her head against the window. The car ride home was even quieter than the silence between them in the nail salon. When her mother pulled up alongside Ben's truck, Amanda quickly grabbed her bags from the backseat and hurried ahead of her mother towards the condo. Once they were in the apartment she sat her bags down and kicked off her sandals. She headed straight to her room, closing the door before sprawling across the bed and drifting off to sleep.

The loudness of the television in the front room woke her out of her sleep. She looked up and reached into her bag to retrieve her cell phone. No missed calls. She scrolled through her call log and stopped on Reggie's number as butterflies gathered in the pit of her stomach while she debated on making the call. She crawled out of bed and held the curtain to the side as she peeked out of the window, the day had grown darker. She looked back at the center of the bed where her phone was laying and thought Fuck it, as she scrolled down the contact list again and dialed Reggie's number. Her nervousness intensified with every ring.

"Hello," she heard Reggie's voice say on the other end.

Her bedroom door flew open and her mother stood in the doorway with a menacing look on her face as she threw the cordless phone on the bed hitting Amanda on the thigh.

"Ouch." Amanda wailed, quickly hitting the end button on her phone.

"How could you?" her mother yelled.

Amanda sat confused as her mother made her way towards her. "What are you talkin' about? How could I do what?" Amanda looked down at her cell phone as it vibrated in her lap with Reggie's name flashing across the screen.

"Maybe you go ahead and answer that, Amanda. You never know, it might just be your boss's husband!"

Amanda body thickened as she slowly looked up at her mother who towered above her with her hands on her hips demanding a response. The look in her eyes was of anger and disbelief.

"I—"

"Stephanie told me everything! She kicked you out of her house because she was so disgusted with you. Amanda, I am so fed up with you I don't even know what to do!" she cried out.

"Well you can decide while I pack my shit," Amanda challenged her, already making up her mind that she was hopping on the first flight back to Chicago. Her mother looked at her as she threw the clothes that were hanging neatly in the closet on the bed.

"You're just gonna leave without tellin' me what the hell is going on?"

Amanda rolled her eyes as she reached into the closet to grab another handful of hangers.

"What is there to tell? I'm pretty sure Stephanie filled you in on everything." Amanda said sarcastically as she brushed pass her mother and grabbed her suitcase. She removed the clothes from their hangers and began stuffing the clothes in the suitcase. Her mother's facial expressions soften from anger and disbelief to worry.

"Amanda, I tried as hard as I could to reach out to you, but you never wanted to talk."

"And so you go behind my back and talk to Stephanie? It has nothin' to do with you mom!"

"I just wanted to be there for you."

"Great, you can be there in the airport watchin' my plane take off."

"So you're just gonna leave instead of talking this out? This doesn't change what you did, Amanda. You just can't keep running from it."

Amanda struggled to close her suitcase. "Who said I was runnin'?" After she succeeded in closing it, she lifted it off of the bed and sat it on the floor. She rummaged through her bag for her flight information.

"What would make you do such a wicked thing?" her mother asked frustrated.

Amanda looked up from her purse to her mother who stood with her head cocked to the side.

"The same thing that made you run off to California with a married man!"

Her mother eyes widened in surprised. She bit her bottom lip, unsure how to respond. Amanda shook her head in disgust and continued searching through her purse. A hush filled the room.

"Ben was separated from his wife when I took interest in him."

"He was still married! Try again."

"Look, I'm not perfect, but—"

"Well stop attackin' me like you are!"

"I never said I was, Amanda. I just hate I had to hear about everything from your cousin. I don't see why my own daughter couldn't come to me about—"

"Mom, I'm ready to leave when you are," she interrupted as she grabbed the handle of her carry-on and rolled it out of the room leaving her mother alone. She headed towards the front door and gathered up the rest of her things. Ben quickly sat up on the couch.

"You're leavin' already?" he asked with a perplexed look on his face.

"Yeah," her mother answered as she joined the two in the front room.

"What's goin' on?" he asked his wife while his eyes remained on Amanda.

"She—"

"She'll explain all of the hearsay to you when she gets back," Amanda said as she opened the front door and walked out.

"I just don't understand it," she heard her mother say before closing the door behind her. Ben opened the door and followed after them. Amanda began placing her belongings in the trunk of the car. She opened the passenger side door and slid in. Ben grabbed the door before she could close it and looked down at her with pleading eyes. Amanda looked away, staring straight ahead.

"Sweetheart, your mother and I would really appreciate it if you stayed a little longer.

"I have to go," she mumbled without looking at him.

Her mother hopped in on the driver's side. "If she wants to go, let her go," her mom responded angrily. Amanda looked over at her mother and rolled her eyes.

"Excuse me Ben, I have a plane to catch."

Ben stepped back as Amanda took hold of the door and slammed it shut. She folded her arms in front of her. Her mom reversed out of the parking spot and quickly sped off towards the airport.

CHAPTER 18

"I hope I didn't inconvenience you or anything."

"Its cool," Reggie said, speeding off from Midway airport. "Why you didn't tell me you were goin' out of town for a couple of days?"

"I was gonna tell you when I called you, but me and my mother got into this huge over the top argument and I hopped on a flight with the quickness."

Reggie chuckled. "About what?"

Amanda smiled with delight as she observed every inch of him. He was just as handsome as she left him and his crisp clean low hair cut made him look even more mouthwatering. He glanced over at her waiting for an answer.

Amanda looked out onto Cicero. "Nothin' much. It's personal."

"Everything's personal with you?"

Amanda waved him off and smiled. "Whatever…and why you call Tiffany's house the other day?" she asked, changing the subject.

"Shit, I was just returnin' your call."

Amanda sat up and looked over at him. "Returnin' my call? I didn't call you."

Reggie raised an eyebrow in confusion. "Well somebody did." He kept one hand on the wheel and scrolled down his call log with the other. "This is the number, right?" he asked as he handed Amanda his phone to view the time and date of the incoming call.

"Eleven o' clock at night!" Amanda blurted out, staring Reggie down.

"So who called me if you didn't?"

Amanda slouched down in her seat not wanting to know the answer. "I'm not sure."

"What's up with the attitude? I didn't do anything, but return a phone call that I thought you made."

Amanda looked over at him. "I'm not upset with you, baby. I'm just confused."

"So you think it was your girl?" Reggie asked after a moment of silence.

Amanda rolled her eyes. "Let's change the subject."

"Why couldn't Stephanie pick you up from the airport?"

"Please don't say that woman's name in my presence," Amanda snapped.

Reggie laughed. "Which one, Tiffany or Stephanie?" He teased.

Amanda sighed and continued staring out her window.

"So why did you ask me to pick you up?"

"Because no one else was available."

"That's mighty hard to believe. I was around your cousin's place today and saw her truck parked outside. I seen that dude she been kickin' it with too…you know, the one that was all over you."

Amanda's face grew red with madness. "Whatever, Reggie. Keep it to yourself."

Reggie shook his head as he hopped on I-55.

"You still got that nasty ass attitude, I see."

Amanda rolled her eyes in irritation. "I guess I do."

"Look, you called me, I didn't call you. If you got a problem I could pull over to the side of the E-way and you can hitch a ride home."

Amanda sat quietly with her arms folded. She looked over at Reggie who remained focused on the road.

"I'm sorry, Reggie."

Reggie looked over at her surprised. He reached for her left hand, held it up, and kissed it.   "You know I wouldn't do that to you."

Amanda cracked a smile. "I know I deserve it."

"I like you. Maybe a little more than I should."

"I like you too."

"You don't act like it. You—"

"I know, I just have so much shit goin' on and I need to get myself situated."

"What's the deal with your livin' situation? What's up with you and yo' cousin?"

Amanda exhaled. "Reggie, that's between me and her."

Reggie shook his head as he exited on King Dr. "I just don't understand you."

"I hope she's home," Amanda said changing the subject.

"I thought you called her."

Amanda wanted to smack herself. "I did. I know how she likes to run around," Amanda said quickly covering her lie.

When Reggie pulled up in front of her house Amanda looked him over once more. He turned his head and when he caught her eyeing him he smiled.

"You like what you see?" he flirted. Amanda grinned. "I see you blushin'," he added.

"I'm not blushin'," she laughed, shielding her face with her hands. Reggie grabbed her chin as she lowered her hands from her face, leaned over and kissed her. She returned the kiss.

"So what's up? You just gone call me whenever you need a favor, or—"

"I do not call you only when I need favors."

They laughed. Amanda's laughter quieted when she saw Tiffany's car pull up behind Reggie's.

"Is that yo' girl?"

Amanda rolled her eyes. "Yeah." She leaned over and kissed his cheek. "I gotta' go. I'll call you." Both Amanda and Reggie opened their doors and climbed out. Amanda walked around the car while Reggie grabbed Amanda's luggage out of his trunk and placed it on the sidewalk. He embraced Amanda who kept her eyes narrowed on her friend. Tiffany had already hopped out of her car and was headed towards them. "Thank you," she said before kissing his lips once more.

"You should let me take you out tonight," Reggie said with his arms still wrapped around her waist.

"That sounds cool. I'll call you later."

"Well, well, well, I see California didn't last too long."

Both Amanda and Reggie turned towards Tiffany. He chuckled while Amanda sighed and rolled her eyes as Tiffany outstretched her arms towards Amanda. Reggie released her and started to walk off towards the car. Tiffany quickly grabbed his hand. "You better give me a hug, long time no see." Tiffany said after hugging Amanda, surprising both her and Reggie. Tiffany hugged Reggie who stood with an uncomfortable look on his face. Amanda stood paralyzed with shock, but kept herself from going upside Tiffany's head.

"All right ladies," Reggie said quickly heading towards his car. "Call me later, sweetheart."

"All right," Amanda called out to Reggie as she grabbed the handle to her luggage and headed inside.

"So what's the deal with ya'll?" Tiffany asked once they were inside her apartment.

"What you mean what's the deal with us?"

"Seeing how you went out of your way to have him pick you up from the airport when you could've just called me."

Amanda sat on the couch and twiddled her thumbs. She looked up at Tiffany who stood over her with her hands on her hips waiting for an answer.

"Maybe I didn't want to call you."

Tiffany chuckled and walked off towards her room. Amanda shot up and followed after her friend. "And what's up with you callin' him?"

Tiffany turned to face her. "Callin' who?"

"Reggie, the same guy you went out of your way to hug a few minutes ago!"

Tiffany chuckled. "Girl you makin' a big deal out of nothin'. I was just bein' friendly."

Amanda folded her arms and tilted her head sideways. "Well you be friendly with somebody else's man!"

"Oh, so now he's your man?"

"Why did you call him?"

"I mistook his number for somebody else's."

"Why didn't you tell me you called him?"

"It wasn't a big deal."

"So what was the point of tellin' me he called when you knew he was simply returnin' your call?"

"Look, enough with the questions. I don't want to be bothered about it anymore." Tiffany sat on her bed examining her fresh manicure. "Ugh, why did I choose this color?"

Amanda hadn't moved. She shook her head in disappointment. "You can't have everything I got."

Tiffany looked up at Amanda with a twisted look on her face. "What did you just say?"

"You heard me!"

Tiffany stood up and took a couple of steps towards Amanda. "I don't think I heard you correctly. That comment just came from a bitch that ain't got shit! Bitch, you just came back to my got damn apartment. So who's—"

"Calm the hell down talkin' to me like you crazy," Amanda said taking a step closer.

"I'll talk to you however the hell I want to talk to you!" Tiffany took another step forward. "You not gonna come up in here talkin' to me crazy."

"Whatever, Tiffany! What you did was out of line. You got some low down ways about you. Damn. Don't you have enough men you foolin' around with?"

"Ha, this comin' from the same jobless bitch that screwed her cousin's man!"

"And, so what? What are you gonna do about it besides throw it up in my face every chance you get."

"Keep talkin' and I'll call yo' little boyfriend up again and tell him why your ass is here in the first place." Tiffany challenged.

Amanda stood motionless and silent. Tiffany continued standing in her face with her arms folded in front of her chest waiting for Amanda's response. Feeling confident she had the last word, she turned and walked out her bedroom leaving Amanda dumbfounded in the middle of the floor.

CHAPTER 19

"You sure you want to hang out tonight? You don't sound too excited." Reggie said after Amanda got into the car and closed her door.

"I'm fine. Me and Tiffany got into a little petty argument."

"About what?"

Amanda looked over at him with tears in her eyes. "I don't know what I'm gonna do."

"Do about what?" Reggie asked concerned. "What happened? Is she kickin' you out?"

Amanda shrugged her shoulders as she wiped a few tears away. "I just can't stand bein' around her sometimes. She just acts so—"

"Jealous." Reggie finished. Amanda looked up at him. "What's up with that stunt she pulled earlier? I don't even know that girl."

Amanda shrugged her shoulders again. "I don't know what her problem is. I really—"

"Why did you move out of your cousin's house in the first place?"

"We weren't gettin' along."

"Ya'll surely fooled me. I thought ya'll were pretty close."

"Well, we aren't," Amanda said looking out the window.

"Do you want to sit here in the car all night, or do you want to actually go somewhere?"

Amanda shrugged her shoulders once before looking over at Reggie who eyes were on her thighs that peeked out from under her short black cotton dress. Amanda couldn't help, but laugh. "You like what you see?"

"Hell yeah," Reggie said while nodding his head.

Amanda giggled as she twirled her hair around her finger. She looked out the window and back at Reggie. "How about be we go to your place?"

Reggie chuckled while shaking his head. "Naw, my crib ain't lookin' too hot right now."

Amanda raised an eyebrow. "And why is that?"

Reggie stared out his window. "It's just not clean right now. I mean at least for a first time visitor." He looked at her and grinned.

"That doesn't really matter to me, but whatever." She shrugged the suggestion off.

"Here we go again. Why does everything have to be such a big issue with you?"

"I didn't even say anything."

Reggie reclined his seat, laid back and closed his eyes. Amanda took the time to examine every inch of him. Her eyes rolled over his fitted cap to his white polo, down to his dark wash jeans. Her eyes narrowed in on his crotch as her imagination took over, painting vivid images of them engaged in a wild steamy love session. She barely had time to look away when his eyes shot open. She was busted. She smiled and leaned over to kiss him. He pulled her closer as the kisses grew more intense. She sucked his lips and slipped her tongue into his mouth. He did the same. He reached around her torso and cut the engine off never parting lips as his right hand eased between her thighs. She let out a sensual moan when he slid her thong to the side and slipped his middle and index finger inside of her.

Both of their eyes shot wide open when a pound on the driver's side window startled them. They quickly looked up to see Tiffany's face pressed against the glass. Amanda sighed as she fixed her dress and slid back over in her seat. Reggie looked at Amanda and chuckled. "What's up wit' yo' girl," he asked as he hit the button and slightly rolled the window down.

"Can ya'll not have sex outside my apartment. Amanda, you should be a little classier about where you get fucked. Haven't you already had enough of gettin' screwed in the back of cars?"

Reggie looked from Tiffany to Amanda who sat paralyzed with a look of shock on her face.

"Ain't nobody havin' sex so—"

"Fuck that, you don't have to explain shit," Amanda said as she climbed out. She walked around the car, and without a second thought, slapped Tiffany so hard across the face she fell to the ground. Reggie hurried out of the car and grabbed a kicking and swinging Amanda before she could do any more harm to her friend. Tiffany sat on the cool concrete dressed in a white tank and short bottoms holding her face. One of her flip flops sat a few inches in front of her while the other remained on her foot.

"Get yo' shit out my house!" Tiffany yelled and pointed towards the building in which she lived, still holding her face with her other hand. Amanda looked up to see a few neighbors peeking out their windows. Reggie shook his head before releasing Amanda. "Get all of yo' shit out of my house right now!"

"I heard your sorry ass the first time!" Amanda yelled back at Tiffany as she headed for the house.

"Sorry? Are you callin' me sorry?" Tiffany asked, finally rising to her feet, hopping over to her other flip flop. Reggie let out a laugh as he lowered his head. "Guess who ain't got a place to stay because she fucked her cousin's man?"

Amanda stood frozen with fear. She wanted to turn around and look at Reggie, but her shame kept her eyes lowered to the ground. Reggie lifted his head and looked at Tiffany and then to Amanda waiting for her response. When no response came he closed his passenger side door and walked towards her.

"Amanda, what's the deal?"

"Tell him…tell him what kind of nasty bitch you are. Tell him why you ain't got a damn job. Tell how you fucked your boss's husband in the back of her car. Tell him why Stephanie put you the hell out. Tell him how you came over here sobbin' and cryin' to me for a place to stay." Tiffany continued yelling loud enough for the entire block to hear her.

Amanda lowered her head in embarrassment unable to look Reggie in the face. When he grabbed her hand she snatched it away and hurried into Tiffany's building up to her apartment. She ducked into the bathroom, locked herself in and broke down crying. The knocks from the other side quieted her sobs.

"Amanda let me in, I want to talk to you," she heard Reggie's voice plead from the other side.

Amanda ignored his pleas and continued sobbing, letting the massive flow of tears run down her face. She crouched in the corner, brought her knees up to her chest and buried her head in her lap.

"Open up the got damn door." Tiffany pounded.

"Calm down," Amanda heard Reggie say to Tiffany. "What the hell is your problem anyway?"

"I don't have a problem. She has all the problems," Tiffany responded to him as she pounded on the door again. "Open my damn door," she yelled.

Amanda wiped away a few tears as she lifted her head. She looked at the door and back down again. Tiffany continued banging on the door.

"Amanda, sweetheart, just let me in so I can talk to you."

"Talk to her for what?" Tiffany questioned.

"Mind yo' damn business," Reggie said irritably.

"Excuse me, have you noticed that you're in my got damn house?" Tiffany snapped back. Amanda shook her head. "Maybe you can help her pick all her shit up off the ground when she decides to bring her pathetic ass out." Amanda heard a pair of footsteps walk away from the door. She quickly stood up and unlocked it. When Reggie stepped inside, she locked the door behind him. He looked down at her and wiped a few tears from her face.

"Please tell me that shit she was sayin' out there was a lie."

Amanda looked down as she shook her head. She heard Reggie sigh. She went in to lean against his chest, but he stepped back causing her to nearly stumble against the sink. She looked up with tears in her eyes. He looked away into a corner of the bathroom.

"Reggie, I didn't mean to do what—"

"Save it, sweetheart. I'm out of here." He unlocked the door and walked out. Amanda followed closely behind him. She clinched the back of his shirt.

"Reggie please, just listen to me. Please just let—"

Reggie spun around. "Let me go! Don't touch me and don't put yo' dirty ass hands on me!" He yelled as he smacked her hands away from him and continued out of the building. She followed him out to his car and nearly fainted when she saw all of her belongings spread out on the ground. The sight brought more tears to her eyes. Reggie opened his car and slammed the door shut. She knocked on his car window with pleading eyes as he stuck his key in the ignition, started the engine, and sped off. She brought her hands to her face and burst into more sobs. Onlookers had gathered in front of their apartments and cars to watch the commotion. Amanda looked up to see some people snickering while others shook their heads.

"I don't ever want to see your sorry ass again," Tiffany screamed as she threw another pile of her clothing on the ground. She walked towards Amanda and stood over her. "After all of the shit I did for you, and you—"

"You got three seconds to get out my face," Amanda said calmly. She could smell the alcohol on Tiffany's breath. She stood on her feet, causing Tiffany to take a few steps backward. As bad as Amanda wanted to pick up one of the nearby stones on the ground and heave it at Tiffany's head, she decided against it. Instead she began gathering up her things and piling them in the trunk of her car.

"You better call Stephanie!" Tiffany yelled before walking off towards her apartment.

Amanda ignored her and continued stacking items in her car. When she put everything that belonged to her in the trunk, she slammed it shut, walked around to the driver's side and sat inside the car. She looked up and out of the window examining Tiffany's building for what would probably be the last time. She searched her purse for her car keys hoping they'd still be in there. She was relieved when she pulled them out, sticking her car key into the ignition and starting the engine. Where to? She thought. She put the car into drive and zoomed off down the street full of rage. She circled the blocks uncertain of where she would rest her head during the night.

A few blocks from Stephanie's place she pulled over and put the car into park. She left the engine running while she decided on what action to take next. She picked up her phone and dialed Reggie's number. He was her only hope for the night. When his voicemail picked up she pressed the end button and tossed her phone on the passenger seat. She put the car into drive and sped off, circling blocks once again driving further and further from Tiffany's place. She made a right turn onto a block that was all too familiar. Part of her wanted to put the car in reverse and back up down the one way street, but when another car turned onto the block behind her, she had no choice but to keep forward.

She rolled down the street with ease until the driver behind her honked their horn so hard she pulled over to the side and made a face at the old woman who swerved around her. She backed into a parking spot and looked across the street at the building she once shared with her cousin, cutting off the engine as she reclined back in her seat hoping she wouldn't be spotted by Stephanie. Realizing she was homeless for the night, she adjusted herself in her seat and closed her eyes. The events that transpired minutes earlier forced her awake. She lay still with her eyes wide open, unable to adjust to sleeping in the car on a chilly summer night.

She looked across the street once more, paying closer attention to the cars that lined the street. When she spotted Mike's car in the lineup she shook her head with even more disappointment. Her pride wouldn't let her get out the car to walk across the street and ring the bell. She looked up towards Stephanie's apartment from where she was sitting. There were no signs of life in the midst of darkness. She found herself wondering what Mike and Stephanie were up there doing. Knowing her cousin, she was quite sure they were most likely rolling around in the bed. She shook her head trying to shake the thoughts away, but it was to no benefit. Thoughts of her and Mike returned for a visit and she allowed the images to take hold of her mind as she closed her eyes in delight, unaware she had slipped a hand between her thighs, happy she had worn a dress out that night, although things didn't turn out in her favor. She squeezed her thighs together as she massaged herself, enhancing the pleasure.

Giggling noises outside of her car forced her to open her eyes and look around. Embarrassed, she quickly removed her hand from in between her legs and looked around. She spotted a couple across the street hugged up and smooching and exhaled a sign of relief as she sunk back in the driver's seat. She sat wet and throbbing wanting to unleash her sexual arousal. She dialed Reggie's number again, and again she received his voicemail. She smacked her lips, sexually frustrated and annoyed with him ignoring her calls. She glanced across the street at the couple and watched as the guy and girl slobbered each other down. She quickly turned her head when they looked up. She laid her head against the head rest once more and shut her eyes, this time in an attempt to fall asleep. Within minutes, she was breathing heavily in a deep sleep shifting to a more comfortable position every now and then. The kissing couple had ventured off their separate ways and the noise around her ceased.

A thunderous bang on her car window caused Amanda to hit her head against the glass as she sat up in her seat. She rubbed her eyes in a daze hoping she was still dreaming when she saw her cousin standing outside her car with her face pressed against the passenger side window. Stephanie tapped the windowpane with her key ridding Amanda's hopes of a dream.

"Open up, Amanda. Nice job playin' sleep!" Stephanie bickered from outside.

Amanda sighed and let the passenger side window halfway down. Stephanie reached through the window and unlocked the door and before Amanda had time to react, Stephanie had already climbed in on the passenger side beside her, dressed in a pair of gray slacks and a white collard shirt. She looked at Amanda with a raised eyebrow. "You mind tellin' me what you're doin' sittin' outside my house. You just can't get enough of him can you? What? Are you sittin' around hopin' he'll come out so you can fuck him one last time? Well let me make one thing clear—"

"Shut the hell up!" Amanda said interrupting Stephanie's babble. Stephanie mouth dropped in shock as she combed her fingers through her hair. "Ain't nobody thinkin' about you, or that woman's husband."

"They have a divorce pending," Stephanie said.

"What a poor attempt at defending yourself."

"I'm not defending anything. How about you explain to me why you're sittin' out here?" Stephanie examined her cousin's hair and clothes. "A little black dress for easy access," Stephanie snapped.

"Why are you so on edge about somebody who doesn't belong to you? Are you always in such frenzy over that man?"

Stephanie exhaled and looked out of the window. "No, only when my close cousin fool around with him behind my back."

Amanda sighed. "I'm tired of you runnin' and tellin' everybody my business. Haven't you already done enough to screw up my life?"

"Screw up your life…yeah, right."

"How dare you open your big fat mouth to my mother? Of all the people in the world you go and tell her everything."

"She called me first of all. Furthermore, don't think I'm gonna sit up and protect your little triflin' ass."

"I have nothin' because of you, Stephanie!"

"That's right Amanda, blame me. Blame me for puttin' you in the backseat of Mike's car for you to fuck his brains out," Stephanie yelled sarcastically. "You're such a fuckin' victim. Cry me a fuckin' river!"

"It was an accident!"

"An accident? Really? So somehow you just fell on top of his dick and went for a ride, right?"

Amanda shook her head in frustration. "Whatever Stephanie, nothin' I say makes a difference anyway," Amanda pointed to Mike's car. "As we can see."

"As you can see, he's someone I'm madly in love with."

"To bad he doesn't feel the same way about you," Amanda said slightly under her breath, but loud enough for Stephanie to hear.

"Oh yeah, well why else would he be here?"

"Because you went to his wife's place of work and told her he was a cheatin' bastard. At least she had the sense to drop him. Maybe you could learn a thing or two from her."

"Why are you sittin' out here in the first place?"

"Because I wanted to."

"What now...let me guess...Tiffany caught you with her man?"

Amanda chuckled to keep from knocking her cousin upside the head. "Wrong answer."

"And just how long have you been parked outside my building?"

"Why does it matter? Are you gonna let me inside? Are you gonna help me out if I tell you that because of you I have no where else to go."

"Amanda, I'm not your problem."

"You sure as hell caused a lot of them," Amanda said, turning her head to face her cousin.

"No, I'll tell you what caused your got damn problems...you! You're an ungrateful ass deceitful little bitch, and until you learn to treat people with respect and be appreciative of the things people do for you, nobody...and I mean nobody is gonna put up with you."

"Who the hell are you to call me a deceitful bitch?"

"I know my situation with Mike and I'm fine with it."

"No you're not. Stop foolin' yourself. There's no fun in havin' a man that doesn't belong to you. It's just problem after problem."

"Yeah, tell me all about it," Stephanie said mockingly.

They sat silent in Amanda's car until Amanda started the engine. Stephanie looked at her watch.   "Time for me to go, unlike you, I have a job to get to," she said, tossing Amanda an evil smirk as she let herself out of the car and climbed into her truck. Amanda quickly sped off down the street and made a right turn onto the block before Stephanie's and pulled over. She sat in her car with the engine running staring at her radio clock. It was twenty minutes after six in the wee hours of the morning. She was quite familiar with her cousin's work schedule and knew Stephanie had to be at work by seven. When she felt confident that Stephanie had left, she sped off, hit the corner and circled Stephanie's block twice before pulling up behind Mike's Jaguar. She shut off the engine, grabbed her keys out of the ignition, and hopped out of her car, walking swiftly towards Stephanie's apartment.

She rang Stephanie's bell, keeping her head lowered.

"Who is it?" Mike's sleepy voice responded.

"Baby, it's me I forgot my keys, and I—"

Before Amanda could complete her sentence in her best imitation of Stephanie's voice, Mike had already buzzed her in. She quickly ran inside the gate and up the stairs. Mike had left the front door open a crack. Amanda smiled to herself as she walked in and gently shut the door behind her then tip toed through the semi dark apartment, past Stephanie's bedroom where Mike was laying facedown across the bed. She ducked into the washroom and closed the door behind her. She used the toilet and checked herself in the mirror, running her fingers through her head before reapplying lip-gloss. When she was done she opened the door and walked towards Stephanie's room and she stood in the doorway. Mike's naked muscular body sent tingling sensations up her spine, conjuring up all the sensual thoughts she tried so hard to suppress.

"I hope Stephanie wouldn't mind me using her bathroom," she said no longer disguising her voice. Mike lifted his head, squinted his eyes before widening them. "Yeah it's me, Amanda." She laughed seductively as she slowly entered the room making her way over to him.

"What you doin' here?" he asked not bothering to cover his exposed body. He quickly sat up in bed with his manhood standing erect.

"You happy to see me again?" she asked smiling.

"Where the hell is Stephanie?"

"Relax…she's on her way to work. You should know her schedule by now."

"Why are you in here, what are you doin'?"

"I'm not doin' anything…yet." Amanda tossed her bag on the chaise near the bed. She stood directly in front of Mike, who zoomed in on her thighs. "I see you lookin'," she teased.

"I see you lookin' too," Mike said letting his eyes roam up to her breast. "I guess you want to go for another round."

"Or is that what you want to do?"

Mike chuckled. "What is this? Some little ploy to set me up?"

"Set you up for what? I have nothin' to lose," Amanda said as she raised her arms and lifted her dress over her shoulders and dropped it to floor in front of her. She took a few steps closer while undoing her black lace bra. Mike sat staring at her, hypnotized once again by her full curves. He reached up, grabbed her arm, and pulled her onto the bed. She giggled as she crawled on top of him. He quickly slid her underwear off as she mounted herself on top of him. He knew he was deep inside when she let out a soft moan.

Amanda let herself loose while enjoying the ride, moaning, giggling, and caressing his body. She took full advantage of the space they had available now compared to their romp in the backseat of his car. They found themselves on every part of the bed, rolled around on the carpeted floors, stood against the walls, and positioned themselves on the chaise lounge. After their third session they laid in bed cradled, panting, and rubbing each other's body parts. The house phone on the nightstand rang. Mike looked at Amanda and then at the phone. She nodded her head as an okay to answer it, she figured it could only be Stephanie calling this early.

"Hello," Mike answered the phone pretending to be awakened from his sleep. Amanda snickered quietly as she struggled to hear who was on the other line. "Yeah...look...I'll call you a little later." he mumbled and then ended the call.

"She checkin' up on you, huh?" Amanda teased as she started putting her clothing back on.

Mike nodded his head as he sat up in bed and swung his feet to the floor. He slipped his huge feet into a pair of house slippers and walked to the bathroom. When Amanda heard the shower running she quickly picked up the phone and dialed star six seven. The phone rang twice before a woman's voice answered.

"Hello," a familiar voice answered. "I'm sorry I called the house, it's just that you weren't pickin' up your cell phone. I just want you to come back home, and—"

"I'm sorry, honey, but he's a little busy right now."

Amanda's mouth dropped after she hung up the phone. Melanie, she mouthed as she shook her head and snickered. The phone rang again, startling her. She quickly answered.

"Hello?"

"Amanda?" Stephanie nearly yelled though the phone.

"Oh, hi Stephanie. How's work goin' for you?"

"What the hell…where's Mike? Why—"

"Oh, he's busy showering."

Amanda heard Stephanie gasp.

"What is—"

"Yeah you might want to throw your bedding into the washer."

Stephanie remained quiet on the other end too stunned to talk. "How could you?" were the only words Stephanie could manage to muffle.

"Well, I needed somethin' to do, you know, considerin' I don't have a job anymore," Amanda continued. "Enjoy work." She hung up the phone. The phone continued to ring as she finished dressing and gathered up her things. Mike was too engrossed in his shower to hear anything. She knocked on the bathroom door then cracked it opened. Mike opened the glass shower door.

"You want to join?" he asked grinning.

"Naw, I'm out of here," she returned a smile. "Oh, you might want to get those sheets washed…Stephanie's on her way home." Mike's grin faded. Amanda closed the door and let herself out of the apartment. She walked briskly to her car, hopped in, started the engine, and raced down the street. She removed her phone from her purse and placed it on her lap as she drove. As she continued heading North on King Drive, her mind wandered as she thought about where she'd lay her head that night. She knew she couldn't sleep in her car with her belongings for too long.

At a red light she scrolled through her call log, hoping a person would be willing to let her crash at their place for a little while. A loud horn caused her to shriek and look up. The light had turned green. She was nearing the McCormick place, heading towards the South Loop. She quickly turned down Indiana and pulled her car over to the side, unable to both drive and look through her phone at the same time. The last thing I need to do is get pulled over by some stupid cop, she thought. It was an early weekday morning. She looked up every now and then to see pedestrians rushing down the street heading to wherever they needed to be for the day, or the school kids giggling and laughing walking at a much slower pace than the brisk walking adults. She was still staring out her window when her phone vibrated in her lap. She quickly looked down at the name on her screen. Reggie.

"Hello," she quickly answered.

"Yo' cousin was nice enough to let you stay with her last night, huh?"

"What?" Amanda asked surprised. "What are you talkin' about?"

"I drove past this morning and saw your car parked outside not too long ago."

Amanda exhaled after realizing she had been holding her breath during Reggie's response.

"Why does it even matter? You sure as hell didn't answer your phone," she said swiftly changing the focus.

"Aren't you busy fuckin' someone else?"

She looked around as if someone else could have heard him. His outburst surprised her and she leaned back in her seat unsure of what to say.

"I don't need this right now." She hit the end button on her phone and let it fall back onto her lap. It instantly vibrated. Reggie's name flashed across the screen again. She let it ring a little while before answering. "What?"

"Where you at right now?"

"Reggie, seriously, what's the deal?"

"The deal is I hate you so fuckin' much right now! You played me, Amanda. You really fuckin'—"

"Wait, hold on, you're losin' your mind. I haven't done a damn thing to you. I—"

"Why you even bother callin' me back if you were messin' around with somebody else?"

Amanda took note of the concern in his voice. She took a deep breath to calm her nerves. She found herself at another loss for words. She closed her eyes as she pressed her hand against her forehead. "Because...I...I guess I just...I don't know." She opened her eyes in time to see a police car pull up along side her. She abruptly lowered her window and flashed a smile at the middle aged officer.

"You know you're sitting in a no parking zone, right?" He pointed up to the sign from where he sat in his squad car.

"I'm sorry, officer. I just didn't want to talk and drive, you know, since it's against the law and everything." She shrugged her shoulders.

He smiled. "So is sittin' in a no parking zone."

"I'm about to move right now."

The officer flashed another smile before driving off. Amanda stared off at the squad car, rolling her eyes.

"Hello," Reggie said as she placed the phone back up to her ear. "Where you at?"

"I'm drivin' around."

"Drivin' around? Why you drivin' around?"

Amanda sighed becoming a bit overwhelmed with all of the questioning. "Because I have nowhere to go."

Silence interrupted the conversation for a few minutes.

"Come over here," he said after he exhaled.

"No, I don't want to be a bother."

"Amanda, damn, stop bein' so difficult," Reggie snapped.

Amanda rolled her eyes. "What's the address?"

CHAPTER 20

"Why did you invite me here?" Amanda asked Reggie as she walked through the freshly cut grass over to the park bench where he sat, wearing a pair of dark denim jeans and a white graphic tee. His straight face soften into a smile when she stood over him looking down. "Don't start smilin' at me." Amanda said, revealing a smile of her own.

"Ugh, I see somebody has on the same thing they had on yesterday."

They both exploded with laughter. Amanda playfully shoved him.

"Shut up."

"I still like you, come here," he said as he pulled her down on his lap. "Smelly and all."

They laughed in union.

"Do I really smell that bad?"

"Nah, I can't smell you, I'm just teasin'."

"Are you lyin' to me? Does my breath stink?" Amanda asked cupping a hand over her mouth and blowing into her palm.

"I hope not."

She leaned forward and kissed his lips.

"What was that for?"

"I just wanted to see if you were lyin' to me about my breath."

Reggie chuckled. Amanda took in her surroundings, gazing at the green grass and tall trees. She looked out further East towards Lake Michigan.

"So I'm assuming you stay somewhere in Hyde park."

"Why, because we sittin' in a park that's in Hyde Park? Who knows maybe I was just in the area."

Amanda smirked. "Whatever, I'm not gonna sweat you about your secrecy."

They sat silent for a few minutes.

"So where you stay last night?"

Amanda looked away. "With my cousin."

"With your cousin, or with the dude she fuckin' with?"

Amanda rose to her feet and looked down at him with her hands glued to her hips. "Fuck you, Reggie."

"Amanda, real talk, was you seriously messin' around with that dude from the restaurant?"

"It's none of your business what I was doin'. You are not my man."

"So I guess that's a yes?"

"It's a mind your fuckin' business!"

Reggie shook his head. "I need to holla' at dude so he could put me on to his game."

Amanda rolled her eyes. "Is this what you called me over here for, to bask in his glory?"

"Wow, so you really did fuck dude, huh?" Reggie shook his head in disbelief, disappointed.

"Yeah I fucked him, and you know what else, I fucked him this morning too, real fuckin' good! Fuck you, fuck Tiffany, fuck Stephanie, and fuck him too!"

Reggie eyes widened in shock. Amanda turned away and headed towards her car. Reggie hastily grabbed her arm. She spun around and stared him in his eyes with tears in her own. "Just give it up Reggie, I'm no good."

Reggie sheltered her as she burst into sobs.

"I just don't get it," Reggie said as she continued to cry. "It doesn't make sense at all."

Amanda looked up with tears still racing down her red face. "I don't know why I did it. I really...I fucked up...I—"

Reggie hugged her again. He led her back over to the park bench where they sat until Amanda found the courage to look up and stare him in the face.

"I'm ready to listen when you ready to talk." He looked towards the lake. Amanda could see the hurt in his face. She wiped away a few of her tears.

"I'm so sorry, Reggie. I really wanted—"

"Just get on with the story," he said trying to disguise his hurt feelings and frustrations.

Amanda looked away sheepishly. She bit her bottom lip and wiped away more tears before speaking.

"The first time was an accident...well, I...I knew it was wrong, but I wanted it so bad. What was so good about Mr. Michael that kept Melanie...his wife, and Stephanie so on edge about him...I—" Amanda lowered her head before continuing, "I never wanted to hurt my cousin. I love her so much...I just couldn't control myself that night, and—"

"What night?" Reggie interrupted.

"My job had a dinner for the entire department. He was there...with his wife...my boss." Reggie shook his head. Amanda ignored the gesture and continued, "Long story short he ended up givin' us a ride home, and after he dropped Tiffany off...me and him ended up at a park not to far from my...Stephanie's place...and we...you know...we—"

"Fucked each other," Reggie finished, shaking his head in disbelief.

"I swear if I could take it all back I would," Amanda said in between sobs.

"That's bullshit."

Amanda looked at him and then looked away. "Reggie, I don't know—"

"You fucked him again this morning? You think I believe you feel sorry for what you did to your cousin and your boss?"

"But I do! She just pissed me off so bad this morning—"

"So you go up there and fuck to even the score?" Reggie asked sarcastically.

Amanda sighed. "No...look...I can't take back what I did. I'm just so fed up with everybody right now. I was wrong and I wish I could go back in time, but I can't.

"Amanda, you fucked him this morning. I mean as much as I want to console you, I can't. I felt bad when yo' girl threw yo' shit out on the streets, but the more I sit here and listen to you...the more I feel that's where you belong."

Amanda gasped and more tears rolled down her face. She knew there was no getting around the damage she had done to her reputation. She looked away and scooted towards the opposite end of the bench. She sat with her arms folded and her legs crossed with a pout on her face.

"I don't know what to do...I lost everything."

"Was it worth it?"

Amanda looked to her left. "What do you think, Reggie?"

"Hell, you went back again, I'm a little uncertain."

Amanda smacked her lips and sighed. "He got away with everything. And after all that Stephanie continued on with him, like what he did didn't even matter...and even his wife wants him back...she—"

"Well it's not like he raped you, you fucked him! He did what any normal asshole would do. You offered it and he took it. I mean can you blame him? Besides, he was already married so why would you think that him fuckin' you would make any difference to your cousin. He didn't betray her, you did."

"I understand that, but—"

"Look, what you did was wrong, and I'll be damned if you think you about to sit here and play a victim. I'd have more respect for you if you just kept it real with yo' self. Seriously, all of this victim shit is drivin' me crazy. You fucked...you were wrong...you fucked him again...and you're still shady as hell."

Amanda looked away in anger. "I—"

"Why did you fuck him again?" Reggie interrupted her.

Amanda looked at him. "Because it was so fuckin' good that I just wanted it one more time." She shrugged her shoulders as Reggie's mouth nearly dropped to the floor. "I'm just, as you suggested, keepin' it real."

Reggie sat shaking his head, this time with a grin on his face. "So now what?"

"What you mean now what?"

"So where you gone lay your head tonight? I mean it certainly won't be with me. I can't have all that shit around my daughter."

"Daughter?" Amanda snapped.

"Yeah, my daughter."

"Which means you have a baby mama'...which means you probably got a chick at home right now."

"Wrong answer," Reggie said in a game show host voice. "I have a daughter that stays with me from time to time. And no I don't mess around with her mother anymore."

Amanda rolled her eyes in disappointment. Reggie examined her reaction to the news.

"Oh, so now I'm the bad guy?"

Amanda looked at him. "You could've told me, Reggie, a lot sooner than now."

"What difference does it make? I don't think me and you have much of a future anymore."

"You had no reason to think we ever did," Amanda said heatedly.

"Now that's a lie. If you didn't like me you wouldn't be sittin' here next to me."

"Luckily for you I had nowhere else to go."

"Now you sittin' here frontin'."

Amanda lowered her head and stared at the pavement beneath her feet. She rubbed her hands through her hair as she tilted her head back and sighed.

"I'm just so frustrated right now."

"And that's my fault?"

"I never said it was your fault. Can you just shut up?"

"Can you just learn to tell the truth?"

"Some nerve of you, Reggie. I can't believe you hid the fact that you had a child."

"I didn't hide anything. I just didn't tell you. And it might've been worth it."

"Well now you can leave me be. You don't have to worry about me any longer."

Reggie looked away momentarily before hostilely responding, "You never deserved all the trippin' I did over you. You want to sit up here and act like I did somethin' wrong to you. I'm not sittin' here right now because I need you, I'm sittin' here because I had feelin's for you. But you so busy out here fuckin' peoples' men and makin' excuses for it, that you too stupid to realize what's in front of you." He stood up with a frown on his face. Amanda had never seen him so distressed. "Lose my number."

Surprising Amanda, Reggie walked off towards his car leaving her sitting on the park bench by her lonesome, mulling over his words. When his car sped off down the street she exploded with tears all over again. She pulled a napkin from her purse and patted her eyes dry as she sniffled. She sat with her arms folded, legs crossed, and her face red from crying. She looked around hoping no one was staring at her. The park was nearly empty since it was so early in the morning.

She stood up and walked sluggishly towards her car uncertain of where her next destination would be. The mountain of clothing and other belongings sat piled high in the backseat. She shook her head at the ridiculous sight. Once seated in the driver's side she scrolled through her phone until she came across her Aunt Sheryl's number. She pondered over whether to make the call or not, wondering if Stephanie had revealed all of her dirty ways to her aunt. Fed up with driving around with all of her things and headed nowhere she made the call.

"Hey sweetheart," Aunt Sheryl cooed into the phone.

Amanda exhaled, releasing some of her tension. "Hi Auntie, how are you?"

"I'm doing well. Isn't it nice to hear from you. How is everything going?"

Amanda leaned her head against the window. "Not so good," she responded realizing Stephanie hadn't filled her mother in on any of their drama.

"Well what's the matter, baby? It better not be over a nappy headed little fool."

Amanda cracked a smile. "Well…no…that's not it."

"Well what is it, Amanda?"

"Can I just come over for—"

"Honey, you know I'm always here for you. If you feel you need to come on over to get away for awhile then come on. You know good and well my doors are always open."

Amanda sighed. "Thanks Auntie. I really needed that. I'll be there in a little bit."

"Great, now I have someone to go to the grocery store with."

Amanda rolled her eyes. "I'll see you soon." She hung up, started her engine and headed towards the Dan Ryan expressway.

CHAPTER 21

Amanda walked in her aunt's restored 3-story Tudor home, greeted with open arms. Her Aunt Sheryl looked her over as she always did after she hugged her.

"Hey honey, how's everything?" she asked after squeezing one of Amanda's cheeks.

"I hate it when you do that," Amanda giggled, following her aunt towards the large micro fibered sofa in the spacious living room. Amanda looked up at the coffered ceilings and then down at the hardwood floors before turning her attention to her smiling aunt. "I absolutely adore this house," Amanda said returning a smile.

"Well, maybe it'll be yours one day."

"Yeah right. We both know Stephanie has first dibs."

"Stephanie is way too snooty."

"Well who do you think she learned it from?"

"Her father," Aunt Sheryl teased. "So how's everything going? Is Stephanie still dating that mystery man?"

"I guess you can call it datin'.'"

Aunt Sheryl sat up with raised eyebrows. "And what is that suppose to mean?"

Amanda looked down at the hardwood floors before lifting her head. "It means that Stephanie needs to find someone that doesn't belong to someone else."

Aunt Sheryl lowered her head in disgust. "Not again. I know that—"

"I really don't want to bring that up." Amanda sighed.

"Well it's pretty relevant, Amanda. I don't know what's gotten into that girl. I raised her better than that. You'd think that she learned her lesson by now. It just doesn't make any sense. I know what she did to you a few years back must still hurt you. Knowing that she—"

"Yes, knowin' that she dated one my ex's behind my back still hurts me. I don't care how long ago it was. She—"

"She needs get her act together before I get it together for her. I knew she was keeping that man a secret for a reason. She makes him out to be such a gentleman. No wonder she hasn't brought him over to meet me yet. He probably already has in-laws!"

Amanda rolled her eyes. "He still calls me every now and then…apologizing."

Aunt Sheryl eyes widened. "Who still calls you?"

"Shaun, the infamous Shaun that Stephanie just had to have. Even if it meant pickin' me up from school in his car." Amanda watched as her aunt's eyes widened. "You did know she picked me up from school in his car?"

Aunt Sheryl shook her head apologetically. "It was so long ago, sweetheart. You girls were still in high school."

"I never forgot that, Aunt Sheryl. I swear I try so hard to put that behind me. We've grown so much closer since then, but that still hurts me. Why does she feel the need to have it all?"

Aunt Sheryl looked down as she bit her bottom lip. "You got to get over it, honey. You two live together and if you're gonna be upset with her over it then you need to address it. Let her know that her actions right now trigger past emotions for you. Let her—"

"Aunt Sheryl, I didn't come over here to talk about this," Amanda rolled her eyes waving the issue off. She hated when her aunt started talking sappy. Besides, as far as Amanda is concerned the score is very much even.

"Don't roll your eyes at me."

Amanda twiddled her thumbs glancing in every direction of the house. "Its been awhile."

"Since you've come to visit, I know."

"Beverly is still a beautiful area."

"Tell me about it. It was either here, Hyde Park, or the South Loop."

"The South Loop is way too congested and it's hard to find parkin'." Amanda said as she combed her fingers through her head.

Aunt Sheryl jumped up in time to see her cellular phone vibrating across the coffee table. She picked it up and glanced over at her niece. "Stephanie," she said to Amanda before pressing the talk button. Amanda smacked her lips and sighed when her Aunt looked away. She wondered if she had made the right decision to come over, she certainly wasn't ready to face her cousin if she decided to drop by. She became so engrossed in her thoughts she hadn't realized her aunt was now off of the phone.

"What was all of her babblin' about this time?"

"She's on her way over and sounded really distraught about something."

Amanda crossed her legs and exhaled. "So do you want me to leave?"

Aunt Sheryl looked at Amanda with a concerned expression. "Why would you ask me a question like that? When have I ever asked you to leave my house while Stephanie was here?"

"I'm just sayin'. You said she sounded distraught. I figured maybe she'd want a little mother-daughter time."

"No, we can sit right here and wait for her. What's going on with her? I'm surprise you don't know."

Amanda uncrossed her legs and shrugged her shoulders. "Maybe it's somethin' he did."

"Well, she said it was something you did."

Amanda body went numb and her eyes widened as she looked over at her aunt. "Somethin' I did...well...like what?"

"I was hoping you would tell me. Is that why you're here?" her aunt asked, crossing her legs and folding her arms against her bosoms, with an unyielding look on her face.

Amanda sat quietly rummaging through the thoughts in her head. She was speechless. She wasn't sure what to say to her aunt at that moment though she was certain that Stephanie was on her way to let the cat out of the bag. She couldn't move herself to open up to her aunt.

"I don't have much to say right now."

"What do you mean you don't have much to say? What exactly is going on between you two, Amanda?"

Amanda shrugged her shoulders once more, unwilling to look her aunt in the face.

"Look at me when I'm talking to you dammit!"

Her aunt's outburst had surprised her and she quickly looked over at her aunt in shame. Aunt Sheryl's stern expression remained the same as she stared her niece down drawing her own conclusions. "If you have something to say to me, you better say it now."

Amanda turned away once again, this time with tears in her eyes. Her aunt gently placed a hand on her shoulder, startling her. "What is it, Amanda. It can't be that bad."

"Auntie I can't…."

"You can't what?"

"I can't even begin to tell you the awful things that's goin' on between me and Stephanie." Tears raced down her cheeks.

Aunt Sheryl sighed and nodded her head. "Does it have anything to do with that man?"

Amanda nodded her head. "Yes."

"Well are you gonna tell me what happened, or are we about to sit here and play a guessing game," Aunt Sheryl asked, loosing her cool.

Amanda rolled her eyes upset with herself. "What would you do if you found out your cousin slept with someone you were head over hills for?"

Aunt Sheryl head dropped in disappointment. "Please don't tell me you did that to her."

Amanda looked away unable to look her aunt in the face any longer. "I don't know what came over me."

"Amanda!" Aunt Sheryl shouted as she got up and stood over her. "How could you?"

The two heard house keys being inserted into the lock. Stephanie had a spare key to her mother's place. Aunt Sheryl and Amanda shared one last look at each other before Stephanie bombarded through the door and launched at Amanda with a pointed high heel in hand. Before Amanda had time to jump off the couch, Stephanie was already on top of her drumming her in the head with the shoe. Luckily for Amanda, the heel of the shoe was facing up. Aunt Sheryl yelled for her daughter to stop as she struggled to pull Stephanie off of Amanda. Amanda wrapped her hands around her cousin's throat tightly, causing Stephanie to gasp for air. Finally, Stephanie and her mother fell back onto the other end of the couch with all three breathing heavily.

Amanda quickly stumbled up from the couch holding a badly bruised face. Her head and face were throbbing from pain. She crouched down in a corner of the room.

"I don't know what the hell has gotten into you two!"

"Ask her," Stephanie yelled, pointing at her cousin. "She sure in the hell does! Was he good to you, Amanda?"

"Was Shaun good to you?" Amanda yelled back catching Stephanie off guard.

"Are you fuckin' kiddin' me? Don't bring up that nonsense, it's so irrelevant!"

"It's irrelevant only because you want it to be, Stephanie."

"Don't try to use what happened in the past to justify the present!"

"That still hurts me!"

"Amanda, you're so ridiculous. You'll go to great lengths to paint yourself a victim. Guess what…you're not."

"Cut it out…both of you!" Aunt Sheryl said angrily.

"Well you aren't either! Besides, he was married!"

"Bitch please! Like you give a damn about him bein' married. That didn't stop you from fuckin' him…twice!" Stephanie said, trying to make her way around the couch before her mother could stop her. Aunt Sheryl grabbed her daughter's shirt in an effort to save her niece from another beating. She stood with her eyes widened in shock, as she looked from her daughter to niece in disgust.

"Somebody tell me what the hell is going on! I am so disgusted right now!"

"She betrayed me! She slept with him, mom. The guy I loved so much."

"You sound ridiculous," Amanda rolled her eyes still holding her face.

"No…you look ridiculous! I can't wait for you to see yourself in the mirror," Stephanie taunted.

Amanda stood up and cringed. Although her face and torso throbbed from the pain, she was too afraid to look in the mirror to examine the damage her cousin had done to her.

"Get up and put you some ice in a zip lock. This doesn't make any damn sense!"

Amanda quickly walked out of the room. Aunt Sheryl and Stephanie heard a loud shriek from the other room. Stephanie let out a low chuckle. Amanda appeared in the living room a few minutes later holding a cold pack against her half swollen face. She ran a finger across her swollen lip as she stared at Stephanie sitting on the couch with her head turned in Amanda's direction.

"His wife called the house this morning." Amanda watched her cousin's body become rigid. She looked away. "Hope you didn't think you finally had him to yourself."

"Hey…hey…stop it you two!"

"It doesn't matter anymore. He's out of my life…just like you." Stephanie smirked, keeping her composure.

"Yeah right, if you—"

"I said cut it out!" Aunt Sheryl stood up raising her voice. Stephanie and Amanda both closed their mouths. Only the noises of the house sounded. They could even hear the faint tunes of jazz music playing from the small radio in the kitchen.

"I can't take another minute of her," Stephanie stood up. "I'm out of here."

"Sit down!" her mother instructed. Stephanie looked down at her mother's firm expression before glancing behind her at Amanda. She settled back on the couch and let out a long sigh. Aunt Sheryl looked backed at Amanda who stood leaning against a wall still holding a zip lock bag full of ice cubes pressed against her bruised face. "Come on over here."

"I don't want to be anywhere near her!"

"Are you fifteen all over again? I said—"

Amanda rolled her eyes as she walked around the couch and sat on the opposite side of her aunt.   "There's nothin' you can say to make me change my mind about her. I am—"

"I'm doing all of the talking now," Aunt Sheryl interrupted.

"Mom, really I'm an adult. I can handle my own garbage."

"Can you really," her mother questioned. "Because from the looks of things neither one of you are doing a very good job."

The room fell quiet once more.

"I seriously can't believe you went into my house this morning and had sex in my bed! That's seriously low down. Why did you do it, Amanda?"

Aunt Sheryl and Stephanie both turned their heads towards Amanda who sat with her legs folded and arms crossed. She looked over at them.

"I don't know," she shrugged.

Stephanie exhaled obviously annoyed with her cousin's response. "Here we go again."

"Why would you do something like that, Amanda?" Aunt Sheryl asked concerned.

Amanda shrugged her shoulders again. "I was mad...upset...I just wanted her to feel how angry I was with her."

"Angry at me for what?" Stephanie asked looking past her mother at Amanda.

"I lost my job because of you."

"No...you lost your job because of you."

"Excuse me? Were you not the one who went into Melanie's office and made up some—"

"It doesn't matter. You were gonna lose your job anyway. It would only be a matter of time before she found out."

"Are you telling me that you haven't been working all of this time?" Aunt Sheryl asked confused.

"I also don't have anywhere to stay."

"I wonder why," Stephanie said sarcastically.

Aunt Sheryl looked from Amanda to Stephanie, shaking her head disgustedly. "This is just ridiculous. I would have never expected this kind of childish behavior from you two."

"It's not like Stephanie's so innocent."

"You know what, Amanda, give it a rest. Nobody wants to hear your little sob stories about me and Shaun! It happened and it's over! It was years ago…good grief. And besides you two weren't together."

"And neither were you and Mike, so you get over it."

"Oh honey I was with him, contrary to what you may believe."

"Both of you sound stupid." Aunt Sheryl butted in. "I don't want to hear anymore of this nonsense. You both were raised a hell of a lot better than this."

Both women rolled their eyes in nuisance.

"Does your mother know about this?" Aunt Sheryl asked. Her voice filled with curiosity.

"She's aware." Amanda snapped after shooting her cousin a menacing look.

"Yeah, wait until she finds out you went back a second time!" Stephanie threatened.

"Stephanie, do what you want. I'm satisfied."

"I bet you are."

Aunt Sheryl stood up and looked from one girl to the next with her hands placed firmly on her hips. "You two are an embarrassment to this family." She shook her head again as she exited the room. Amanda and Stephanie sat in an uncomfortable silence absorbed in their own thoughts. Both women had their legs crossed and arms folded in a mere reflection of the other. Amanda combed her hand through her hair as she always did while Stephanie twirled her ponytail around her left index and middle finger.

"I can't believe you had the audacity to go into my house this morning and fuck him in my bed," Stephanie blurted. "After all I've done for you!"

"Exactly what have you done for me?"

"Oh, what happen? Did you bang your against my headboard while you were fuckin' him and forget that I let you stay at my place after Tony left your sorry ass hangin'!"

Amanda smacked her lips. "Stephanie, I'm very grateful for your hospitality."

"You're such a fuckin' smart ass! You need to figure out who's gonna take care of your broke ass now."

"If you don't watch it, it might be Mike!" Amanda snapped.

Stephanie chuckled as she shook her head. "Honey, that cheap talk doesn't faze me. As much as you'll like to see me hurt by it all, I'm not. I sent him home to his little wife. You can take it up with her. Hey, maybe you should've asked her for your job back when you spoke to her this morning."

"I was occupied…sorry."

"Amanda, I'm not about to sit here and go back and forth with you. It's pointless. You totally screwed it all up. I will never forgive you for what you did."

"I could care less—"

"You know, what bothers me the most is how unfazed you are about what you did. I mean, you clearly weren't under the influence this morning."

"I was remorseful, but after you went as so far as to get me fired from my job I totally—"

"You were never remorseful about it, Amanda!" Stephanie said, uncrossing her legs. "You went and fucked him again without the slightest care in the world."

"I just wanted you to feel how I felt!" Amanda said rising to her feet and hovering over Stephanie, still holding the cold icepack to her face. "You took my job from me…you put me out, and you paraded around with him like nothin' was wrong. He was just as guilty, Stephanie."

"That doesn't justify what you did this morning. You're a self centered, jealous bitch!"

"Oh, is that what you think, that I'm jealous of you?"

Stephanie stood to her feet directly in front of Amanda. "You have every reason to be." Stephanie snatched up her black leather bag and stormed out the front door, slamming it shut behind her. Aunt Sheryl appeared in the living room startled.

"What in the hell is going on? Where's Stephanie?"

Amanda turned and shamefully faced her aunt. "She left."

Aunt Sheryl sighed and returned to the kitchen. "I need you to run to the store and grab a few items for me," her aunt yelled. Amanda sunk into the couch and sulked wishing she could be somewhere else for the moment. Her Aunt appeared in the living room again. "Did you hear me?"

"I heard you." Her aunt handed her a short list of items she needed from the store. Amanda scanned the list. "A spare key?" Amanda questioned with a raised eyebrow.

Aunt Sheryl handed her a set of keys. "You need some way to get in when I'm gone, right?"

Amanda forced a smile. "Right."

CHAPTER 22

Amanda, dressed in a pair of hip hugging jeans and white crew neck top, pushed her shopping cart down the baking aisle in search of flour, the last item on her aunt's shopping list. She stood looking over her many options until she finally decided on one and placed it into her cart. Again she continued down the aisle eyeing the products on the shelf until she reached the end of the aisle. She glanced over at a few customers gathered by the meat section before looking down at her list. She double checked it, crossing out the items she had in the cart. When she was certain she grabbed all of the necessities, she stuffed the list inside of her black hobo purse.

She turned into the cookie and cracker aisle headed towards the checkout stand. She stopped mid aisle in search for a bag of chips to snack on and decided on a flavor of Doritos and threw them into the cart.

"Amanda is that you?" she heard a familiar voice ask just as she placed her hands on the handle of the cart. She quickly spun around. Jessica. A look of surprise swept over both girls' faces. "Wow, it is you…hi," Jessica said extending her hand. Amanda forced a smile, but kept her hands firmly placed around the handle of the buggy. Jessica awkwardly let her hand fall back to her side.

"Hey Jessica, how's work?"

The question caught Jessica off guard. She smiled. "Oh, everything is…fine."

"You don't sound too convincing."

"Well, I mean, Melanie hasn't been herself lately. She's still trying to pull herself together."

Amanda raised an eyebrow in interest. "Oh…really, from what?" Amanda kept her eyes fixated on her former coworker anxious to hear her response. Jessica folded her arms across her chest, tilted her head sideways, and looked towards the floor.

"I'm pretty sure you don't need a reminder," she said to Amanda, after raising her head to stare her in the face.

"A reminder," Amanda repeated leaning forward against her cart with inquisitiveness. "Please…by all means, remind me," she said with intimidation in her voice.

Again Jessica lowered her eyes to the shiny white square tiled flooring. "Amanda I'm really not here to make a scene."

"Who's makin' a scene?" Amanda questioned, lowering the tone of her voice.

"You know exactly what you did, Amanda. The entire office knows what you did. How could you do such a God awful thing to someone? What possessed you to sleep with her husband?"

Amanda stood motionless lost in her thoughts while Jessica stood waiting for a response.

"Look, whatever happened…I didn't mean for it to happen." Amanda said, replaying her and Mike's first rendezvous in her head.

Jessica shook her head. "You don't sound too convincing."

Amanda sighed. "There's nothin' I need to convince you about. It wasn't your man."

"I'm not concerned. My boyfriend wouldn't be caught dead with someone like you."

Amanda chuckled. "Don't be too sure about that."

"I don't know what's gotten into you, or why you've become the slut that you are, but just remember, what you do to others will most certainly come back around." Jessica shot her a devilish look before swiftly walking off. Amanda stared off at her backside until she turned out of the aisle. She continued with the rest of her shopping mulling over Jessica's words, still surprised that they ran into each other.

After loading the groceries in her car she quickly hopped in and sped back towards her aunt's house. She gathered as many bags as she could manage and walked up the few stairs before inserting her newly made key into the lock then opening the door. Her aunt walked into the front room, drying her wet hands with a paper towel.

"I just finished making the salad," her aunt said as she lifted a few bags and headed towards the kitchen. Amanda followed closely behind. "Were the lines long?"

"Not really," Amanda said nonchalantly.

Her aunt glanced back at her. "Girl what's wrong with you? Fix your face. Why are you so down? I already offered my home to you. You need to learn to be a little more grateful and—"

"Auntie...please...I'm just not feelin' really good about myself right now." Amanda said surprising both herself and her aunt.

"Feeling a little remorseful, huh?"

Amanda nestled herself in a chair and plopped her elbow on the table with her head resting against her hand. She widened her eyes in an attempt to stop the flow of tears. They ran down her face the minute she squeezed her eyes shut. She burst out in sobs and lowered her head against the table. "Awwww, honey," her aunt said as she rushed over to comfort her weeping niece, gently rubbing her back. "It's All right, honey. Let it all out. You can only run from your pain for so long."

"I feel absolutely horrible," Amanda muffled as she lifted her red, wet face. Her aunt handed her a paper towel. Amanda struggled to pat her face dry as the tears continued to pour. "I really messed up."

"Is this about what happened between you and Stephanie?"

Amanda nodded her head as she reflected on Jessica's last words at the grocery store. "It's about everybody. I lost everybody over this stupid situation," Amanda said, wiping away more tears.

"What do you mean you lost everybody? I just—"

"Stephanie...Tiffany...my mother...Reggie...my job!"

Aunt Sheryl rested her chin in hand. "Tiffany? Reggie?"

Amanda waved a hand in the air. "I don't want to talk about either one of them right now."

"Amanda, you can't go on avoiding issues. Talking is exactly what you need to do. Go and talk it out. Hell, talk to your boss about—"

"Are you out of your mind? I'm not talkin' to that woman."

"Why not?"

"What am I suppose to say to her. Oh, I'm sorry for fuckin' your husband."

Aunt Sheryl slapped her hand against the dark wooden kitchen table. "Watch your mouth."

Amanda lowered her head and shrugged her shoulders. "Talkin' to her wouldn't make any sense. That's all I'm sayin'."

"Well, you're a grown woman and I'm sure you'll figure it out," Aunt Sheryl said rising out of the chair and walking over to the stove to check on dinner. Amanda exhaled as she brought her head back up and looked towards her aunt.

"I ran into a coworker at the store."

"Really?"

"Yeah, thanks to you."

"See, that's your problem. You like to blame everyone else for your mishaps."

Amanda contorted her face. "I was jokin'."

"And I wasn't."

"As I was sayin', I saw someone I really didn't care too much for before I left the company." Amanda said as she filled her aunt in on an edited version of her and Jessica's conversation in the store.

"Well baby girl, I hate to admit how right she was. Everything that goes around comes around. You can't go around denying the truth."

"I'm not denying the truth."

"Will you stop being so got damn defensive and listen to what I'm saying? Good grief. Denial is simply that act of you walking around here acting like what you did doesn't bother you, or the people around you. Making excuses for everything. You continuously try and justify everything to yourself for the sake of saving face, or just to keep from admitting how wrong you were."

Amanda sat quietly at the table with her arms folded across her heaving chest staring straight ahead lost in her aunt's words. "Are you hungry?" her aunt asked, setting a plate of salad, tilapia, and garlic bread in front of her. Amanda shrugged her shoulders and looked down at the food.

"I'm done talkin' about it. I'll figure it out."

"Very well," Aunt Sheryl said as she seated herself at the table across from Amanda and lifted a fork full of salad into her mouth.

CHAPTER 23

"You said you wanted to talk, so talk," Tiffany said heatedly without looking in Amanda's direction.

"With him in the room?" Amanda asked, staring at Tiffany's other guest. He sat on the opposite couch wearing only pair of boxer briefs and a white ribbed tank, his eyes was glued to the television. Tiffany was seated on the same couch with her legs outstretched across him.

"Oh, if ya'll want me to leave, that's cool with me," he said. Tiffany sat up, placing her legs on the floor.

"You can stay, sweetheart," Tiffany cooed to him before leaning over to plant a kiss on his lips. Amanda sat awkwardly on the opposite couch watching their heated kissing session.

"Naw, Imma' head out of here," he said, rising to his feet. He was tall with an athletic build and caramel complexion. Amanda's eyes drifted to his midsection that stood erect through his boxer shorts. Cute, she thought to herself, nearly cracking a smile. She quickly turned her head so Tiffany wouldn't catch her staring. He walked out of the sunny living room, leaving the two girls alone. Tiffany tightened the wrap tie on her red silk robe cover her nakedness underneath and combed her fingers through her wild mane.

"Whew, what a night," she said leaning her head against the back of the couch as she closed her eyes, basking in the moment.

"Who is he?" Amanda questioned trying to rid herself of the awkwardness.

Tiffany eyes reopened right as the guy reappeared in the living room, fully clothed in a pair of jeans and a graphic shirt.

"You leavin', baby?" Tiffany asked him, ignoring Amanda's question. She grabbed his arm as he leaned down to kiss her once more.

"Yeah, I gotta' head out. I had fun with you. I'll give you a call a little later."

Tiffany stood up and followed him to the door like a little puppy dog trailing its owner. Amanda rolled her eyes when neither one of them were looking. When the guy finally made it out of the apartment Tiffany walked towards the couch smiling.

"He's this guy I met a couple of weeks back. Isn't he sexy, girl?"

Amanda forced a laugh, not sure how to answer the question. There was already enough tension between the two. "Girl, he does his thing in the bedroom. Damn, he makes me wet just thinkin' about him." Tiffany continued, spreading herself out across the couch.

"That's good," Amanda said dryly before quickly rolling her eyes.

"So, how are things between you and the love of your life?" Tiffany asked chuckling.

"The love of my life?" Amanda asked confused.

"Reggie," Tiffany blurted out, sitting up on the couch, waiting for Amanda's response.

Amanda forced a smile, hiding her irritation. "He's most certainly not the love of my life."

"Humph, well, how's he doin'?"

"Fine, I guess," Amanda answered wondering where the pointless conversation was headed.

"You guess? What happened this time?"

"Tiff, seriously, I didn't come over here to talk about Reggie. And speakin' of Reggie, I still don't appreciate you tellin' him my business."

"He would've found out anyway. You know what they say...what's done in the dark always comes to the light."

"Thanks for your words of wisdom," Amanda said as she crossed her legs. "Maybe you should focus more on what you do in the dark and not so much on what I do. You had no right to do what you did to me. You're supposed to be my best friend."

"You know if I could go back and erase it all I would, but—
"

"You are such a liar. Don't pretend to care. I—"

"Look, if you came over here to argue, you can leave. I'm really not up for it. I just let a damn good piece of dick walk out of here for you, so you—"

"Please, he was practically scrammin' out of here."

"Yeah, probably just as fast as Reggie."

"You don't know anything about me and Reggie...new subject."

Tiffany rolled her eyes and stood up. "Lock the door on your way out."

Amanda jumped up and followed Tiffany to her room. "Not so fast."

Tiffany climbed on her bed while Amanda seated herself at the edge. "Amanda seriously, what do you want? You're such a bitch. I don't even know how I stayed friends with you for so long."

"I came over here to talk to you."

"Well talk...you're doin' more arguin' than talkin'."

"I deserve an apology, Tiffany."

"Are you fuckin' kiddin' me? You deserve everything you're goin' through, you screwed up so many people lives."

"Who are you to punish me? You had no right to do what you did."

"Ok, fine I had no right, I was a little intoxicated. You knew I had a few glasses of wine that day. Things slipped out."

"Right. You were dyin' to spill the beans. How come? I mean I know he's a handsome guy, but—"

"Amanda you weren't even interested in him!"

"What are you talkin' about?"

"That night, the first night he introduced himself you acted like a total bitch!"

"Oh, so this is about that night? The night you threw your drink on me and left me in the club?"

"You deserved it!"

"Big deal, yeah I acted like a bitch that night and he was still nice enough to take me home. You know how I am when I meet guys, I—"

"You're a stuck up bitch."

"Is that what you think of me? Should I learn to be a little looser? I think you're just jealous."

"You want me to be jealous, but I have no reason to be."

"Well why else would you betray me and tell Reggie all of my business? Why would you call him behind my back and why did you give him that ridiculous hug?"

"All of that means nothin'. You're blowin' things out of proportion."

"Whatever honey, deny it all you want. You and I know the truth."

"Yeah, that you're a low down dirty slut who likes to portray a victim."

"Tiffany you're such a hater, it's so ridiculous. Let's just put it all out on the table."

"Put what on the table? I said what I had to say. I mean, I don't get it. If you're a slut, you're a slut, admit it and stop denying it. What you did to your cousin was beyond anything I could ever imagine doin'. It was pretty low down don't you think?"

"Yeah…it was. And you know what else I think?" Amanda asked rising to her feet, "I think if you had the chance to bang Mike in the backseat of his car, you certainly would've. But no, he wasn't interested."

Tiffany chuckled shaking her head. She buried her face in her pillow and let out a loud scream as Amanda to let out a few giggles of her own. Tiffany lifted her head and flung the pillow at Amanda, causing her to stumble a bit.

"I'm so tired of you. I'm wonderin' why you're even standin' in my face right now. Why are you here?"

"Tiffany I came over here to talk to you. Yes, I'm extremely upset with you for what you did to me, but I guess I—"

"Need me in your life because no one else likes you," Tiffany interrupted as she laid her head on another pillow. "Like I said…I was a little tipsy that day. I'm sure it wouldn't have happened any other day," she continued, shrugging her shoulders.

Amanda shook her head. "I'm not quite sure I believe you."

"That's your problem, not mine."

"I don't want our friendship to end," Amanda said as she sat on the bed. Tiffany raised her head from the pillow again.

"What did you just say?"

"You heard me," Amanda said as she rolled her eyes. Tiffany sat up in bed, studying Amanda's facial expression.

"I'm sorry…I just don't get it."

"You don't get what? Me wanting to continue a friendship with you even after all the bullshit?"

"Yeah…I just find it a little weird. I mean, I know we have our little spats, but I didn't expect you to recover from this so soon. What's really goin' on?"

Amanda screwed up her face and shrugged her shoulders. "I'm not gettin' what the big deal is. You should be excited."

"I mean I appreciate you comin' over, but I don't now...somethin' feels weird."

"What's weird, Tiffany?"

Tiffany continued to stare at Amanda with a puzzled look on her face. Finally she shrugged her shoulders. "I guess...it's cool with me. I mean I'm really—"

Amanda held up a hand silencing Tiffany. "I feel horrible. I am so ashamed about everything. Stephanie has always been there for me and we were so close. It wasn't worth it." Amanda closed her eyes and lowered her head in shame. "It really sucks. I screwed up everything. The talk I had with my Aunt a few days ago really hit home and I just..." Amanda began to sob. "I just can't take it anymore. I wish—"

"You wish you didn't do it?" Tiffany finished. Amanda looked up nodding her head in agreement as she wiped a few tears with the back of her manicured hands.

"Tiffany, I wish I had an answer for it all. Like...seriously I don't know what convinced me to lay down with him a second time."

"A second time?" Tiffany asked loud enough for the neighbors in the surrounding apartments to hear. "Wait, are you tellin' me you slept with—"

"Yes! Yes! I had sex with Mike the other day. I...she made me so mad that...I just wanted to get back at her."

"Stephanie?"

"Yes!"

"What did she do? Did she—"

"She just has it so fuckin' good." Amanda blurted out. Tiffany raised an eyebrow, but remained silent. "She's selfish and spoiled. I still have trouble gettin' over the fact that she dated Shaun."

"Amanda, I thought you both buried that situation. Is he really still that significant, or is this just another one of your validations?"

"I was pregnant!" Amanda exploded.

Tiffany's mouth dropped leaving her at a loss for words. She lifted her hand to Amanda's back and rubbed it to sooth her. "Pregnant? Amanda, how could you keep that secret from me?"

"Tiffany, it was enough to be humiliated by the fact that she would do that. I was so tired of hearin' everybody whisperin' about it. I couldn't tell anyone that I was two months pregnant. It was no point. I did what I had to do to put it all behind me, but..." Amanda exhaled, "Sometimes it resurfaces."

Tiffany lowered her head while Amanda wiped her face. They sat quietly listening to the flow of traffic outside Tiffany's window. Amanda laid beside Tiffany and closed her eyes, hoping to rid herself of her throbbing headache. Tiffany laid with her eyes wide open staring at the white ceiling immersed in her thoughts as Amanda drifted off to sleep.

A loud thump caused Amanda's eyes to shoot open and sit up in bed. She looked around the room, rubbing her eyes with the back of her hands. Tiffany walked into the room fully dressed in a pair of jeans and a flirty top.

"Don't mind me. I tried to be as quiet as possible."

Amanda exhaled and lay back down. "Where you on your way to," Amanda asked shielding her eyes from the sun outside Tiffany's bedroom window. "It's so bright in here." Tiffany walked over towards the window to close the blinds. "You're fine...leave them open, I need to get up anyway." Amanda sat up, pulled the sheets back and swung her feet to the floor. She looked back down at the spot she had been lying in. "Eeewww."

"What?" Tiffany asked looking over at her.

"I fell asleep in your bed." Amanda teased.

Tiffany laughed. "Girl, you know what kinds of things go on in that bed."

Amanda smiled. "Where you headed?" she repeated.

"Nowhere. What's on your agenda for the evening? No Reggie?"

Amanda shook her head as she yarned. "I wish. He pretty much told me to lose his number."

Tiffany eyes widened. "Really?" Tiffany mumbled, feeling blameworthy as she sat besides Amanda on her unmade bed. Amanda playfully shoved her, easing the awkwardness. "Girl, I still can't believe you held that in for so long. Did you ever mention it to Shaun?"

"Nope," Amanda shook her head. "There was no reason to. I wasn't keepin' it. I was absolutely humiliated."

"So Stephanie has no idea either...I'm assuming."

"Just me and the clinic."

Tiffany looked away, twiddling her thumbs. "I feel so bad, Amanda. We've been friends for so long and—"

"I know, I know. I wanted to tell you, but I couldn't. Can you imagine bein' pregnant by someone you were head over hills for and seein' your close friend or relative ridin' around with him, datin' him...like its cool?"

Tiffany shook her head in astonished. "And we know how in love you were with Shaun."

Amanda rolled her eyes. "Don't remind me."

Tiffany playfully reached over and rubbed Amanda's stomach. "Aawww, you had a little Shaun in there," she said laughing. Amanda playfully slapped her hand away.

"Stop…before I start cryin'."

Tiffany wrapped an arm around Amanda's neck and pulled her towards her, embracing her. "It's ok…let it out." Amanda smiled as a few tears trickled down. She cradled her face in her hands. "You'll be fine, Mandy."

"I have to live with that every single day of my life," Amanda muffled between sniffles.

Tiffany looked down at her. "Maybe you should have a talk with Stephanie."

Amanda quickly pulled away shaking her head, looking Tiffany in the face. "I don't want her to know. I don't want anyone to know. I'm scared I told you."

"I won't say anything about it."

"Besides, tellin' Stephanie wouldn't matter. She'd probably laugh in my face."

"I doubt she'd laugh about it, Amanda," Tiffany said reassuringly.

"And do you know his wife called the house while I was there? He's still seeing her," Amanda said, changing the subject.

"I'm not surprised. I mean, she was the one married to him."

"If I apologized to anybody, she'd be the one."

Tiffany raised an eyebrow. "Are you kiddin' me? She hates your guts. She hated you even before you slept with her husband. And she—"

"I know...I know," Amanda interjected. "I feel so bad for her. She was the one that offered us a ride home that night."

"Yeah, she pretty much handed him over to us," Tiffany cracked. "Dummy."

Amanda laughed. "Tiffany, I'm serious."

"So what are you gonna do about it, Amanda...apologize?" Tiffany asked sarcastically after she stopped laughing.

"I was thinkin' about it."

Tiffany's face hardened. "Girl, you're losin' it."

"I just need to do somethin'. I feel like I caused so much trouble."

"He caused all of the trouble," Tiffany said, referring to Mike. "He needs his ass kicked. And trust me, I'm sure he has plenty of other bitches on his roster. He was creepin' way before you and Stephanie came into the picture."

Amanda nodded her head in agreement. "Yeah, well, I can't speak for all of his other women, but I am thinkin' about sayin' a few words to Melanie. I don't even know if she knows the truth. Stephanie pretty much screwed me over."

Tiffany sighed, shaking her head in disapproval. She buried her face in the palm of her hands. "Just leave it be, Amanda," she said, bringing her hands down from her face.

"So how should I go about it?"

Tiffany stood up. "You shouldn't."

"Why not, I don't see any harm."

Tiffany shook her head in annoyance. "Ok, do as you wish," she said waving the issue off with a hand.

Amanda smiled. "You're comin' with me."

"I don't want anything to do with that woman, or her husband."

"You sure about that," Amanda teased.

"I'm certain."

Amanda chuckled. "I'm hungry."

"Well let's eat."

CHAPTER 24

"Mom, seriously, I don't even know why you insist on havin' her here," Stephanie whined as she poured herself a glass of orange juice.

"Don't you have a job you need to get to? Why are you here?" Amanda asked furiously.

"Oh honey, don't worry about me and my job. I'm fine. You worry about getting your triflin' ass out of my mother's house."

"Stephanie, don't start." Aunt Sheryl said growing frustrated.

"Thank you." Amanda rolled her eyes.

"I'm not startin' anything. Mom, has she even applied to a job since she's been here?" Stephanie turned around in her chair to look at her mother. Aunt Sheryl didn't bother looking up from her Chicago Tribune newspaper. Stephanie turned back around heatedly, rubbing her face with her manicured hands.

"Mind your business." Amanda snapped.

"My mother is my business."

Amanda snickered. "Really, Stephanie?" She got up from the kitchen table and carried her empty bowl to the sink. "Don't worry, I won't cause her any trouble. And you know what else…I'm tired of bickering back and forth with you. I'm really sick and tired of it. I know you don't really care for me right now and there isn't much I can do to fix what I did—"

"You're absolutely right! There isn't a damn thing you can say to me that will stop me from hatin' your guts," Stephanie said, cutting her cousin's speech short.

Amanda shrugged her shoulders before placing her dish in the sink. "Well, I'm sorry."

"I agree."

Amanda threw her hands in the air. "It's not even worth it."

"Because I know you aren't sorry. You're just ashamed."

"Whatever, I'm done talkin' with you."

Stephanie looked away. Aunt Sheryl closed her newspaper and sighed.

"What's wrong?"

"I have a slight headache," she answered as she stood up and pushed the barstool in place. "I'll be in my bedroom."

"You need anything, mom?"

"Yeah…I need for you two to grow up and stop all the fussing. I'm sick of it." She walked out of the kitchen clutching her newspaper to her chest.

Amanda and Stephanie looked at each other and then looked away. Amanda leaned against the counter with her arms folded across her chest.

Stephanie sighed as she slid her chair back from the table, shaking her head. "I mean what does she want me to do, forgive you?"

Amanda shrugged her shoulders. "Do what you want. It's out of my hands."

"A few lousy apologies won't make up for fuckin' Mike."

"Of course not, but—"

"And you did it twice!" Stephanie yelled to her face as she pounded her fist against the table. Amanda looked away in shame.

"I'm sorry." Amanda looked her cousin in the face as Stephanie contorted hers in anguish. "What…I don't know what else to say or do anymore. What do you want from me, Stephanie?"

"I want you out of my life."

"You didn't want him out of your life! What about me? What about all the cruel things you did to me in the past? What about you and Shaun? I forgave you!" Amanda said, fighting back tears as her voice began to crack.

"We've already discussed Shaun, it's in the past."

"But it still bothers me!"

"Is that why you slept with Mike?" Stephanie asked sarcastically. "Amanda, give me a break."

"Mike isn't your man. He's still fuckin' his wife and who knows how many other women."

Stephanie placed her hands on her hips. "Thanks for the information, I really fuckin' appreciate it!"

"You can count on me," Amanda smirked as she headed out of the kitchen.

"You know what, forget about it," Stephanie said as she grabbed Amanda's arm and spun her around, catching Amanda off guard. "Forget about it."

"What's that suppose to mean?"

"I'm done with it. I don't want to discuss it anymore."

"Fine."

"That doesn't mean I don't still hate you. I'm so done with you."

"Whatever."

Stephanie rolled her eyes. Amanda snatched her arm out of Stephanie's grasp and continued to the living area with Stephanie following closely behind. "I want you out of here. I don't want my mother callin' me about any of your bullshit. I swear I will kick your ass."

Amanda chuckled before turning around to look her cousin in her face. "Stephanie, get over yourself."

Stephanie snatched her hand bag from off of the couch and swung it across her shoulders. "Your broke ass need to find yourself a job."

"Don't worry about me, honey, I'll be fine. You worry about that lady's husband you runnin' around with."

Stephanie threw up her middle finger as she opened the front door and slammed it shut behind her. Amanda paced the floor back and forth before picking up her cellular phone to scroll through her stored numbers. She flopped down on the couch, staring at Reggie's number. As much as she wanted to call him, she decided against it, and tossed her phone to the side. She slapped her hand against her forehead and closed her eyes.

"Where's Stephanie?"

Amanda opened her eyes as she turned her head to face her aunt who had quietly crept up on her. "She left...thank goodness."

Aunt Sheryl took a seat next to her niece and crossed her legs. "You two straighten everything out?"

Amanda shook her head. "There are no straightening things up with Stephanie."

"That's not true. Your cousin has a good heart. She just needs time to let a few things blow over."

"How much time can she possibly need?"

"Amanda, not everything works on your time. You slept with a man she was seeing for Christ sakes...married or not married, it doesn't excuse what you did."

"I'm fully aware of that."

"I thought you were just about done playing the victim role." Aunt Sheryl said raising her voice a pitch or two as she shook her head.

"I'm not playin' a victim role. I've taken responsibility for my actions, and I'm fully aware of what I've done. I—"

"Are you really, Amanda? What exactly have you done to fix the situation?" Aunt Sheryl asked staring Amanda in the face. Amanda looked away, rubbing her hand against her chin.

"I've apologized to her numerous times. I even apologized to Tiffany."

"And just what does Tiffany have to do with anything?"

Amanda shrugged her shoulders as she turned her head to stare at her aunt. "She and I had a pretty bad fallin' out."

"What about your mother? What about that lady?"

Amanda shrugged her shoulders again. "What about them?" Amanda challenged.

"If you don't fix your situation, God will," Aunt Sheryl warned as she got up from the couch and headed towards the kitchen area. Amanda immediately stood up, following close behind her.

"What?"

"You heard what I said to you."

"I heard you, but I don't understand you."

"Is it that you don't understand me, or do you not like what I said?"

Amanda sighed. "Everything will be fine. My mother and I will be fine as well as—"

"You don't have to convince me of anything, sweetheart. I'm certainly not the one."

"So what do you suggest, auntie? That I storm back in to my old job that your daughter got me fired from and apologize to my boss?"

"I suggest you do whatever the hell you want to—"

"What am I suppose to say to that lady? What about Stephanie? Isn't she just as guilty as I am?"

"Amanda, you're an adult and I'm confident you'll find the right solution to your problem. In the meantime, I don't want to hear another word about this from you or Stephanie." Aunt Sheryl opened the refrigerator, grabbed a bottled water, and slammed it shut. "All of it really sickens me. It's disgusting to even think about it. I'm sure your mother feels the same."

Amanda watched her aunt as she gulped half of her bottled water down. "Thirsty," she teased, trying to ease the tension.

"Tired," her aunt said as she placed the top back on the bottle and walked out of the kitchen, leaving Amanda leaning against the counter. She walked back into the living area and retrieved her phone off of the couch. She dialed her mother's number, secretly hoping she wouldn't answer.

"Hello," her mother answered happily.

Amanda sighed before replying, "Hey."

CHAPTER 25

What is she doing here?" Melanie asked the receptionist, Lisa, one of Amanda's former coworkers. Lisa shrugged her shoulders as she looked from Amanda to Stephanie with raised eyebrows. "What do you mean you don't know?" Melanie snapped, frowning.

"Look, I just wanted to talk to you about—"

Melanie held up her hand to silence Amanda. "My office."

Amanda followed Melanie back into her office with a lowered head. She didn't want to mistakenly make eye contact with any of the pairs of eyes that were cast upon her. Melanie, on the other hand walked briskly in front of her with her head held high. When they entered Melanie's office, Amanda quickly closed the door behind her. Melanie leaned her backside against her desk with her arms folded against her chest. Her black seamless camisole peeked out from underneath a gray blazer. Her hair hung loosely about her head, a bit disheveled. Amanda couldn't help but notice the striking similarities between her and Stephanie as she continued to examine Melanie's ensemble, a sexy professional with a snooty demeanor.

"Are you gonna talk, or stare at me all day?"

Amanda sighed. "I'm just feelin' a little—"

"Guilty?" Melanie finished, rolling her eyes and twisting up her face. She shook her head. "I don't believe you had the audacity to even show your face around here." Amanda bit on her bottom lip to keep from saying something she'd regret. "This entire office knows about what you did to me. You ruined my life, my marriage, everything!"

"Mike ruined your marriage," Amanda said loudly. "I know you're upset with me, but I really didn't mean—"

"Amanda, it's really nothing you can say to me to make me feel any differently about you. The damage is done."

"I understand. I know I can't go back and undo the damage I've caused, but if I could...I would. Melanie, you deserved better than him."

Melanie chuckled, throwing Amanda for a loop, as she swung her hair over her shoulders. "Just stop...please just leave before I have you escorted out of here."

Amanda didn't budge. Instead she pulled out a chair and took a seat.

"I'm not leavin' until you hear me out," she challenged. Melanie eyes widened with disbelief as she unfolded her arms and let them fall to her side.

"Fine, you have two minutes and then I'm calling security," Melanie threatened as she walked around her desk. Amanda rolled her eyes as Melanie nestled herself in her large black leather office chair and stared her in the face. "So talk." When nothing came out of Amanda's mouth for a full two minutes, Melanie stood up. "All right I'm—"

"Wait, wait, wait," Amanda pleaded as she motioned for Melanie to take a seat. "This is just a little difficult for me, Melanie. It's not easy looking' you in the face."

"I'm sure it isn't," Melanie said as she sat back down. "After all, you and that cousin of yours made a complete fool out of me. You know, I don't know how you two sleep at night."

"Maybe you should ask your husband," Amanda blurted, wanting to smack herself afterwards.

Melanie eyes widened in utter shock. "Get out!" She pointed towards her office door as she stood up and began making her way towards the door. Amanda quickly stood up from her seat and threw herself against the door before Melanie could open it.

"No...no...I didn't mean—"

"Amanda you have two seconds. I'll call the cops."

"Melanie, please just let me explain myself."

"I gave you a chance and instead you chose to insult and humiliate me," Melanie said, practically breathing in Amanda's face. "I want you out. I have an office to run." She struggled to reach around Amanda to grab the door knob. Amanda kept herself planted firmly against the door leaving Melanie no choice but to walk back to her desk and pick up the phone to dial security.

"Wait...no, no, no," Amanda said, finally stepping away from the door to grab the phone from her former manager. "Melanie, please, five minutes."

"Let my hand go," Melanie said before shoving Amanda's hands away causing Amanda to drop the phone on the desk. Melanie quickly picked it up and slammed it on the receiver. She flopped down behind her desk, her face red with anger. Amanda returned her bottom to the chair after she felt certain Melanie wouldn't bolt for the door. Silence found its way into the office, both ladies looking at some corner of the room without making eye contact. After what seemed like an eternity of silence, Amanda finally tuned in on Melanie, who kept her eyes on the plant in the corner.

"I truly apologize for what I did to you, Melanie. If I could go back and change the hands of time, I would."

"Were you the one who picked up the phone when I called that lady house that morning?"

Amanda took a deep breath and exhaled. "Yeah, it was me."

"So it's safe for me to assume that you were there that day with—"

"Yes, I was there with Mike."

"Don't refer to him as Mike…you don't know him! You don't know anything about him or me. Your cousin is gonna get what she deserves! She has—"

"Why are you two the defending that asshole?" Amanda yelled loudly interrupting Melanie's rant.

"Because that asshole happens to be my husband! You have no idea how much my marriage means to me. If you think that I'm gonna let you or any of your got damn family ruin my marriage, you're sadly mistaken."

Amanda shrugged her shoulders. "What happens between you and your husband is none of my business," Amanda said, rising from the chair. "I simply wanted to apologize to you about everything and—"

"What a waste of time. Your apology means nothing. If you don't mind, I have an office to run."

"Not a problem. I wish—"

A knock on Melanie's door caused both ladies to stare at the door as if staring at it would reveal the identity of the person knocking.

Melanie cleared her throat before replying, "Come in."

Lisa, the receptionist, opened the door with a huge smile on her face. Amanda's body froze when Mike appeared in the doorway holding a bouquet of peach colored roses. His smile faded when he saw Amanda. Nonetheless he casually walked over to Melanie and kissed her on the cheek before extending his arm to hand her the flowers. Melanie giggled like a preschooler as she took them from him and laid them on the desk. Amanda looked from the couple back to Lisa who still stood in the doorway and wondered what she was smiling about.

"Sweetheart, what's she doin' here?" Mike asked Melanie while casually glancing over at Amanda. "I thought we already sorted this mess out."

"We did," Melanie said as she cleared her throat. "She was just leaving." Melanie pointed to the door.

Amanda frowned as she reached into her purse for her phone. She pretended to be dialing a number while searching for a perfect angle to snap a shot of the seemingly picture perfect couple. When she was sure she had the best view of Melanie, Mike, and the roses she snapped the picture.

"What are you doing?" Lisa asked from behind.

"Mind your fuckin' business." Amanda said heatedly quickly putting her phone back in her purse. Mike and Melanie stood together with perplexed looks on their faces.

"Lisa, do you mind showing—"

"Don't worry, Melanie, I'll leave you to your pathetic husband." Amanda said as she turned and headed out of the office.

Mike chuckled. "You have a nice day, sweetheart."

Mike's words caused Amanda to stop in her tracks right as Lisa was pulling the door up behind them. She quickly pushed Lisa out the way causing her to stagger to the floor and grabbed the handle before the door had completed shut. She swung the door opened, walked back into Melanie's office, grabbed the roses, reached across the desk, and immediately started smacking Mike across the face with them. Petals fell to the floor with each slap across the face. Mike held up his arms to shield himself, but Amanda continued to hit him wherever she could. Melanie stood helplessly looking on. A pair of arms came from behind and dragged her outside of the office. She let the nearly empty stems fall to the floor.

"Get off of me," she said as she broke free from the grasp, turning to see who had the man power to handle her. It was a former male coworker. "Get the fuck off me, John," Amanda said, breathing heavily, adjusting her shirt. By now, the entire department had gathered around Melanie's door to witness the commotion, staring at Amanda with wide eyes and gaped mouths. She pushed herself through the crowd of people that she once giggled, worked, and had lunch with, out of the door and onto the elevator. On the ride down to the first floor she pulled out her phone and sent the picture she snapped of Melanie and Mike to Stephanie's and Tiffany's phones then quickly exited the building and rushed to her car.

CHAPTER 26

"I figured maybe it'd help her get over him."

"Perhaps, perhaps not," Tiffany said as she dipped the paint brush into the bottle of red nail polish for a second coat. She chuckled to herself once more and she shook her head in surprise. "I still can't believe you hit that man in the face with his wife's flowers. That's absolutely hilarious. What was the expression on their faces?"

"Girl, I don't know. I was so focused on knockin' him upside the head. My mind was gone." Amanda laughed as she folded her legs underneath her.

"Obviously. I'm surprised she didn't get security involved," Tiffany said as she twisted the top on the nail polish and blew on her nails. She extended her hand out in front of her. "I hate this color."

"And you painted ten nails before you realized it."

"Maybe it might grow on me."

Amanda sighed as she picked up her phone. "Wow, Stephanie responded to the message," she said as she held her phone out towards Tiffany. Tiffany quickly grabbed the phone from her and scanned over the text message. She looked up with raised eyebrows.

"Are you kiddin' me?" Tiffany said with a wide grin on her face. "She actually wants you to come over to her place."

"I know."

Tiffany laughed. "That picture must've got her ass right together." Tiffany snapped her fingers for emphasis. "I know she's devastated."

Amanda shrugged her shoulders. "I don't know why. I mean, I know she wasn't naïve enough to think that he wouldn't go back to Melanie."

"People in love can think quite foolishly at times."

"Stephanie knows better."

"What do you think she wants to talk about?"

Amanda shrugged her shoulders. "Mike."

"Honestly, what were your intentions on sendin' her that picture?"

"I just wanted her to see what an asshole he was."

Tiffany twisted her mouth to the side. "Yeah right."

"What you mean yeah right?" She cocked her head to the side.

"Did you secretly want her to be jealous?"

"Jealous of what?"

"Of seeing him with his wife."

"I didn't know what to expect from her. I just felt that she should see it. I figured maybe it'll help her move on from him."

"And why are you so concerned with her movin' on from him?" Tiffany challenged cocking her head and folding her arms as well.

"What are you gettin' at?"

"Just answer the question."

Amanda looked at Tiffany with squint eyes, examining her face as if it would reveal the reasoning behind her question. Amanda combed her hand through her hair. "I really don't know what you're getting at. I sent the picture to her so she could see what an asshole he is."

"What's the point? Why are you so—"

"I hate him," Amanda said, cringing. "I hate how he got away with everything. It really pisses me off. He walks around so fuckin' high and mighty without a care in the world! Stephanie had—"

"Why are you surprised?"

"It really hurts, Tiffany. I feel like such a fool for what I did to Stephanie. I mean, I know we had our problems in the past, but she didn't deserve it," Amanda said with her voice cracking. "I feel horrible. I really wish I could erase everything I did because it just wasn't worth any of this. Everyone looks at me like I'm this horrible home wrecker and I'm not. Both my cousin and Melanie hate my guts, and I just think it's so unfair that they won't take the time to see that he's just as guilty. Why are they so blind to everything he did?" Amanda asked as she wiped a few tears from her face before fidgeting with her hands. She shook her head in confusion. "Why do we let them get away with everything?"

Tiffany continued to sit quietly, not taking her eyes off her friend.

"You know," Amanda continued. "When I found out about Tony secretly cheatin' on me and goin' so far as to have a baby on me I completely flipped out. I kept askin' myself what was wrong with me? I compared myself to that girl, I was so angry with her. I dropped out of school because I couldn't stand to see the sight of her. I hated her! Meanwhile, I was blowin' up Tony's phone, beggin' him to work things out, to not leave." Amanda sobbed. "Why did I do that? Tiffany, he laughed in my face!" Amanda said, crying. Tiffany sat next to her friend.

"Amanda, sweetie, I know what that fool put you through. I was there with you through it all." Tiffany reminded Amanda as she placed her arms around her. "You have to move past it. Its been so long and you've done so well for yourself. You can't let what Shaun and Tony did to you affect you so much. Nor can you use them as excuses for your actions."

Amanda looked up, wiping her wet face. "Stephanie was there with me too and I betrayed her. Tiffany, it wasn't worth it. I hate guys."

Tiffany let out a chuckled. "Girl, don't even start. Girls are not an option."

"Do you understand where I'm comin' from?"

"I totally understand you. I think Mike deserves neither one of them. But if they're foolish enough to tough it out with him, let them. I think you need to have a talk with Stephanie. It may not change things right away, but it damn sure is a start." Tiffany released Amanda from her arms and stood up. "She already invited you over. That should make goin' over there a little easier."

"It's never easy talkin' to her, especially when it comes to him."

"Girl please, one day you'll both be sittin' back laughin' about it all. Hell, I laugh about it just about every day."

"You make it sound so peachy," Amanda said crossing her legs. "You know damn well this isn't a laughin' matter. I can barely stand to be around her anymore."

"I don't know why. It's not like she has a clean past."

"I know, but it's just not the same. We came so far and I ruined it."

Tiffany sighed. "Girl, I can't stand it anymore. Shut up and talk to her!"

Amanda smacked her lips as she uncrossed her legs. "You want to come with?"

"No, because if you two get into some type of brawl, I'd hate to have to choose a side," she teased.

"You're my friend."

"Yeah, but I still don't agree with some of your ways." They laughed in union.

"I need you there for moral support."

"Moral support my ass. I just sat here and had a therapy session with you. I should've charge you."

"I don't have a job." More laughter. "I'm still mad about that. She really went out of her way to get even with me, but let him completely off the hook."

Tiffany threw her hands in the air. "I don't want to talk about this. I'm fed up with it all. Fix it or shut up talkin' about it. Both of ya'll were petty. The only one who deserves a little remorse is that man's wife, and hell, even she's a dumb ass, so I don't really care. In the end you and Stephanie are family, so I—"

"I just got another text message," Amanda said holding a finger in the air as she reached over to pick up her phone. "She's really actin' urgent about this."

"Girl, just go over there and call me later."

Amanda picked up her bag and swung it over her shoulders. "I'm out of here. If anything happens to me, you know where I was," she teased.

"She probably has another ass whoopin' up her sleeve," Tiffany said chuckling as she walked off towards her room.

Amanda threw up her middle finger and left Tiffany's apartment. She hopped in her car and drove the short distance to her relative house. Stephanie's truck was parked directly in front of the building. Amanda pulled up behind it and checked out a few other cars to make sure she didn't see the familiar Jaguar parked anywhere. She examined herself in the rearview mirror and combed her hands through her hair. Butterflies gathered in the pit of her stomach as she made her way to the large black ironed gate that surrounded Stephanie's building. She rung the bell and before she was able to identify herself she was buzzed up. More butterflies. Stephanie answered her door wearing a pair of leggings and a tank top. Her hair was pulled back into a ponytail.

"It took you long enough," Stephanie said after closing the door behind Amanda.

"Where's the fire," Amanda said sarcastically as she took a seat on the couch.

Stephanie forced a smile. "I'm sorry. I get a little impatient."

Amanda was taken aback by how friendly her cousin suddenly seemed. She raised an eyebrow in curiosity. "Did you get my text?"

"Yeah I got it. I could barely maintain my composure. The sight of them together makes me sick to my stomach."

"Are you still foolin' around with him?"

"Amanda, it's not like I didn't know he had a wife in the first place."

Amanda rolled her eyes. "So you're still gonna continue your little rendezvous with him? Are you insane?"

"No. I'm in love. I really care about him. I know what the situation is and I'm fine with it. He has a wife, that's his problem, not mine. He gives me everything I want."

"Pretty soon he'll be givin' you crabs, gonorrhea, or syphilis!"

Stephanie contorted her face. "Could you not talk like that, it's disgusting."

"He's disgusting!"

"Amanda, get over it! He's with me the majority of the time anyway."

"Wow, you got yourself a real winner."

Stephanie shrugged her shoulders. "You know how good he is…I mean after all, even you went back for more!"

Amanda looked away. She couldn't argue with that. "So what's the deal? What's the urgency?"

Stephanie sat on the couch besides her. Weird, Amanda thought.

"I talked to him after I saw the picture. I mean although I know his wife ain't goin' nowhere it still pisses me off to see them together—"

"Or Lord, what are you gonna do, kill her?" Amanda joked.

"Ugh…no." Stephanie said rolling her eyes annoyed. "You won't catch me on one of those criminal mastermind shows."

"You're no mastermind."

"I'm a hell of a lot smarter than you." Stephanie teased with a smile on her face.

"Anyway, finish what you were sayin'," Amanda said, feeling the awkwardness.

"That picture made me call him up and curse him out!"

"Wow, you really taught him a thing or two."

"Chill out with all of the sarcasm. Its annoyin'."

"Sittin' here listenin' to you go on and on about this man is just as equally if not more annoyin'."

"I was so upset that I called him and let his ass have it."

"And then what?"

Stephanie bit her bottom lip. "He flipped it on me as usual. Why did you hit that man across the face with a bunch of roses? I—"

"If I had them here I'd probably smack yo' ass across the face for askin' me that stupid question! Look, I don't care about what's goin' on between the two of you anymore. It's obvious you're still idiotic enough to look past all his bullshit. I don't like him and I'm not gonna cover for you. I hate him!"

"Is that why you fucked him again?" Stephanie challenged letting her smile fade. "You know I'm still highly pissed about that!"

"I'm sorry, Stephanie, but you're just gonna have to get over it."

"I am over it! I'm so over it that I finally let you step foot in my house!"

"Why did you call me over here anyway?"

"Because I need you."

Stephanie's reply caught Amanda off guard. She looked at her cousin confused. "What?"

Stephanie sighed and replaced her smile. Her voice softened again as she spoke. "Let's just put this all behind us. You made your point, you apologized, and I forgive you. I just need you to do me a little favor."

"Humph, I should have known this was—"

"Mike takes really good care of me in and out the bedroom. It's so hard to just give that all up. Come on, Amanda, you see how fine the brother is," Stephanie playfully nudged her cousin on the arm.

Amanda finally smiled. "What's the favor, Stephanie? I hope it's not money, I'm broke."

"I can help you out, if you help me out…a favor for a favor."

"Sounds like a plan so far. What's the deal?"

"I know Mike is on the fence about me sometimes and I just wanted to do a little somethin' that…you know…might get him off the fence and back into my yard."

Amanda sat confused. "Okay."

"I want to have a threesome," Stephanie revealed.

Amanda eyes widened as she jumped to her feet. "Are you fuckin' kiddin' me?" she yelled. "You actually have the nerve to sit there and ask me to participate in a threesome with you? How disgusting can you—"

"No, not with you!"

Amanda placed her hands on her hips, feeling a little foolish. "Well with who?"

"I need you to see if maybe...Tiffany might be interested."

Amanda's mouth dropped. "You're absolutely insane!" she said shaking her head in surprise and disgust. "Stephanie, what is with you?"

"Fine, I'll ask her," Stephanie said, rising to her feet and walking off towards the kitchen. Amanda followed closely behind still yapping away.

"Stephanie don't you have any class about yourself?"

Stephanie reached into the refrigerator for a bottle of water. "Yeah right, this was the exact same hoopla you were talkin' right before you let Mike put it on you. Either you're gonna ask her, or I'll do it myself."

"Tiffany wouldn't go for it. I mean she's—"

"Not too different from you."

"What is that suppose to mean?"

"Amanda, you'd go for it if I were any other chick."

"Not true. I can't even believe you called me over here for this shit. Actin' all phony and shit." Amanda turned and walked out of the kitchen. "I'm out of here. I can't even stand to be around you right now."

"Hell, you need to be tryin' to make you some extra money. Have you even started lookin' for another job?"

"Don't worry about what's goin' on with me. If it wasn't for you I would've still had one."

"Well get over it because now you don't, broke ass!"

"Yeah, well, I'd rather be broke than spendin' money on bitches to help me screw somebody's husband."

Stephanie trailed Amanda to the front door. Amanda turned to her cousin after she opened it.

"I'll talk to Tiffany myself," Stephanie said smiling.

"Good luck." Amanda walked out shaking her head. She quickly pulled her phone out of her purse and dialed Tiffany's number.

"What happened," Tiffany asked eagerly.

"Just stay put I'm on my way back over. My cousin is officially one crazy bitch."

Tiffany laughed on the other end. "Hurry up!"

Amanda pushed the metal to the floor and reached Tiffany's apartment in a matter of minutes. Tiffany buzzed her up. Amanda walked in breathing heavily. She sat on the couch and closed her eyes, struggling to regain her composure.

"She wants to have a threesome!"

"What?" Tiffany yelled, wide eyed with both hands over her mouth. "A threesome? With his wife?"

"With you!"

Tiffany fell to the floor in laughter. "Stop playin'...you're jokin', right?"

Amanda shook her head. Tiffany laughter came to a halt. "I'm fuckin' serious."

Tiffany scrambled from the carpeted floor onto the couch next to Amanda. "Wait, this just doesn't make any sense. Please break it all down for me and let me know exactly what happened when you went over there."

Amanda let out a long winded exhale before passing the conversation that occurred between her and Stephanie along to Tiffany, who sat listening intently. After Amanda finished her tale of events, Tiffany roared with more laughter. Amanda didn't join in. Instead she sat with a serious expression on her face rolling her eyes.

"I told her you wouldn't do it. I mean she'd have to be absolutely nuts to even think that you'd—"

"Exactly how much money was she talkin'?" Tiffany asked curiously.

"What do you mean how much money?"

"I'm just sayin'."

"You're just sayin' what?"

Tiffany frowned and stood to her feet. "Don't start that holier than thou shit with me. Bitch...you fucked him too!" she said as she stood looking down at Amanda with a hand on her hip.

"So you're actually gonna to do it? You're gonna have a fling with him and my cousin?"

Tiffany rolled her eyes and sighed. "Don't make it sound so bad. I didn't say I was gonna do it."

"Good, because you're not!" Amanda stared her in the face as she stood up. "I'm leavin'. I'll talk to you later." She pushed past Tiffany to the front door. When she opened it, she turned back to her friend who had her arms folded across her chest. "If she calls you, just don't answer. As simple as that."

"Whatever, I'll talk to you later," Tiffany said irritably.

"Tiffany, I'm serious. This thing has been dragged out long enough. If Stephanie wants to be a dummy then let her. I'm sure she could find plenty of other stupid women out there who'd fall all over his nuts," Amanda said slowly pulling the door close behind her while waiting for a response. When Tiffany didn't reply, she slammed the door shut.

CHAPTER 27

"Amanda, chill out! I'm at work. I told you I'll call you back," Stephanie whispered over the phone.

Amanda sighed. "You said that last night and you never called me back. You haven't called me back in four days."

"That's because you're irritating the shit out of me. Do I have to go back to not speakin' to you again?"

"You can do whatever you want once you let me know what's goin' on."

"Goin' on with what?" Stephanie asked anxiously.

"Between you and Tiffany."

Stephanie let out a chuckle. "Aw, is this what you've been stalkin' me about? Well, since I'm a bit occupied you should hang up with me and call her."

"Oh my goodness, does that mean you two actually—"

"Amanda, call me later. I have—"

"Dammit, Stephanie, stop horsin' around and just fill me in. Tiffany hasn't responded to any of my calls so I know somethin' is up."

"Well, sweetheart, go with what you know," were Stephanie's last words before hanging up the phone.

Amanda let the phone fall from between her ear and shoulder onto her pillow. Her aunt had left the house a few hours earlier, mostly to run errands. She lounged around lazily, only getting up to either eat or release what she ate. She spent the majority of her afternoon ringing Stephanie's and Tiffany's phones back to back. Bored, she scrolled through her phone, flipping through previous text messages from her inbox and sent folders. An old message from Reggie redirected her thoughts. She thought about calling him, but hurriedly dismissed the thought as quickly as it emerged. She placed the phone beside her hoping someone would call and break her from her trance as she stared up at the spinning ceiling fan. She hated being alone with her thoughts, there were some she'd rather not dwell on. Thoughts of Reggie, her exes, and sometimes him, drifted into her head at moments like this. She let out a long winded exhale to shake the feelings as she sat up in bed with the sheets wrapped around her torso.

She reached for the robe beside her and covered her naked body. Sh moved the sheets from around her and swung her feet to the warm carpeted floor. The sound of the doorbell alarmed her. She hurriedly fastened her robe and rushed towards the front door, wondering who had decided to come for a visit. She looked through the peephole and excitedly opened the door for Tiffany. "I've been callin' you all afternoon!"

Tiffany grinned as she entered the house and made her way towards the couch. Amanda closed the door and plopped down beside her friend. Tiffany looked away with a wide smile still stuck to her face. "I don't even want to know what that stupid smile is for."

"So you're not mad at me?"

Amanda raised an eyebrow as she twirled a strand of her hair. "You really went behind my back and did it?"

"Did what?" Tiffany asked shamefully, shielding her face with her hands.

Amanda pried her hands from her face. "You know what you did!"

"I just want to make sure we're on the same page here."

"Wipe that stupid smirk off your face!"

"Amanda, are you mad at—"

"You ignored me for the past week. So you—"

"It hasn't exactly been that long, maybe a couple of days at the most," Tiffany whined.

"Ugh, stop it. I hate it when you do that."

"I know you bugged the hell out of your cousin already."

"I didn't!"

"She already told me how you've been blowin' her phone up."

"Aw, so you guys are best friends now? Since when does Stephanie pick up the phone to call you?"

"Only to rant and rave about…you know."

"I don't know! I don't even think I want to know!"

"I think you do."

Amanda shook her head. "I'm in complete utter shock."

Tiffany reached into her handbag and pulled out a blank disk. A naughty grin formed on her face. Amanda quickly snatched the CD from her and held it up. "What is this?"

Tiffany giggled. "How about we name it tag team."

"Tag team, eewww, you're so disgusting. Tiffany, you slept with him? You actually went behind my back and had a threesome with my cousin and him?"

Tiffany sighed as she buried her face in her hands. "Are you upset?"

Amanda shook her head. "How much did she pay you?" Amanda asked, not taking her eyes off her friend.

"Five hundred."

"Five hundred?" Amanda repeated as she jumped up from the couch. "Are you out of your mind? You slept with them for five hundred measly dollars?"

Tiffany lifted her head. "Well at least I didn't do it for free!"

"You might as well. What the hell is five hundred dollars? I mean come on, that isn't even a week's worth of pay."

Tiffany remained quiet then let out a pretend yawn. "Go on," she said sarcastically.

"It kills me, Tiffany! All the bullshit you said to me about what I did and you basically went behind my back and did the same exact shit. Hell, I don't even think Stephanie needed to give you any money. You probably would've done it for free. Am I Right?"

Tiffany screwed up her face. "Wrong!"

"Right."

Tiffany slammed a hand on the armrest of the couch. "What are you upset about?"

"You slept with him!"

"And so did you!"

"How could you sleep with someone I've slept with?"

Tiffany raised an eyebrow. "The same way you slept with someone you knew your cousin was sleepin' with."

Amanda chuckled. "Stop throwin' that in my face." She shook her head.

"I'm just sayin'," Tiffany said after sliding a stick of chewing gum in her mouth. "It is what it is." She shrugged her shoulders.

"And you don't even care!"

Tiffany stood up. "What am I suppose to be carin' about?"

"You don't think it's kind of weird that you slept with him and my cousin. That's just plain sick! And then you sit here and try to make me feel like crap when you wanted him all along."

"I didn't want him all along. I did it for the money."

"You didn't need five hundred dollars that bad!"

"You don't know what I need. You're just jealous."

"Right, now I'm jealous. Are you kiddin' me?" Amanda rolled her eyes. "Forget it. I don't even want to talk about it. It's over and done with. I hope you're happy. You finally got a piece of him."

Tiffany sighed and threw up a hand. "Whatever."

Amanda picked up the disc and looked it over. "So this is it, huh?"

Tiffany laughed, putting aside her irritation for the moment. "Girl yeah, I don't know if you can handle it. It's definitely hardcore."

Amanda's mouth dropped. "So disgusting," she said shaking her head. "I don't think I can watch this," she said standing up and sliding the CD into the DVD player.

"Wait, where's your aunt? I don't need her walkin' in on—"

"She's gone and won't be back for awhile, thank goodness," she sighed and slapped a hand across her forehead in exaggeration.

"I take it she's not so fun to be around."

"She drives me up the wall!"

"Well, you're welcome to come and crash at my place every now and then."

Amanda looked in Tiffany's direction. "Why, so you can ruin my next so called relationship?"

Tiffany let out a loud chuckle, slapping her hand against her thigh as she spoke. "Girl please, that wasn't a relationship. Hell, you had more relations with Mike than you did with Reggie. So get over it."

"I really cared about Reggie." Amanda stood up, slowly backing away from the TV not wanting to miss any scene of the supposedly raunchy video. She took a seat next to her friend.

"Like I said, get over it."

Amanda shoved Tiffany. "You get over it," she teased. "Keep talkin' to me and you're gonna have a lot to get over."

Tiffany opened her mouth to argue back until she appeared on the television screen alongside another familiar face. The site of Tiffany and Stephanie taking turns swapping spit and stroking a long hard penis made Amanda gasp like a little school girl. Tiffany sat smiling like a proud mother watching her kid walk cross the stage.

"He was packin'," Tiffany said as if reading Amanda's thoughts.

"Damn ya'll didn't waste no time. No role playin' or anything."

Tiffany raised an eyebrow. "Aw…and what kind of role playin' did you get into?"

Amanda ignored her and kept her eyes glued to the screen as Mike laid down on his back while Tiffany slowly crawled towards him and mounted herself on top. Amanda frowned inside while watching Tiffany on screen thrust herself back and forth on him like a wild stallion. Tiffany sat just as still, examining her every move, letting out a laugh or clap every time Mike threw his head back in utter satisfaction.

"Look at him," Tiffany said pointing at the TV. "He loved every bit of it." Tiffany threw her head back in laughter.

Amanda did all but crack a smile as she curled up on the couch engrossed like she was viewing a Lifetime movie. She wanted to turn her head away when Stephanie positioned herself on Mike's face with Tiffany still doing her thing between his thighs, moaning at the top of her lungs.

Amanda rolled her eyes and sighed. "You are so dramatic," she said, propping her elbow on the armrest and leaning her head against the back of her hand.

Tiffany looked over at her with a smirk. "Don't be jealous."

Amanda waved her off and redirected her focus on the video just in time to see her cousin and friend switch positions on Mike. Amanda sat fuming inside, uncurling herself and sitting up on the couch. A smiling Tiffany looked over at her.

"Girl, he ate some good cookie! You didn't tell me he—"

"Will you shut up?" Amanda said jumping up, cringing as she walked over to the television and cut the homemade video off.

Tiffany let out a laugh. "What's your dilemma, honey?"

"I can't watch the damn thing because of your loud ass!" Amanda lied. She folded her arms across her chest.

"You couldn't take it, huh?"

"Whatever, I could care less. Do what you do, Tiffany."

"Oh believe me, I definitely do what I do," Tiffany cracked, amused by Amanda's reaction.

"Tiffany, you're so annoyin' sometimes."

"Or are you annoyed by what you just saw?"

"I'm glad you gettin' a kick out of this. Trust me, I'm not fazed. You can continue fuckin' them both for all I care."

Tiffany smiled. "Who knows, there may be a second video, maybe an entire collection."

"Have fun, sweetheart."

"Oh, I did."

"If you're tryin' to crawl under my skin you're not doin' a good job." Amanda said to Tiffany with squinted eyes.

Tiffany chuckled for the umpteenth time. "I'm not," she said trying to keep a steady face.

"Get out," Amanda said animatedly.

Tiffany laughed. "Ok, fine. I have things to do anyway." Tiffany said gathering her belongings. "You suck!" Tiffany smirked as she practically skipped towards the front door in delight. "I might head over to your cousin's."

Amanda bit her lip and shook her head as Tiffany let herself out. Amanda quickly locked the doors behind her. She walked hurriedly towards the oversized sofa, nestled herself with a comfy throw pillow, and held the remote towards the television clicking the video back on. She managed to watch it long enough to see both girls lick around their lips as Mike let himself loose on their caramel faces. Amanda nearly burned a hole into the TV as she sat wide eyed. Raunchy was an understatement.

When the screen went black signifying the end of the movie, she hopped off the couch and removed the disc from the DVD player. She examined it, wondering if Tiffany had any idea she left it behind. She was angry. Envious. Jealous. Hell, Mike hadn't even eaten me out and there Tiffany goes sitting herself on his face, Amanda thought. She walked into her aunt's small room, converted into an office and placed the disc into the computer. She quickly saved the video onto the desktop and brought up her Yahoo email account. She grinned to herself as she typed her former boss work email address in the address box. She then attached the raunchy video of Stephanie, Tiffany, and Mike to the email. She could feel the butterflies gather in the pit of her stomach as she dragged the cursor over to the top left corner and let it rest on top of the send button. Now she sat smiling at the computer screen, like a proud mother watching her kid walk across the stage.

She skimmed over the empty white box under the attachment. In it she simply wrote: Enjoy. She chuckled to herself as she clicked the send button. She would definitely have the last laugh.

CHAPTER 28

"I really would like to see you again, honey. We ended on such a bad note last time. I love you dear."

Amanda smiled and blew a kiss through the receiver. "I love you too, mom. I just don't know when I'll be able to make it out there. I've been a little busy."

"Busy doin' what?"

"Well for one, I've been job hunting. I had a job interview yesterday. It seems promising."

"Honey, we have plenty of opportunities here. At least I'd be able to help you get on your feet."

"Mom, that's the problem. I'm an adult. I can't run to you for everything. I just need a little time to get things together."

"Honey, I know how your Aunt is. She gets fussy. How are things working out there?"

"Everything is fine between us. She has her moments, but things aren't so bad."

"How are you and that cousin of yours?"

Amanda shifted her legs on the sofa. She sent the raunchy video of the threesome to her former boss two days ago and ever since then Stephanie had been calling Amanda like crazy.

"I guess she's fine," Amanda chuckled to herself. You know her and Aunt Sheryl aren't speakin' to each other."

"Really? Why is that?"

"In regards to some video Aunt Sheryl found of her and some chick with that guy," Amanda grinned, rubbing it all in. She heard her mother gasp. "I'm not really sure," she lied, not wanting to go into anymore details. "Maybe Stephanie can fill you in."

"I don't think I want to know. I've heard enough. I don't think that cousin of yours can get any more ridiculous."

Amanda rolled her eyes. "You never know with her." Amanda shrugged her shoulders. "Anyway, I'll talk to you later. I have more job applications to fill out."

"Well good luck, honey. Call me if you need anything. I'm here for you."

"Talk to you later, mom," Amanda said quickly hanging up the phone.

Almost immediately after she hung up the house phone her cellular phone vibrated. She rolled her eyes anticipating seeing her mother's number flash across the screen. Her eyes nearly bulged out of their sockets. It wasn't her mother. Her eyes were glued to the familiar number on the screen of the phone. It was a number that belong to an employer she once worked for. The same employer she resigned from weeks earlier. When she finally mustered up the courage to press the talk button, the call had become a missed call. She contemplated on calling the number back as she tapped her fingers on the desk in disbelief. Who was on the other end? she wondered. Her eyes darted from the phone back to the computer screen until her phone danced across the desk again. She quickly looked down and scooped the phone up in her hands staring at another number that belonged to her former boss. She tapped the talk button.

"Hello."

"Amanda?" Melanie asked in a faint whisper.

"Melanie?" Amanda questioned in surprise, as if she didn't know who the number belonged to.

"I just called you from the work...I mean the—"

"I get what you're tryin' to say," Amanda said, trying to speed the conversation along. "What is it?"

She heard Melanie exhale and pause on the other end. "Why did you do it?" Melanie muffled.

"Do what?" Amanda questioned.

"The video you sent a couple of days ago. I—"

Amanda remained quiet as Melanie let out a few stifled sobs. "Melanie?"

"I'm sorry, I just can't help it. I don't know what to feel right now. I'm just so confused. I'm so angry...hurt...I loved him. I loved him more than any of you ever could," Melanie managed to say as she wept.

Amanda exhaled and closed her eyes to rid herself of the guilt that was flooding through her. "I know," was all she managed to say.

"Know what?" Melanie asked.

"I know how you feel."

"Amanda, have you ever been married?"

"No," Amanda answered, caught off guard.

"Well, you have no idea what I feel."

Amanda bit her bottom lip. She couldn't argue with that. "Well, I guess I—"

"Look, as much as I hate your guts, I just called to thank you."

"Thank me?" Amanda asked with raised eyebrows. She definitely wasn't expecting a call from Melanie, let alone a thank you.

"That video pushed me over the edge. I am done with that man for good. I will not sit around and tolerate that fool, or any of his lies anymore. My life is a living hell because of him. I will never ever want anyone to go through all he's put me through."

Amanda sat feeling awkward as Melanie cried and suddenly the other end went dead. Amanda twisted her face as she lowered the phone from her ear and glanced at it. Her home screen appeared. She placed it on the desk and rested her head in her hands as she mulled over Melanie's words. Then the phone rang again. She lifted her head and answered.

"What happened?"

"I got a little choked up. Amanda, I can't even look these people in their faces anymore."

"Look what people in the face?"

"The entire department! I can't leave the office without everyone looking at me and throwing a big pity party. It's embarrassing."

"Who cares about what they—"

"That's why I'm quitting."

Amanda's mouth dropped. "Quittin'? Are you kiddin' me? Why would you do—"

"You'll understand when you become a married woman."

"This has nothin' to do with your marriage."

"He was my life. My life as it is right now reminds me of him. I don't want to be reminded of him…or you…or any of the things that took him away from me." More sobs.

"Melanie…I'm sorry."

"You're not sorry. You're just feeling guilty. Look, I didn't call you for an apology. My marriage ended long before you came along, and long before this video appeared on my screen."

"I only sent the video because I—"

"Wanted to get back at me and your cousin?" Melanie finished. Amanda remained quiet. "I know you could care less about me," Melanie continued.

"I don't know why I did it," Amanda finally spoke up. "I wanted everybody to—"

"Amanda, there are no victims."

Melanie words quieted Amanda's rambling. She took a moment to let the words sink in.

"Look Melanie, I know there's not much I can say to you right now. I wish there was a way to prove how sorry I really am. I wish I never did what I did."

"Its fine, Amanda. I don't want to go back and forth about this anymore. I just want to get on with my life. I wish you well."

"Thanks," Amanda replied feeling a little relieved.

"Look, I don't know what your situation is, but I know someone who's looking for someone with a little work experience right up your alley."

"I don't know about that."

"Oh, so you have a job?"

"No, I'm fillin' out applications as we speak. I just don't want you doin' anymore favors for me."

Melanie chuckled. "Perhaps you have a point. My last favor placed you on top of my husband."

Amanda didn't laugh. "All right, well, I guess I'll be goin' now."

"Keep this between us."

"Who am I gonna tell, your husband?" she chuckled.

"You never know."

"I know I want to get on with my life as well."

"Good luck with that. I'm hanging up now. I have visitors."

"Ok, well I—"

Melanie's end went silent. Amanda pressed the end button. She shook her head, still in shock that she had just had a conversation with Melanie.

She sighed after staring at the job application on the computer screen and quickly closing out of the site and logging off the computer. She had enough of filling out online job applications. It had been her early morning routine for the past couple of days. She figured she could use a little excitement in her life as she pushed herself away from the computer, grabbed her bag, and headed out the door.

She walked slowly towards her car, phone in hand, scrolling through her contact list. She stopped on his name. Reggie. She smiled to herself, her hand shaking as she pressed the talk button. She forced herself to think positive thoughts as the phone rang on the opposite end. When his voicemail answered she quickly ended the call. Her Smile faded along with all of the positive thoughts. She sighed as she opened the driver's side door and climbed in. After tossing her purse on the passenger seat, she stared blankly out the front window in a daze. Her head quickly turned towards the passenger side and her eyes narrowed in on her bag. She could hear her phone vibrating. She lifted her bag and dug through her purse frantically. Buried at the bottom, she finally retrieved the cell phone and stared at Reggie's name on the screen. Butterflies gathered in the pit of her stomach and lingered there until her status changed from an incoming call to a missed one.

She let out a long winded exhale and leaned her head back against her seat. She was happy he had at least returned her call. She opened the miss call and hit the talk button once again. Her hand shook uncontrollably as she brought the phone to her ear.

"What's up," Reggie answered quicker than she expected.

"Hey," she replied, caught off guard. A few awkward seconds of silence passed. "Um, how's everything," she asked closing her eyes to calm her heavy breathing. She rested a hand on her chest.

"Everything's cool. I'm a little surprised to hear from you."

Amanda bit her bottom lip before responding. "Yeah, I was just wonderin' how you were doin'."

"I'm cool, nothin' much, how about you?"

"Uh, I'm fine. I've been in Beverly, at my Aunt's place."

"Oh really, how you like bein' over there?"

"It's All right. It's home for now."

"For now?" Reggie repeated. "You plan on movin' again?"

"Well, I need to get my own place. I've been busy lookin' for another job and all."

"I hear you. It'll all work itself out. Just stay focused."

Amanda let out another winded exhaled. "Yeah, I guess," she said awkwardly. The conversation went dead again.

Reggie cleared his throat. "Well, I'm about to head out. I promised my daughter I'd take her to the park."

Amanda ran her hands through her hair. "Okay...yeah, well...have fun."

"All right, sweetheart, take it easy," he said before hanging up.

Amanda squeezed her eyes shut, banging her fist against the steering wheel. Why did I even bother calling, she thought. Again, she sat staring out of the window lost in thought. She shook her head in disappointment when she realized all attempts at rekindling the connection her and Reggie once shared was over. She squeezed her eyes shut again, only this time a tear trickled down her face, followed by another and another. She sniffled as she quickly wiped them away with the back of her hand. She mulled over the brief conversation she just had, wondering what she could have said differently. She stuck the key into the ignition and started the car. She griped the steering wheel firmly with both hands still uncertain as to where she was going. The talk she had just had with Reggie stole her excitement to seize the day. Part of her wanted to shut off the car and run in the house to lounge in her bed and sob all day. She shook her head to rid herself of the thought and the suddenly drab mood she was in. When her phone rang again she quickly picked it up.

"Hello," she said with barely any enthusiasm at all.

"What's your problem?"

Amanda sighed. "Hey girl, what are you up to?"

"That sounds better," Tiffany said. "I'm headed back home. Just came from the nail shop. A sister's feet were lookin' a little jacked."

Amanda snickered. "Finally, you realized it."

"Don't even go there with me. My feet are pretty."

"How long will it be before you get home?"

"I'll be there shortly. Are you headin' over? Don't come over actin' all moody."

"Don't do or say anything to make me act moody."

"Is it your time of the—"

"I'll see you in a little while, Tiff." Amanda hit the end button and headed off in the direction of Tiffany's house. Once there, she sat in her car with the engine running. The block was filled with people loitering on their front porches engaged in conversations. Music was coming through a raised window from the building next to Tiffany's. Amanda cut off her engine and climbed out of her car when Tiffany stepped out on her porch.

"What the hell were you sittin' in the car for?" Tiffany asked coming down the steps meeting her friend halfway. She wrapped her arms around Amanda. Surprised, Amanda took a few steps back and gave Tiffany the once over.

"Uh, what was all that for?"

"Oh hush, it was just a hug. As crabby as you sounded earlier, I'm sure you could use a little tender lovin' care."

Amanda forced a one sided smile. "I could use a lot of things right now," she said as they sat on the concrete steps.

"Still fillin' out job applications?"

"Yeah, I had an interview the other day for a receptionist position at the hospital."

"Which hospital?"

"Northwestern."

"Cool, I'm pretty sure you'll hear back from them."

Amanda looked over at Tiffany. "I hope so, girl. I am so ready to get out of my aunt's house."

"Is it that bad?" Tiffany asked.

"I just need a peace of mind. I want to walk around butt naked for a change."

The two girls laughed. "You know my aunt found the video of you and Stephanie?"

Tiffany stopped laughing and her eyes widened in surprise. She nudged Amanda's shoulder.

"Why are you just now tellin' me this? That's why Stephanie hasn't been answerin' my calls!"

"What were you callin' Stephanie about?"

"That's none of your business. What's goin' on, Amanda? What happened between her and your aunt? What did you do? You know I wasn't supposed to show you that video. Where is that video? Oh no, please don't tell me your aunt has it!" Tiffany asked rising to her feet.

"Shut up already with the twenty one questions! You're givin' me a headache."

"Amanda, did you show your aunt that video?"

"Tiffany, why would I show my aunt the video?"

"I don't know, maybe to get back at Stephanie, or to—"

"I don't care about gettin' back at her. I don't care what either one of you do anymore."

"Well how did your aunt get a hold of the disc that I accidentally left with you?"

"I accidentally left it in the comp—"

"The what?" Tiffany asked curiously with raised eyebrows. "The computer?"

"Yes, the computer."

"Why was it in the computer, Mandy?"

Amanda sighed and looked away. "None of that matters, Tiffany. She found it and it's over with."

"Oh my goodness, how could I be so stupid. I knew I should've came back for it. I know Stephanie is highly pissed. I thought I could trust you, Amanda!"

"Just as much as I trust you," Amanda yelled rising to her feet as well. "What is goin' on between you and Stephanie that's so got damn important? What are you three doin' that I don't know about?"

"Things that don't always necessarily involve Mike," Tiffany snapped.

Amanda gasped. "I'm so done with both of—"

"Amanda, call her from your phone. I just want to explain what happened. Maybe I should—"

"What are you now, her girlfriend? You two just became lesbians all of a sudden? I'm not callin' her for—"

"I knew somethin' was wrong," Tiffany whined.

"I can't believe you're actin' all—"

"Just call her for me, Amanda."

"No…I'm not doin'—"

"Where's your phone? I'll call her myself," Tiffany said as she reached for Amanda's purse. Amanda forcefully shoved Tiffany's hands away. Tiffany shielded her eyes from the sun with her hand and sighed. "Forget about it."

"Already forgotten."

Both girls stood motionless, shielding their eyes from the bright sunlight. Tiffany shook her head after folding her arms.

"Why was the video in the computer?"

"Because I was watchin' it on the computer."

"Oh, it was so good you had to watch it on the computer?" Tiffany asked sarcastically. "Did you set that up between your aunt and cousin?"

"And if I did, what are you gonna do about it, whoop my ass? I guess that makes you the butch."

"Whatever, Amanda."

"I can't believe you and—"

Amanda stopped mid-sentence when she felt her phone vibrating in her bag. She dug in her purse and retrieved her phone. "Speakin' of the devil."

Tiffany launched at her snatching the phone out of her hand before Amanda had time to react.

"Hello," Tiffany said answering the call. "No, it's me, Tiffany," she continued. Amanda shook her head and walked off towards the curb, uninterested in the conversation. She leaned her backside against the hood of her car. She quickly jerked up when the heat from the engine and the blazing sun nearly burned a whole through her jeans. "She did what?" she heard Tiffany yell. She quickly shifted her attention towards her friend now coming down the steps towards her. Amanda quickly straightened her stance. She had an inkling as to what Tiffany probably had heard. Tiffany quickly hung up the phone and tossed it in Amanda's direction. She caught it just in time.

"You definitely would've been buyin' me a new one."

"Really, you stooped that fuckin' low, Amanda?"

"What are you talkin' about?" They stood face to face.

"Come on, Amanda! You know damn well what I'm talkin' about!" Tiffany yelled throwing her hands in the air. "What would possess you to email that lady?"

Amanda smirked. "She deserved it. Even after I was nice enough to go up there and apologize she—"

"Don't give me that bullshit! You didn't do it to get back at her. You did it to get back at us! You were jealous, just admit it already. Its written all over your face."

"That's not true," Amanda said defensively backing away.

"Why did you do it?" Tiffany took steps forward.

"I did it because of him! I did it because he just doesn't deserve to get away with everything he's done."

Tiffany glared at her. "He didn't do anything to any of us that we didn't allow him to do."

Amanda looked away long enough to see Stephanie's truck pull up.

"Aw, so what is this? Why is she here? Why didn't you tell me she was comin' over here?" Amanda asked, turning back to Tiffany.

"She's here now, so it doesn't matter."

Stephanie hopped out of her truck and approached the girls wearing a smirk on her face. She stood in front of her cousin and placed her hands on her hips.

"You didn't think your little scheme would stop us, did you?"

"Stop what?" Amanda asked, playing clueless.

"You sent that damn video to his wife only to have her file for a divorce."

Amanda squinted up her face. "At least she has sense."

"And you have none. If you think he's gonna get rid of me, Amanda, you're sadly mistaken. Now I'll have him all to myself. Hell, I can't even be mad at you."

"You think I actually care about you and him bein' together? Trust me, he will grow weary. He's stretched you far enough, believe me."

"So what did he say?" Tiffany asked concerned.

Stephanie turned her head in Tiffany's direction. "He's pissed off. She's takin' everything that sucker has. But after he cools down, he'll realize that he was better off with me all along." Stephanie loosened her ponytail and shook her hair out. "I was always the hotter one."

"And the stupid one," Amanda interrupted. "You still want his ass, broke and all, huh?"

"That's what you call love."

"No, Stephanie, that's what you call stupid!"

Tiffany chuckled. "Ladies, stop with all the foolishness."

"Aw, look at you defendin' your girlfriend…how cute," Amanda teased.

Stephanie looked from Tiffany to Amanda and back to Tiffany. "What is she talkin' about? Did you tell her about that one night? Stephanie asked cocking her head.

Tiffany stood looking guilty. "I'm not the one makin' it a big deal."

"Well don't. And don't tell Mike about it either. You know how jealous he is," Stephanie smiled.

Both Tiffany and Amanda rolled their eyes. All three girls stood in awkward silence, scoping out the surroundings.

"I guess everybody decided to sit out on the porch and be nosy today, huh? Stephanie asked breaking the silence.

"Yeah," Amanda answered nonchalantly.

Stephanie turned towards her truck. "Well, off I go. I have things to do."

"Hey Stephanie, Where's he now?" Amanda asked, surprising herself and the others.

Stephanie looked back over her shoulder. "He's with her I suppose. Why?"

"I was just wonderin'."

Stephanie smiled. "He'll be with me soon enough."

"What did she say to him? Did she—"

"Why don't you call her up and ask her, since you're so concerned."

Amanda bit her lip. Although they talked, she would have really gotten a kick out of the expression on Melanie's face when she opened the video. It surely would have been more appeasing than the smile on Stephanie's.

"I just figured he told you somethin'," Amanda shrugged, keeping the conversation she had had with Melanie earlier to herself.

"I don't talk to that man about his wife. I could care less." Stephanie said trotting off towards her vehicle. She opened the driver's side door. "You find yourself a job yet?" she yelled as she climbed in the driver's seat.

"I'm workin' on it," Amanda answered irritably, looking over at Tiffany who stood with her hands on her hips checking out a guy across the street.

"You know she's ready to have her place to herself."

"I don't want to talk about it, Stephanie. I already know she's—"

"I'm just sayin'," she continued as she closed her door and started the engine. She rolled down the driver's side window. "You know you were wrong for showin' her that video," she said, catching both Amanda and Tiffany off guard.

"I didn't do it on purpose. I left the video in—"

Stephanie shook her head. "She basically hates me now!"

"Well, I guess we're even."

"I wouldn't say that. You don't have a job...or a man." Stephanie chuckled at her cousin's expense.

Amanda rolled her eyes and shrugged her shoulders. "I'll live."

"You don't have a man either!" Tiffany said in Amanda's defense.

Stephanie looked over at them cheesing, raising her phone in the air. "Ha, look who's callin' me as we speak, ciao ladies!" She rolled up her window and drove off.

Both girls looked at each other.

"Well, that didn't go too bad."

"I thought she was gonna get out of the car swingin'."

"Who side would you have taken mine or hers?" Amanda asked shifting her weight to one leg and tilting her head.

Tiffany laughed. "That's a stupid question."

"No it's not. Not with how infatuated you were actin' with her before she pulled up."

"I was not. I'm not gay or anything. I just wanted to have a little fun again, and—"

"Don't be in denial," Amanda teased, giggling.

"Whatever."

"Now that she thinks she has him to herself, she tossin' you to the birds."

Both girls erupted with laughter.

"You know bitches ain't shit!" Tiffany laughed, shaking her head at the thought.

Amanda nodded her head in agreement.

The End

ABOUT THE AUTHOR

Veronica E. Kelly is a graduate of Columbia College Chicago with a degree in Fiction Writing. She currently resides in Chicago, Illinois, and enjoys letting her imagination run wild.

25629032R10184

Made in the USA
Charleston, SC
09 January 2014